Martial Law

Book Three
The Boston Brahmin Series

A novel by

Bobby Akart

Copyright Information

Other Works by Amazon Top 50 Author, Bobby Akart

The Doomsday Series

Apocalypse
Haven
Anarchy
Minutemen
Civil War

The Yellowstone Series

Hellfire
Inferno
Fallout
Survival

The Lone Star Series

Axis of Evil
Beyond Borders
Lines in the Sand
Texas Strong
Fifth Column
Suicide Six

The Pandemic Series

Beginnings
The Innocents
Level 6
Quietus

The Blackout Series

36 Hours

Zero Hour

Turning Point

Shiloh Ranch

Hornet's Nest

Devil's Homecoming

The Boston Brahmin Series

The Loyal Nine

Cyber Attack

Martial Law

False Flag

The Mechanics

Choose Freedom

Patriot's Farewell

Seeds of Liberty (Companion Guide)

The Prepping for Tomorrow Series

Cyber Warfare

EMP: Electromagnetic Pulse

Economic Collapse

DEDICATIONS

To the love of my life, you saved me from madness and continue to do so daily. Thank you for loving me.

To the Princesses of the Palace, my little marauders in training, you have no idea how much happiness you bring to your mommy and me. Seeing your wiggly butts at the end of a long day behind the keyboard makes it all worthwhile.

To my friends and readers, please heed the warning of this series. A cyber attack can strike in an instant. No bombs, no bullets, no swordfights. Just a few keystrokes on a computer, and we're done. I write this book to entertain you, but also to get you ready for the coming cyber war. And make no mistake, Martial Law is a distinct probability in the event of a catastrophic event. The President's power to wield this authority transcends party affiliation or political ideology. Any President will use it as necessary.

To the Founding Fathers, whose vision and bravery built America. My apologies for what we've become.

ACKNOWLEDGEMENTS

Writing a book that is both informative and entertaining requires a tremendous team effort. Writing is the easy part. For their efforts in making The Boston Brahmin series a reality, I would like to thank Hristo Argirov Kovatliev for his incredible cover art, Pauline Nolet for her editorial prowess, Stef Mcdaid for making this manuscript decipherable on so many formats, Joseph Morton for bringing my words to life in audio format, and the Team—whose advice, friendship and attention to detail is priceless.

Thank you!   Choose Freedom!

ABOUT THE AUTHOR

Bobby Akart

Author Bobby Akart has been ranked by Amazon as #55 in its Top 100 list of most popular, bestselling authors. He has achieved recognition as the #1 bestselling Horror Author, #2 bestselling Science Fiction Author, #3 bestselling Religion & Spirituality Author, #6 bestselling Action & Adventure Author, and #7 bestselling Historical Author.

He has written over twenty-six international bestsellers, in nearly fifty fiction and nonfiction genres, including the chart-busting Yellowstone series, the reader-favorite Lone Star series, the critically acclaimed Boston Brahmin series, the bestselling Blackout series, the frighteningly realistic Pandemic series, his highly cited nonfiction Prepping for Tomorrow series, and his latest project—the Doomsday series, seen by many as the horrifying future of our nation if we can't find a way to come together.

His novel *Yellowstone: Fallout* reached the Top 50 on the Amazon bestsellers list and earned him two Kindle All-Star awards for most pages read in a month and most pages read as an author. The Yellowstone series vaulted him to the #1 best selling horror author on Amazon, and the #2 best selling science fiction author.

Bobby has provided his readers a diverse range of topics that are both informative and entertaining. His attention to detail and impeccable research have allowed him to capture the imaginations of his readers through his fictional works and bring them valuable knowledge through his nonfiction books.

SIGN UP for Bobby Akart's mailing list to receive special offers, bonus content, and you'll be the first to receive news about new releases in the Doomsday series:

eepurl.com/bYqq3L

VISIT Amazon.com/BobbyAkart, a dedicated feature page created by Amazon for his work, to view more information on his thriller fiction novels and post-apocalyptic book series, as well as his nonfiction Prepping for Tomorrow series.

Visit Bobby Akart's website for informative blog entries on preparedness, writing, and a behind-the-scenes look into his novels.

BobbyAkart.com

Previously in The Boston Brahmin Series

Dramatis Personae

THE LOYAL NINE:

Sarge – born Henry Winthrop Sargent IV. Son of former Massachusetts Governor, Godson of John Adams Morgan and a descendant of Daniel Sargent, Sr., wealthy merchant, and owner of Sargent's Wharf during the Revolutionary War. He's a tenured Professor at the Harvard-Kennedy School of Government in Cambridge. He is becoming well known around the country for his libertarian philosophy as espoused in his New York Times bestseller—Choose Freedom or Capitulation: America's Sovereignty Crisis. Sarge resides at 100 Beacon Street in the Back Bay area of Boston. Sarge is romantically involved with Julia Hawthorne.

Steven Sargent – younger brother of Sarge. He is a graduate of United States Naval Academy and former platoon officer of SEAL Team 10. He is currently a contract operative for Aegis Security—code name NOMAD. He resides on his yacht — the Miss Behavin'. Steven is romantically involved with Katie O'Shea.

Julia Hawthorne – descendant of the Peabody and Hawthorne families. First female political editor of The Boston Herald. She is the recipient of the National Association of Broadcasting Marconi Radio Award for her creation of an internet radio channel for the newspaper. She is in a romantic relationship with Sarge and lives with him at 100 Beacon.

The Quinn family – Donald is the self-proclaimed Director of Procurement. He is a former accountant and financial advisor who works directly with John Adams Morgan. He is married to *Susan Quinn* with daughters *Rebecca* (age 7) and *Penny* (age 11). Donald and Susan coordinate all preparedness activities of The Loyal Nine. They reside in Brae Burn Country Club in Boston.

J.J. – born John Joseph Warren. He is a direct descendant of Doctor Joseph Warren, one of the original Sons of Liberty. The Warren family founded Harvard Medical and were field surgeons at the Battle of Bunker Hill. J.J. was an Army Battalion Surgeon at Joint Base Balad in Iraq. While stationed at JBB, J.J. saved the life of a soldier who was injured saving the lives of others. He later became in a relationship with former Marine Second Lieutenant Sabina del Toro. He finished his career at the Veteran's Administration Hospital in Jamaica Plain, where he also resides. He is affectionately known as the Armageddon Medicine Man.

Katie O'Shea – graduate of the United States Naval Academy who trained as a Naval Intelligence officer. After an introduction to John Adams Morgan, she quickly rose up the ranks of the intelligence community. She now is part of the President's Intelligence Advisory Board. She resides in Washington, D.C. Katie is romantically involved with Steven Sargent.

Brad – born Francis Crowninshield Bradlee, a descendant of the Crowninshield family, a historic seafaring and military family dating back to the early 1600's. He is the battalion commander, achieving the rank of Lieutenant Colonel, of 1st Battalion, 25th Marine Regiment based at Fort Devens, Massachusetts. Their nickname is *Cold Steel Warriors*. He is an active member of Oath Keepers and the Three Percenters.

Abbie – Abigail Morgan, daughter of John Adams Morgan. She is the first term United States Senator from Massachusetts. Elected in 2008, she is politically independent, with libertarian leanings. She resides in Washington, D.C. She has been chosen as the running mate of the Democratic nominee for president.

THE BOSTON BRAHMIN:

John Adams Morgan – lineal descendant of President John Adams and Henry Sturgis Morgan, founder of J.P. Morgan. Morgan attended Harvard, obtaining a master's degree in business and a law degree. Founded the Morgan-Holmes law firm with the grandson of Supreme Court Justice Oliver Wendell Holmes, Jr. Among other concerns, he owns Morgan Global, an international banking and financial conglomerate. Extremely wealthy, Morgan is the recognized head of The Boston Brahmin. His inner circle consists of Walter Cabot and Lawrence Lowell.

Walter Cabot – direct descendant of John Cabot, shipbuilders during the time of the Revolutionary War. Wealthy philanthropist and CEO of Cabot Industries. He is part of Morgan's inner circle.

Lawrence Lowell – descendant of John Lowell, a Federal Judge in the first United States Continental Congress. Extremely wealthy and part of Morgan's inner circle.

Paul and Millicent Winthrop – Descendants of John Winthrop, one of the leading figures in the founding of the Massachusetts Bay Colony, their family became synonymous with the state's politics and philanthropy. The Winthrops and Sargents became close when Sarge' grandfather was Governor of Massachusetts, and his Lieutenant Governor was R. C. Winthrop. The families remained close and became a valuable political force on behalf of The Boston Brahmin. They have a French bulldog called Winnie the Frenchie.

Arthur and Estelle Peabody – Dr. Arthur Peabody is a plastic surgeon in private practice. He is the youngest of the Boston Brahmin at age fifty-five. His wife is Estelle, affectionately called Aunt Stella. They are Julia's Aunt and Uncle. They are direct descendants of the Hawthorne and Peabody lineage.

ZERO DAY GAMERS:

Andrew Lau – MIT professor of Korean descent. A brilliant mind that created the Zero Day Gamers as a way to utilize his talents for personal financial gain.

Anna Fakhri – MIT graduate assistant to Professor Lau of Arabic descent. She prides herself on her "internet detective work". She speaks multiple Arabic languages.

Leonid "Leo" Malvalaha – MIT graduate assistant to Professor Lau of Russian descent. He is very adept at creating complex viruses, worms, and Trojans used in cyber attack activities. He speaks fluent Russian.

Herm Walthaus – newest member of the Zero Day Gamers. MIT graduate student. Introverted, but extremely analytical. Stays abreast of latest tools and techniques available to hackers.

AEGIS TEAM:

Nomad – Steven Sargent.

Slash – Drew Jackson. Former SEAL Team member who worked briefly the private contractor firm—Blackwater. Born and raised in Tennessee where his family farm is located. He has excellent survival skills. He is currently assigned to Senator Abigail Morgan's security team and heads her Secret Service detail.

Bugs – Paul Hittle. Former Army Special Forces Medic, who left the Green Berets for contract security work. He owns a ranch in East Texas, provided to him as compensation for his service to Aegis.

Sharpie – Raymond Bower. Former Delta Force, who now operates a lucrative private equity fund venture with former classmates from

Harvard. He resides in New York City.

OFFICERS OF 1ˢᵗ BATTALION, 25ᵗʰ MARINE REGIMENT

Gunny Falcone – Master Gunnery Sergeant Frank Falcone. Under Brad's command for years. A Loyal member of The Mechanics. Stationed at Fort Devens. Primary on base recruiter of soldiers to join The Mechanics.

Chief Warrant Officer Kyle Shore – Young. Expert in sniping. Recorded two kill shots in Afghanistan at just over 2,500 yards. Stationed at Fort Devens. Also recruits members of The Mechanics.

First Lieutenant Kurt Branson – Boston native. A Loyal member of The Mechanics.

SUPPORTING CHARACTERS:

Malcolm Lowe – John Morgan's trusted assistant. Former undersecretary of state during Morgan's tenure as Secretary of State. He *handles* sensitive matters for Mr. Morgan.

J-Rock – Jarvis Rockwell, leader of the unified black gangs of Dorchester, Roxbury, and Mattapan in South Boston. He rose to power after the death of his unborn child during a race riot in Copley Square in April 2016.

Joe Sciacca – Boston Herald's chief editor.

Sabina del Toro – former Marine Second Lieutenant deployed to Iraq, assigned to the 6th Marine Regiment under the 2nd Marine Division based at Camp Lejeune. The 6th was primarily a peacekeeping force deployed throughout the Sunni Anbar province, which included Fallujah, just west of Baghdad. Sabs, as she prefers to be called, was seriously injured protecting children from a car bomb blast. She lost her left arm and left leg as a result of her heroics. She is in a relationship with J.J.

Previously in The Boston Brahmin Series

Book One: The Loyal Nine

The Boston Brahmin series begins in December and the timeframe of *The Loyal Nine*, book one in The Boston Brahmin series, continues through April of the following year. Steven Sargent, in his capacity as Nomad, an Aegis deep cover operative, undertakes several black ops missions in Ukraine, Switzerland, and Germany. The purposes of the operations become increasingly suspect to Steven and his brother Sarge. It is apparent that Steven's actual employer, John Morgan, is orchestrating a series of events as part of a grander scheme.

Sarge continues to teach at the Harvard-Kennedy School of Government. He begins to make public appearances after publishing a New York Times bestseller, Choose Freedom or Capitulation: America's Sovereignty Crisis. During this time, he rekindles his relationship with Julia Hawthorne, who is also celebrating national notoriety for her accomplishments at The Boston Herald newspaper. The two take a trip to Las Vegas for a convention and become unwilling participants in a cyber attack on the Las Vegas power grid. Throughout The Loyal Nine, Sarge and Julia observe the economic and societal collapse of America.

The chasm between the haves and have-nots widens, resulting in hostilities between labor unions and their employers. There are unintended consequences of these actions, and numerous deaths are the result.

Racial tensions are on the rise across the country, and Boston becomes ground zero for social unrest when a beloved retired bus driver is beaten to death during the St. Patrick's Day festivities. In protest, a group of marchers descend upon Copley Square at the end of the Boston Marathon resulting in a clash with police. The protestors are led by Jarvis *J-Rock* Rockwell, leader of the unified black gangs of Dorchester, Roxbury, and Mattapan in South Boston. The protest march quickly got out of hand, and J-Rock's pregnant girlfriend was struck by the police, resulting in her death and the death of their unborn child.

The Quinn family, Donald, Susan and their young daughters, are caught up in an angry mob scene at a local mall relating to the Black Lives Matter protests. Donald decides to accelerate The Loyal Nine's preparedness activities as he gets the sense America is on the brink of collapse.

The reader gets an inside look at the morning security briefings in the White House Situation Room. Katie O'Shea becomes a respected rising star within the intelligence community while solidifying her role as a conduit for information to John Morgan.

John Morgan continues to act as a world power broker. He manipulates geopolitical events for the financial gain of his wealthy associates—The Boston Brahmin. He carefully orchestrates the rise to national prominence of his daughter, Senator Abigail Morgan.

As a direct descendant of the Founding Fathers, Morgan is sickened to watch America descend into collapse. Morgan believes the country can return to its former greatness. He recognizes drastic measures may be required. He envisions a reset of sorts, but what that entails is yet to be determined.

Throughout The Loyal Nine, the Zero Day Gamers make a name for themselves in the hacktivist community as their skills and capabilities escalate from cyber vandalism to cyber ransom to cyber terror. Professor Lau and his talented graduate assistants create ingenious methods of cyber intrusion. At times, they question the morality of their activities. But the ransoms they extract from their victims are too lucrative to turn away.

The end game, the mission statement of the Zero Day Gamers, is succinct:

One man's gain is another man's loss; who gains and who loses is determined by who pays.

Book Two: Cyber Attack

But who else loses in their deadly game? *Cyber Attack*, book two in The Boston Brahmin series, begins with the Zero Day Gamers testing their skills by taking over control of an American Airlines 757. Throughout *Cyber Attack*, conducting various hacker activities including compromising a nuclear power plant in Jefferson City, Missouri. But one of the Gamers, in an attempt to impress a young lady, makes a mistake. His cyber intrusion into the laptop of Abbie Morgan following the Democratic National Convention is discovered.

Meanwhile, over the summer, The Loyal Nine increase their preparedness activities. Through some legislative maneuvering, John Morgan acquires Prescott Peninsula at the Quabbin Reservoir in central Massachusetts. He immediately tasks Donald and Susan Quinn with renovating the property into a high-tech bug out location for The Boston Brahmin.

While Donald, Susan, J.J., and Sabs focus their attention on Prescott Peninsula, Sarge is making a name for himself on the speaker's circuit as a straight talk libertarian. His relationship with Julia Hawthorne has grown, and they continue to observe world events with an eye towards preparedness.

After the hack of Abbie's computer, through some excellent cyber forensics on the part of Katie O'Shea, the Zero Day Gamers are located and contacted by Steven Sargent and Malcolm Lowe, acting on behalf of John Morgan. The three orchestrate a ruse upon Andrew Lau and his team of cyber mercenaries for hire.

Morgan has determined that America is descending into collapse, both socially and economically, and is in need of a reset. The Zero Day Gamers are the perfect tool to accomplish this purpose.

Morgan has conducted several private meetings with the President culminating with a face to face discussion in August of 2016. The two agree—a reset is necessary, and each will play a vital role in bringing America to its knees only to build the country back in their respective images. These two powerful political players navigate a complex game of chess, not realizing the unintended consequences on the people of America.

As Cyber Attack closes its final chapter in early September of 2016, Andrew Lau is forced to make a choice. Does he watch his young protégés die by a gunshot to the head at the hands of Morgan's men or does he push the button that will result in the end of life as we know it?

Martial Law begins now …

Epigraph

No bombs. No bullets. No swordfights.
Just a few keystrokes on the computer, and we're done.
~ Bobby Akart, Author
*****

A government big enough to give you everything you want
is strong enough to take everything you have.
~ Thomas Jefferson
*****

The nine most terrifying words in the English language are:
I'm from the government, and I'm here to help.
~ President Ronald Reagan
*****

Civilization is like a thin layer of ice upon a deep ocean
of chaos and darkness.
*****

Gimme back my bullets, put 'em back where they belong.
~ Lynyrd Skynyrd
*****

The end begins tomorrow.
~ John Adams Morgan

Martial Law

Book Three
The Boston Brahmin Series

Prologue

September 3, 2016
9:05 p.m.
U.S. Route 411 Northbound
Near Tennga, Georgia

"Baby, you know I'm pedalin' as fast as I can. I wanna get home to them ribs and your lovin' like nuthin' else on dis earth." Big John Ames navigated his Peterbilt through the small town of Eton, Georgia and continued on his northern route along U.S. 411. It had been a long day as he waited on his load at the Olin Chlor-Alkali plant in McIntosh, Alabama. He should have been home hours ago but he couldn't complain. There was no such thing as overtime pay in the trucking business, but Olin did pay their independent drivers for wait time. Detention pay was not typical but it was one of the perks Big John negotiated with Olin. At this hour, traffic was light, and he was making up time.

The Olin plant in Charleston, Tennessee was only twenty minutes from their home in Etowah. His wife of forty-two years, Patty worked for the McMinn County Clerk's Office and their four kids moved away to big cities like Atlanta and Memphis. It was just the two of them now and Big John was eyeing retirement. He still loved to drive but late Saturday nights like this one was not what he had in mind.

He checked his mirrors constantly, out of habit. His eyes were always roving the road — seemingly everywhere at once. Big John was a safe driver with a nearly impeccable driver safety record. Of course, one misjudgment and he may take out a fender in a parking lot or wipe out the fuel pumps at a local truck stop.

"I'll be comin' up on the state line shortly baby and then straight into Charleston. Dem boys know I'ma comin' and I can drop this tanker real quick like. I'm powerful hungry!" After he passed through the small town of Crandall, the diesel engine whined as he upshifts, working through gear after gear. It takes only a short while to get the rig up to speed. Chlorine gas is only slightly heavier than air. Large tanker trucks carrying gasoline or other liquefied loads can reach ninety thousand pounds when fully loaded. This load was light by comparison, an easy haul for his older M11 400E Cummins Diesel.

Crossing Sumac Creek, he notices the fog settling in for the evening. Then he noticed the time — 9:05 p.m. It was time for the David Webb show. "Now sugar, I've got to get down to bidness here. Let me roll on and I'll call ya when I leave da Charleston Plant. I love ya'."

Big John always told his wife he loved her when they hung up — because he did.

*****

9:03 p.m.
Amtrak/CSX Rail Southbound
Near Tennga, Georgia

The word *Tampa* means *sticks of fire* in the native language of the Calusa Indians who inhabited the area surrounding Tampa Bay in the sixteenth century. The term *sticks of fire* may have referred to the many intense lightning strikes the area received during the summer storms.

Railroad magnate Henry B. Plant brought his South Florida Railroad to Tampa in the late nineteenth century thereby connecting the region to industry and commerce via the nation's railway system. The new railroad link enabled another important industry to enter the Tampa market—cigars. Once the railway link was completed, Vicente Ybor moved his cigar manufacturing operations to Tampa from Key

West. Tampa's close proximity to Cuba made the import of the choice tobacco from Havana easy by ship, and the newly created railroad link allowed shipment of the finished cigars to the rest of the United States.

As a result, Tampa became known nationwide for another *stick of fire* — the cigar. As the cigar industry flourished, so did Tampa and its pristine white sand beaches which became a magnet for visitors. The tourists became accustomed to the surroundings and made the annual trek for their vacations from Midwestern states like Ohio, Illinois and Indiana. As the vacationers reached retirement age, Tampa Bay became a logical location to ride out the winter months in the warm Florida sunshine.

In an effort to boost its profits as government funding of its rail operations began to dwindle, Amtrak partnered with CSX, the largest railroad in the eastern United States, to share the CSX railway system. Amtrak created pleasure routes between major population centers and tourist destinations. The partnership allowed CSX to maximize the use of its railway system between Tampa and the Midwest. CSX already operated the *Juice Train*, the collective name for Tropicana's freight cars that carry fresh juice between Bradenton, just outside of Tampa, northbound to Cincinnati. The Amtrak partnership allowed for the rails to be utilized on the weekends.

For its passenger train accommodations, Amtrak created the *Sticks of Fire Express*. It's nine hundred miles from Cincinnati to Tampa. The *Sticks of Fire Express* leaves Cincinnati on Saturday afternoon and arrives in Tampa on Sunday morning. Like a cruise ship, the train travels primarily at night. The journey on the *Sticks of Fire Express* travels through the heart of America, passing through Lexington, Knoxville, Atlanta and Tallahassee. Passengers enjoy spacious two-level accommodations with private bathrooms and a variety of dining options, including the Cross Country Café which could be reserved for private parties.

When Dominic Ciocia planned his wedding with bride-to-be Melissa, he wanted to create a lifelong memory for his bride, their families, and friends. After the tragic death of his parents in a plane crash, Dom's life revolved around Melissa and his new extended family. He was left a substantial inheritance which allowed him to bury his sorrows amidst the wedding arrangements and plans for a new life. His parents, seasoned travelers, would have approved of this unique wedding and honeymoon.

They would not have approved of the Saturday night bachelor's party. A devout Catholic, Dom and Melissa vowed to remain chaste until after their wedding. He loved her and did not want to disrespect her in any way. When his buddies concocted the bachelor's party during the southbound trip to Tampa, he objected. Melissa, the trusting fiancé, encouraged him to enjoy the moment. Her girlfriends planned a bridal soiree of their own in the lounge car. While Melissa played traditional bridal shower games like *twenty questions* and *what's in the bag*, Dom's *boys* enjoyed too many drinks while discussing sexual conquests that probably never happened.

Through the glass doors connecting Melissa's lounge car with the Cross Country Café, Dom thought about spending the rest of his life with his beautiful girl. Thoughts of babies, and growing old together filled his mind. He resisted the sudden urge to ditch the guys and run to her.

He let out a sigh. *Weddings and parties are for the guests more than the betrothed.*

*****

9:09 p.m.
U.S. Route 411 Northbound
Near Tennga, Georgia

"We have just gone through an evolution in American history. This summer has revealed a nation that has lost touch with itself. Too many Americans are letting themselves be led by the headlines and far-reaching goals of the presidential candidates on both sides while ignoring the realistic challenges our nation faces."

Big John admired David Webb. Fellow conservative black men were few and far between. When Big John first became involved in the tea party movement in 2009, Webb caught his ear with a fiery speech challenging blacks in America to step out of their stereotype and consider what is best for their families. Webb, like Big John, believed the Democrat Party took the black vote for granted and ignored the underlying issue of concern to all Americans — economic stability. When Big John drove at night, AM talk radio and David Webb were always welcome travel companions.

The road was deserted in rural north Georgia which provided a quiet trip to the house. With the cruise control set at a steady fifty-mile per hour speed, Big John rolled along through the swirling mist of fog which hung over Perry Creek as it hugged the highway. He turned off the CB radio. *No bears out this late at night. Even the local yokels will be tucked in already.*

"As citizens, we have many civic duties, not just at election time. We need to be cognizant of our relationship with our fellow Americans. To those who continue to play the race card, know this. I am a black man. I am a Republican. I am an American. I speak from experience. Our culture — the American way of life, is under attack from within. The breakdown of our culture can only benefit those who wish to fundamentally transform America. This failure of leadership can be seen at the local level, all the way up to the White House. It is time for all of us, black and white, to rise up and reject the unlawful behavior and dis—"

Static filled the radio. Big John looked down and adjusted the tuner on the radio. Nothing. He scrolled through the AM stations and found static everywhere. *Did I lose the antenna?* He switched to the FM band. *All static.*

His cell phone was ringing. Big John abandoned the radio and reached for the phone which promptly fell beneath the bucket seats of the Peterbilt. He stretched his arm and fumbled around in the darkness, searching for the phone. For a moment, he took his eyes off U.S. 411. *Just for a moment.*

*****

9:11 p.m.
Amtrak/CSX Rail Southbound
Near Tennga, Georgia

Dom's friends ushered him into a chair in the middle of the Cross Country Café. Shouts of *drink, drink, drink* filled the air as shots of tequila were passed around. Dom downed the obligatory shot, his fourth, and was starting to unwind a little. The guys started staccato clapping as they ushered in a scantily clad girl wearing a sexy train conductor's outfit.

This is just great. A stripper. While his thoughts of Melissa were still there, he decided to enjoy the festivities. This was, after all, his last night as a *free man. I'll do it so the guys will get a laugh.*

"I'm here to punch your ticket sir," she said. "May I check your pockets?" Dom smiled a little as the fairly attractive girl began to run her hands inside his pants pockets.

As she reached to feel his right pocket, she groped his crotch and exclaimed "What do we have here?" This brought a roar of laughter from the guys. As the girl straddled Dom, her tuxedo style jacket popped open revealing ample breasts. *Okay, this is too much.*

Dom tried to gently push her away but accidentally grabbed the girl's breasts instead. Amidst the sound of laughter, and without warning, the lights went out in the train. Everyone was quiet for a moment and then they erupted with hoots and hollers. One of the guys had flipped off the light switch.

Now we can really party.

Do her Dom!

If you won't I will.

The massive two hundred ton diesel locomotive which powered the sixteen car passenger train maintained a steady speed of roughly fifty miles per hour. As the engineer approached the ground rail crossing just south of Tennga, Georgia, he briefly blew the train's whistle at one thousand feet and issued a longer warning at six hundred feet. The trainmen slowed the speed as the *Sticks of Fire Express* approached the crossing of U.S. 411. They noticed in disbelief that the traffic signals and controls for the highway grade crossing were not working.

Because the lights were off in the Cross Country Café, Dom had clear visibility through the tall Georgia pines of the approaching truck headlights approaching the train. They were growing larger as their illumination focused on the lounge car in front of him—the car carrying his Melissa.

*****

9:13 p.m.
Brush Town Road
Cisco, Georgia

Kayla Gold lived in a mobile home on Brush Town Road in the small, close-knit community of Cisco, Georgia. This is the kind of town where everyone knows everyone's business. In a rural community, the sound of trains and highway traffic are commonplace. An explosion is not. She remembered when a methamphetamine lab exploded over on Halls Chapel road. That was a mile away and it nearly shook her trailer off its blocks.

This was different. Just a few minutes before, she was watching television when the power went off after she heard an explosion in the distance. The sound resembled the meth house destruction.

However, a minute later, a second massive blast shook her trailer violently. She immediately looked out of her windows and saw the ball of fire in the sky near the highway. The next — and last—thing she saw was a locomotive sliding on its side along the railroad embankment towards her.

*****

Experts say chlorine gas is arguably the most essential chemical in use. It's produced in large volumes because it is easily combined with other elements and synthesized into plastics, drugs, microchips and other products.

However, chlorine gas is particularly insidious. Small exposures can trigger coughing, choking and burning eyes. Inhaling large amounts constricts the airways by inflaming the lining of the throat and airways. During the ingestion of the gas, fluid accumulates in the lungs, making it doubly hard to breathe. People drown in their own body fluids. At even higher exposures, a few deep breaths can be instantly lethal.

Myrna Navarro, who lived across the way from Kayla Gold, watched the derailed locomotive destroy Kayla's trailer as it careened down the embankment. She immediately crossed herself in a silent prayer for Kayla and to thank God for sparing the Navarro family from the catastrophe.

In the darkness, Myrna couldn't see the giant, greenish-yellow cloud of chlorine gas which filled the air. At first she began to gasp for air. *I can't breathe. I'm being strangled.* Her children came on the front porch to see what happened. She desperately motioned to them to go back inside. *Run. Run. Cover your faces!*

Death came too soon for Myrna Navarro and her family. It was just beginning.

PART ONE

Night of Terror

CHAPTER 1

Saturday, September 3, 2016
9:10 p.m.
73 Tremont
Boston, Massachusetts

"Malcolm, call it off! Call them now," screamed John Morgan, showing sheer panic for the first time in his life. Morgan was a man who insisted upon perfection. His life was full of calculated decisions, comprehensive planning, and flawless implementation. *How could I miss this? How could I overlook the safety of my precious daughter, my only family, my legacy?*

Malcolm Lowe, Morgan's longtime assistant, fumbled through his pockets, clearly overcome with nervousness. Morgan yanked the receiver off his desk phone and hit speed dial in an attempt to call Abigail.

It repeatedly rang—no answer. "Where is she, Malcolm?"

"She's giving a speech in downtown Tallahassee somewhere."

Morgan reset the phone and hit the speed-dial button of Abigail's chief of staff, Rhona Jacobs. After several rings, Morgan heard the sound of applause and the faint voice of Jacobs answering *hello*.

And then the line was dead. The lights went out. Darkness descended over the city of Boston and much of America. It was 9:11, *by design*.

CHAPTER 2

September 3, 2016
9:10 p.m.
Tucker Civic Center
Downtown Tallahassee, Florida

Freshman Senator Abigail Morgan from Massachusetts was fulfilling her role as vice presidential nominee on the *Hillary Clinton for President* ticket admirably. The choice of a running mate was a shady, backroom process that rarely saw the light of day. Abbie's fate was sealed during just such a meeting between her father and former President of the United States Bill Clinton. The agreement between the men was the result of blackmail as much as political expediency.

As Abbie began to perform on the campaign trail, the Democratic presidential nominee was given full credit for making the first great decision of her possible presidency. In short, Abbie was a tremendous benefit and provided a much-needed boost to a floundering campaign. Abbie's libertarian-leaning politics coupled with her spotless report card following a rigorous vetting process allowed her to avoid the rancor and negativity that had surrounded American campaigns in the last several decades. The Clinton-Morgan combination became known as the best-rounded political ticket in several presidential campaign cycles and appealed to those four to six percent of the undecided electorate who determined close elections.

As a result, Abbie became the campaign workhorse. Her carefully choreographed schedule typically involved a breakfast meet-and-greet, followed by a day of campaign activities that traversed several cities or states. This evening was an exception to the rule. Abbie had been scheduled to take the campaign plane back to Boston earlier that afternoon, but a late invitation from musician Jimmy Buffett to say a few words at his sold-out concert in the Tucker Civic Center was an extraordinary opportunity to reach out to a cross-section of Florida voters.

Buffett, an avowed liberal who embraced many environmental issues, was a vocal supporter of Mrs. Clinton's campaign. He offered Abbie the opportunity to share the stage in front of over twelve thousand fans. Following her attendance at a fund-raising dinner hosted by retiring Senator Bill Nelson, Abbie was taken to the Tucker Center by her security detail led by the ever-present Drew Jackson.

Drew, a former Navy SEAL and a member of Steven Sargent's Aegis Team, had become more than a valuable member of Abbie's security team. The two had grown fond of each other, and there was clearly an attraction between them. In public, Abbie and Drew were able to maintain proper boundaries and an appearance of professionalism. In private moments, which were rare, their conversations always turned to more opportunities to steal away and avoid the madness of the campaign trail.

Drew stood toward the back of the stage just to the side of the massive speakers that accompanied the Buffett concert road show. A wall of over one hundred flat-screens provided a larger-than-life image of Abbie as she addressed the concert fans.

"Thank you for that warm welcome, parrot heads!" said Abbie into the microphone, her voice booming through the concert hall. The margarita and marijuana-infused fans responded raucously to the parrot head reference—the nickname of Jimmy Buffett fans since his rise to popularity in the seventies. Drew doubted any of these potential voters would remember Abbie's speech tonight, but he was sure the positive media associated with sharing the stage with the barefoot troubadour who hailed from Key West would be a political coup.

Drew's mind wandered somewhat as Abbie continued her stump speech designed to attract Florida voters.

"As an independent, I opposed the recent legislation proposed by Republicans attempting to prohibit online gambling. I believe this would pave the way for more government control over the Internet," said Abbie. "Moreover, such a bill is an inappropriate and unnecessary use of federal powers that infringes upon the rights of individuals and the states. This ban, if approved by Congress, will push gambling back into the black market, where crime can flourish with no protection for our citizens from predatory behavior."

Drew moved swiftly to knock away a beach ball swatted toward the stage. His actions received cheers and jeers from some of the parrot heads. One young woman toward the side of the stage where Drew was posted flashed her breasts at him. Drew instantly looked away. *They're out of control.*

"I believe states have the right to govern their citizenry. We wholeheartedly support the right of Floridians to legalize and regulate online gambling as well as gaming casinos within their state."

Toward the front of the stage, some pushing and shoving occurred as one concertgoer spilled a drink on another one. The civic center was full of marijuana smoke, and Drew wondered if anyone attending was unimpaired.

Throughout the campaign, Drew overheard conversations between Abbie and her campaign team. As the de facto head of her U.S. Secret Service team, he was privy to confidential conversations about their strategy. Following the policies of the dedicated members of the USSS, Drew never spoke a word of these details. He did know Florida Democrats were very pleased with their success in getting two liberal-friendly initiatives on the November ballot—legalized gambling and marijuana. It would boost their voter turnout.

Abbie continued. "Major newspapers in Florida have issued editorials recently calling for an end to marijuana prohibition. As a libertarian, I have held that position for decades!"

The crowd roared its approval. Drew thought the roof was going to blow off the building. Buffett, clearly enjoying the moment, approached the front of the stage and whipped the parrot head faithful into a feeding frenzy. Holding his right hand to his head emulating a shark fin, Buffett swayed back and forth as Abbie spoke. His fans responded and pressed closer to the stage, tipping over the metal barriers that were designed to create a protective buffer.

Instinctively, Drew stepped towards Abbie. He was never comfortable with this evening's campaign appearance. The secret service team had no time to evaluate the venue and prepare appropriate contingency plans. Abbie was not a rock star. She was going to be the next vice president of the United States and had no business sharing a stage with this circus act.

Abbie paused, waiting for the noise inside the arena to subside. The roar of the adoring crowd was so overwhelming that no one heard the sound of the transformer exploding outside the front entrance at the Donald L. Tucker Civic Center, which was simultaneously thrust into darkness.

CHAPTER 3

September 3, 2016
9:12 p.m.
73 Tremont
Boston, Massachusetts

"Sir, I was not able—" started Lowe before Morgan shouted him down.

"Obviously, Malcolm! Get the pilot ready. We're going to Florida."

"Sir, I believe the planes will be grounded under the circumstances."

Morgan was fuming. He was angry that his carefully orchestrated plans were out of control—placing Abigail in grave danger. He was also annoyed with Lowe because he stated the obvious when the situation called for inventive solutions. Morgan threw the phone at the fireplace.

"Dammit, Malcolm, I know that! Get the Sikorsky ready. Call the pilot now!"

Morgan stared out onto Boston Common. This complication was not what he envisioned. The darkness was expected, but the fact that Abigail was not within his protective grasp was unforeseen. This event—*the reset*—was carefully planned and would achieve the desired result. *History will prove it was necessary.*

I can fix this. There is nothing that time and money can't solve.

"Sir," interrupted Lowe, "the pilot has concerns."

Uncharacteristically, Morgan exploded and cursed. "I don't give a crap about his concerns. Give me the phone!" Morgan walked to the window and pushed against the cold glass with his left hand. His

16

palms were sweaty, and he was feeling some pressure in his chest. He calmed himself as he addressed the helicopter pilot.

"We are going to Florida now. What is the closest military installation to Tallahassee?" Morgan listened to his pilot. He shook his head. "The power is irrelevant—we're going anyway! What are our options?" Morgan rubbed his face and began to flex his left arm that was stiffening slightly.

"Not Eglin—too much activity. Camp Blanding will be better. It's smaller, less conspicuous. I'll make the arrangements. We're on our way to Norwood. Hurry!"

Morgan handed Lowe the cell phone. He closed his eyes and rubbed both temples. *This isn't happening. I don't need this right now.* Sirens from first-responder vehicles could be heard through the darkness. *There isn't much time.*

"Malcolm, get Jacobs on the phone." Lowe dialed and handed the phone to Morgan.

"Hello," said Jacobs, who was on speaker. The roar of the voices was deafening.

"This is John Morgan. Listen to me very carefully."

"Sir, the power just went out in the arena. May I call you back in a moment?"

"No, Jacobs! Listen to me. Tell Abigail to meet me at Camp Blanding in the morning. Do you understand me?"

"Sir, yes, of course. But we have the plane ready to return her to Boston. May I call you back?"

"Dammit, Jacobs! Pay attention! Tell Abigail to be at Camp Blanding tomorrow morning. I will pick her up. Understood?"

"Yes, sir. But why?"

"No questions, Jacobs! Tell her now!" Then the line went dead. He saw he still had a signal as he handed the phone to Lowe. The cell phones wouldn't last much longer. The battery backups installed on most cell towers would only last a few hours under normal circumstances. Morgan suspected much of America would be lighting up the cell phone lines over the next several minutes. He knew the increased activity would drain the woefully fragile wireless communications network rapidly.

"I have the team ready to escort you to the heliport, sir," said Lowe. "Am I going with you to Florida?" It was normally a thirty-minute drive to the Norwood Airport, where his Sikorsky S76 helicopter was kept. Tonight, the travel time could be complicated by *circumstances*. Morgan calmed down and regained his composure.

"I need you to ride with me to Norwood," replied Morgan. "There are arrangements to be made. Get the satellite phone and the briefcase out of the safe. Let's go!"

CHAPTER 4

September 3, 2016
9:12 p.m.
Tucker Civic Center
Downtown Tallahassee, Florida

For a brief moment, Abbie felt like she was having an out-of-body experience. The noise was deafening, with no single voice discernible in the arena. One moment the crowd was cheering—swaying back and forth with their favorite singer. The next moment, there was darkness, except for the faint glow of EXIT signs and emergency lighting inside the arena's concourse. The lights brightened and darkened through the haze of smoke that filled the building.

Over a span of thirty seconds, the sights and sounds of cell phones coming to life calmed the throng. Text messages were received and sent. Cell phone calls were answered and placed. In this interconnected world, the twelve thousand plus flock of parrot heads quickly became a panicked mob.

"We've been attacked!"

"Terrorists!"

"The lights are out everywhere!"

"Get out, it must have been a bomb!"

The voices rang through Abbie's head. The crowded arena, overfilled beyond its capacity, became a Jiffy Pop popcorn popper on a hot stove. When it exploded, the mass of people crushed each other and their beloved leader of the parrot heads as they fought their way towards the exits. It was Drew's firm grasp of her arm and authoritative voice that brought Abbie back to reality.

19

"Abbie, Abbie! We have to go now!" shouted Drew through the pandemonium. Into his communications microphone, he was shouting, "Extract! Extract!"

Snapping back to life, Abbie asked, "Drew, what's happened?" She was now surrounded by two more members of her secret service team as several people climbed the stage towards her.

"Stop them!" shouted Drew, motioning to his associates to intervene. He wrapped his arm around Abbie and pulled her towards the hallway at the rear of the stage where her chief of staff was waiting.

"Abbie," started Jacobs, "we've got to get you to the buses. Something major has happened." Abbie, still disheveled, followed Jacobs through the makeshift hallway into the bowels of the Tucker Civic Center. As they entered the concourse, away from the throngs above, Abbie stopped abruptly.

"Rhona, tell me what's going on!" Two more secret service personnel joined the group. Together with Drew, they formed a semicircle protecting the women.

"Information is spotty, Abbie, but it appears the country has been attacked in some way," replied Jacobs. "The power is out across the nation."

"What? The entire grid?"

"I don't know for certain. My cell phone loses its signal and then it will reappear. When I dial out, I hear *all circuits are busy.* I've only been able to receive a couple of phone calls. Most of my information has come via text message."

Suddenly, the smell of mace filled the air as one of the local police used pepper spray to prevent a mass of panicked attendees from entering the hallway.

"We have to go now!" shouted Drew. He pulled Abbie towards him, and they ran through the darkened hallway towards the service entrance on the south side of the complex. As they burst through the fire escape doors, fresh but humid air filled her lungs. Under the circumstances, this was a welcome change from the marijuana smoke that filled the auditorium. *Why do I want to legalize marijuana?* The thought, or the smoke inhalation itself, relieved some of the tension for Abbie.

As they hustled around a large, now deceased, heating and cooling unit, the screams and shouts of Floridians filled the air. Florida Highway Patrol officers were still manning their posts, maintaining security barricades that blocked the parking lot from vehicles trying to enter from West Madison Street. But there were hundreds of people running in all directions in a panic. All were attempting to use their cell phones, but with little success.

Drew pulled Jacobs aside, and the two shared a rushed conversation. All Abbie heard was Drew asking *are you sure*. When they were finished, he motioned for two agents to join them. Abbie, managing to retain her self-control, approached the group.

"What are we going to do?"

"Plans have changed, of course," replied Drew. Abbie admired his restraint. Over the last two months, Drew confided in Abbie about his career as a Navy SEAL, his duties for Blackwater, and then his work with Steven at Aegis. Eventually, he told her some of the details of the Aegis team's activities in the spring that prompted his request for reassignment. Abbie was certain Drew could be trusted if her father had handpicked him for the security detail. Now, looking into his eyes, not only was she comforted, she no longer felt *alone*.

Drew continued. "Rhona received a call from your father. Before the line went dead, he instructed her to evacuate you to a Florida National Guard facility east of here. He will meet us there in the morning."

"Why don't we take the plane? How is he getting here?" Abbie's mind was racing.

"Abbie, the planes are likely grounded due to the power outage. I suspect your father is bringing his helicopter."

Daddy to the rescue. Abbie didn't resent her father. Of course, she loved him. He provided her everything she needed. He always encouraged her throughout her school years and as she pursued her career. When she moved towards a life in politics, he guaranteed her success.

As Abbie grew older, she learned that her father was adept at manipulation. While he didn't treat her as he would an employee per se, she always understood that John Adams Morgan had a plan for his only child—the daughter he wished was a son. With Drew, she now had two influential men in her life, and she was certain both of them loved her.

"Okay, Mr. Secret Agent Man," said Abbie, breaking the tension. With her unexpected lighthearted tone, Drew seemed to relax as well. "Lead the way."

Drew smiled at her and began to reach for her face, but the shouts from a member of his team stopped him.

"The troopers are telling us to leave. They're losing control of the crowd," said one of the men. Drew took charge.

"Listen up, everybody. We'll never get the bus out of here. I need you to grab essential gear from the buses and stow it in the back of the two Suburbans. Ladies, I need you to change out of your Sunday best and put on something comfortable, like you're going for a jog. We only have a few minutes so chop-chop." Drew gently urged Abbie and Jacobs toward their bus.

"You've got this," said Abbie, making a statement more than a question.

"Nothing will happen to you on my watch, Senator, ever," replied Drew as he started walking towards the Florida Highway Patrol detail. He added, "Wear dark clothes, Abbie, and your best running shoes. We need to be prepared for all contingencies."

Abbie absorbed his words for a moment. *He suspects trouble.* Then, she repeated her words—*you've got this.*

CHAPTER 5

September 3, 2016
9:34 p.m.
I-95 / Southeast Expressway
Neponset, Massachusetts

Morgan was morose as the car took him through his beloved Boston. During the many months of planning, he often wondered if there would be regrets. His sour mood had nothing to do with his decision to conspire with the President. In fact, he relished the opportunity to recreate America in the vision of his ancestor—John Adams. The Founding Fathers would never recognize this America. Not because of its technological advances, but because of its attitude toward life and the freedoms its people were given. The efforts of the early colonists to break away from tyranny had long been forgotten—or taken for granted. History taught in elementary schools focused more on the perceived wrongs done to the Indians than the great things that followed the rise of the original Loyal Nine.

Morgan's brooding came from his failing of Abigail. Through all of his machinations, he'd failed to protect his beloved daughter. *Am I that inattentive as a father?*

"Sir, I have received some details from the pilot," said Lowe, breaking the silence. As the car passed Port Norfolk, a massive explosion on the west side of the expressway caught their attention. Flames rose into the sky towards Dorchester. The driver slowed as the cars ahead began to rubberneck the carnage. Morgan pressed the intercom button.

"Why are we slowing down?"

"There's a traffic jam at the Granite Avenue intersection, sir," replied the driver. "I don't see a way around it."

"Use the shoulder," instructed Morgan. "If anybody attempts to stop you, have your associate deal with it." Both Morgan's driver and his partner were trained members of the Aegis team. Use of force upon Morgan's direction was expected and never questioned. Morgan turned his attention back to Lowe.

"What did the pilot say?"

"The fuel range is the biggest issue, sir," replied Lowe. "The Sikorsky has a normal range of just over five hundred miles based upon its full capacity of thirteen passengers and the single pilot. Norwood to Camp Blanding in Starke, Florida, is about twelve hundred miles."

"So we need to stop twice?"

"No, sir, not necessarily. The pilot has calculated the fuel range with only you and another passenger to be six hundred miles. Reducing the passenger count will allow you to stop one time."

"Where does he suggest?"

"Seymour Johnson Air Force Base, southeast of Raleigh, sir," replied Lowe.

As the driver navigated around the Pilgrims Highway interchange, a man startled Morgan by slapping his hands on the window.

"Hey, rich guy! Give me a ride. I'm outta gas!" Two others joined him in trying to stop Morgan's car from continuing. One of the men attempted to open the door and then angrily pounded the glass with the back of his fist. "C'mon, dude, I know you've got room. Give us a ride!" Morgan rolled down the privacy glass to get a better view of the road ahead. Two of the men ran in front of the car and held their hands up.

"Move them out of the way!" shouted Morgan. "Do whatever it takes!"

The driver was inching toward the men, who stood their ground. "Hold on," he advised his passengers as he launched the SUV towards the men. Although momentarily frightened, the two men counted on the driver's restraint and reluctance to strike them.

They were wrong. The driver lurched again, this time hitting one of the men just above the knees, causing him to fall backward. As he screamed in pain, the other man started pointing his fingers at Morgan's driver.

"Hey, you can't do that! We'll sue you for all you're worth!"

Morgan's driver hit the gas pedal again, causing the potential litigant to land on the hood. Seeing the opportunity for a clear path, he pressed the gas in earnest, causing the plaintiff to roll off the hood onto the concrete pavement while the legs of his co-plaintiff were run over by Morgan's custom-made Cadillac Escalade.

Traffic was moving again, and the car made its way east toward the Norwood Memorial Airport. Morgan breathed in deeply as he thumbed through a black address book retrieved from his safe. The next call was going to be one of the most important in his life.

CHAPTER 6

September 3, 2016
9:49 p.m.
Norwood Memorial Airport
Norwood, Massachusetts

Richard Sears was an early settler of the Massachusetts Bay Colony in the seventeenth century. His descendants populated the original Plymouth colony and branched out across America as philanthropists, business owners, and politicians. The Sears family had an impact on not only the original British Colonies but the United States and the world. Today, over twenty thousand people could trace their lineage back to Richard Sears.

One of those descendants was General Mason J. Sears, USMC, and the current Chairman of the Joint Chiefs of Staff. Born and raised in Quincy, Massachusetts, General Sears graduated from Boston College in 1977 and immediately earned his commission. He furthered his military career by graduating from the United States Army War College, Ranger School, and then the Amphibious Warfare School. By holding a master's degree in government from Georgetown and a second master of arts in international law from the Harvard Kennedy School, Sears was one of the most educated generals in the history of the U.S. Armed Forces.

General Sears earned the respect of his fellow Marines when he led the initial attack into Iraq and on to Baghdad during the first Gulf War in 1991. As a result of his service, and with the help of some strongly worded recommendations, General Sears rapidly shot up the chain of command faster than almost anyone in recent Marine Corps history. He was considered a war-wise general by his peers. In his capacity as chairman of the Joint Chiefs, by law, he was the highest-ranking military officer in the United States Armed Forces and was the principal military advisor to the President. General Sears was also beholden to John Morgan.

"General, this is John Morgan."

"Yes, John. I hope all is well. I wasn't expecting your call—*yet*."

"Mason, I have a situation that will require your assistance."

"How can I help?" asked General Sears.

"I am en route to Florida via my helicopter. Mason, my daughter is stranded in Tallahassee. I've sent word for her to meet me at the nearest military facility. I need you to arrange the necessary clearances for us to get refueled."

"Okay," said General Sears. "Tell me what you need, John."

"We will stop midway at Seymour Johnson, both coming and going. I will pick Abigail up at Camp Blanding, now used by the Florida National Guard."

"I know it well. Very historic facility. I'll make the arrangements for you, John. What else?"

Morgan hesitated before he spoke. Agreements had already been reached, but reiteration never hurt. "Have you heard from the President?" asked Morgan.

"Only briefly," replied General Sears. "As you probably are aware, the President has been in Hawaii for several days. We've discussed the situation, and I've made several calls to the Joint Chiefs in this very short period."

"Go on."

"We've elevated our readiness level to DEFCON 2. This level of readiness hasn't been invoked since the first Gulf War as part of the opening phase of Operation Desert Storm. The only other time before that was during the Cuban Missile Crisis in '62."

"Mason, based upon your intelligence, is there a reason to believe we might fall under attack from Russia, China, or others?" asked Morgan.

"No, not at all. Other than the Russians testing our fences from time to time, our adversaries have been noticeably quiet. It seems the entire world is trying to determine the cause and extent of this outage. With no actionable intelligence that a nuclear-delivered EMP caused the grid-down scenario, I suggested to the President DEFCON 3 was more appropriate. Although the Department of Defense maintains a public posture of normal readiness—*fade out*, as they prefer to say—our forces are prepared to operate at DEFCON 4 at all times. The entire military is maintaining above-normal readiness as a matter of protocol."

"Did the President provide a rationale for the special declaration of DEFCON 2 status?" asked Morgan. Morgan had his suspicions. *The President is getting ahead of himself. Why?*

"He did not, but he is my Commander-in-Chief. I will tell you that the Secretary of Defense disagreed with the status as well. But we're both good soldiers, John. You know that."

"I do, Mason, which brings me to my point. Civilian communications networks are already failing. Our only means of contact will be through the use of my satellite phone. I will be available to you twenty-four seven during this crisis. I expect to hear from you daily or when something of importance arises. Are we clear?"

"Of course, John," replied General Sears. Morgan detected a sharp tone in the general's response.

"Mason, I am very concerned about my daughter's welfare. I have no means of contacting her. I will be less surly when she is safe with me."

"John, I completely understand. My sons are both stationed abroad. We may be calling back our forces to protect American soil. These next few days will be stressful for us all."

"Yes, they will," said Morgan. Lowe exited the car to approach the pilot who was standing ready. Morgan forced himself to relax. "Mason, the next several weeks will determine whether we can make this country great again. It is my hope that the President will share our vision. If not, well, you and I have discussed this ad nauseam. Thank you for your help, and keep me informed."

"Absolutely, John. My aide will generate the necessary clearances for your trip. Now go get your daughter."

CHAPTER 7

September 3, 2016
9:49 p.m.
Tucker Civic Center
Downtown Tallahassee, Florida

"Saddle up, troops," barked Drew as he threw his gear in the backseat of the Suburban. Under standard protocol, the local law enforcement personnel provided the motorcade an escort. Typically, while in Florida, one highway patrol vehicle would travel several minutes ahead of the campaign convoy to assess any potential threats or traffic issues that would delay the vehicles from point to point. Under normal conditions, the motorcade would consist of a lead trooper, followed by a Secret Service Chevrolet Suburban from the local fleet, the two campaign buses and finally the USSS Electronic Countermeasures Suburban—the ECS.

Once only used for the President's travels, the ECS trailed the vice presidential vehicle and was used to counter attacks such as rocket-propelled grenades, vehicle-borne improvised explosive devices, and antitank guided missiles. Under the circumstances, the usual complement of Secret Service personnel and vehicles was unavailable. Drew had to make it work.

"Ripley, you're familiar with Florida more than the rest of us, so you'll lead the way with Miss Jacobs and your partner," said Drew. "Captain will ride with us. Cell phone connections seem to be unreliable and intermittent at best. We still have our two-way comms. Let's use them sporadically to conserve battery power. Everybody clear?"

"Yes, sir."

Drew opened the back door of the SUV on the passenger side for Abbie. She was outfitted in a black velour tracksuit with a silver *J* dangling from its zipper.

"You know I hate that codename," said Abbie, stopping Drew from rushing her into the back of the truck.

"What? Captain?" asked Drew.

"Yes. Come on. Captain Morgan? Give me a break. Shall I strike a pose with one leg up on a rum barrel?"

"It could be worse, *Captain*," said Drew sarcastically. "You know what the guys call your running mate?"

"What?"

"Hilla the Hun." Drew laughed.

Abbie stifled a laugh.

"What's the *J* stand for?" asked Drew, still obsessed with the dangling silver *J*.

"Juicy Couture," replied Abbie with a smile.

"Of course it does," said Drew. "I hope you can run in *couture* in the event we have to hoof it."

"Hilarious. I expect you to carry me, soldier."

"Yeah, right." Drew laughed. "Buckle up. This could get interesting."

CHAPTER 8

September 3, 2016
9:53 p.m.
Downtown Tallahassee, Florida

"Ripley, the troopers have suggested we alter our course," barked Drew into his agency-issued Motorola XTS radio. He was frustrated. On a separate channel, Drew was advised the preferred routes leaving downtown Tallahassee were blocked with pedestrians and traffic. The planned route out of the city was to turn left out of the south parking lot of the Tucker Center and head towards the Florida State Capitol. From there, the caravan would travel northeast on Thomasville Road towards Interstate 10, where they would have a direct route to the east for over one hundred miles. They were now at a standstill in front of the Capitol grounds—after only four blocks. It was obvious to Drew the situation was deteriorating rapidly.

"Which way should we go?" asked Abbie from the backseat. Drew looked left and right before answering.

"We should defer to the locals," said Drew. "But we are stuck like chuck. The Florida State football game was moved from Orlando to Doak Campbell Stadium just to the west of us due to the oncoming hurricane. Everyone is leaving for the suburbs to the northeast, according to the trooper. They need us to change course."

Drew fumbled with the onboard GPS and punched in Exit 199 on Interstate 10. The route appeared on the display. He suggested the change to the highway patrol.

"Ripley, you copy?"

"Go ahead."

"Follow the trooper," said Drew. "GPS is Exit 199. We've lost the front vehicle—" Suddenly a beer bottle crashed against the windshield of their truck, followed by a chorus of angry shouts.

"Hey, fat-cat politicians!"

"Give us a ride!"

"When are you gonna fix the power?"

Drew instinctively reached for his weapon but composed himself before issuing instructions. "Trooper Walker, we need to move now. Go! Go! Go!"

"Ripley," Drew continued his instructions, "we have an angry mob surrounding us. Let's roll!"

The buzz of spinning tires on the rain-soaked pavement filled the air as the trooper quickly turned left on Pensacola Street and back towards the Tucker Center.

"We're going back?" asked Abbie, now sitting on the edge of the bench seat.

"This isn't safe, and the northeast route of the city is at a standstill," replied Drew. "We're going to backtrack slightly to access the interstate. Between the event and the football game, there are nearly one hundred thousand people within a mile of us."

The three-vehicle caravan pushed its way west to Martin Luther King Jr. Boulevard and then turned north at the FSU College of Law.

"This is madness!" exclaimed Abbie. Drew couldn't disagree. Traffic was at a crawl and pedestrian traffic was shoulder to shoulder. Abbie was clicking the keypad of her phone.

"Abbie, our first goal is to extract you from danger," started Drew. "Then we need to gather information so we can better assess the situation. Listen, seat belts, please." Abbie clicked her belt and adjusted it for comfort. She held her phone up for the guys to see her display.

"Well, I might be able to help there. Rhona sent me a text. She said the hashtags *collapse* and *SHTF* are trending on Twitter. Apparently, with limited cell service, information is still being disseminated."

"Our service-issued phones aren't getting any signal. Do you have any details?" asked Drew.

"It's all based on speculation," replied Abbie. "There are allegations of an attack by Russia. Apparently, the BBC reported an EMP weapon may have been used. You know the media. In their quest to be the first with the *breaking news*, they tend to play loose with the facts." They were approaching a major intersection ahead when the state trooper's vehicle abruptly turned left—followed by Ripley.

"Hold on," shouted Drew. The hefty armor-clad Suburban hustled to catch up with the other two vehicles. Traffic was beginning to decrease as they passed a cemetery. Several people stood on the sidewalks as the motorcade sped past, and watched with amusement as it suddenly skidded to a stop at North Macomb Street.

"What the —!" exclaimed Jonesy before he caught himself and nodded to Abbie. "Excuse me, ma'am."

"Ripley, you guys got this?" asked Drew. Drew listened for a moment and then spoke. "Apparently the major cross street up ahead is blocked. The troopers appear hesitant to cross the road." Drew placed his hand to the earpiece.

"We have the lead highway patrol cruiser back with us," said Drew. "They're going to block westbound traffic and our guy will block the eastbound lanes. We'll shoot the gap." Jonesy held the Suburban back for a moment while the troopers positioned themselves for the maneuver. Horns were blaring, and a crowd was gathering in the Popeyes Chicken parking lot.

As the lead Suburban lurched forward, Ripley shouted, "Green light!" The two-truck train screamed through the gap just as an eastbound pickup truck going the wrong way in the westbound lane rumbled past them and T-boned the highway patrol cruiser. The impact of the collision caused the cruiser to spin four times before knocking down a streetlight.

"Keep going, Ripley," instructed Drew. "Jonesy, we can't help them. This is a doggone disaster!"

"To say the least," added Abbie. "Rhona says the power is out nationwide, according to the BBC. She got connected to Washington, but the signal was lost immediately." Two Tallahassee police cars—

sirens and lights blaring—sped in the opposite direction toward the accident.

"I think we've lost our escort," said Jonesy. "According to GPS, it's only a couple of miles to the 10."

"Pay attention," interrupted Drew. "Ripley said to keep our eyes open. We're in Frenchtown, the most dangerous neighborhood in Tallahassee. Wonderful."

In the nineteenth century, settlers from France moved to the Florida panhandle and settled in this area of Tallahassee. Many moved west to New Orleans or eventually back to France. Because the area was considered flood prone and relatively undesirable, Frenchtown became readily available to newly freed slaves after the Civil War. Today, Tallahassee had one of the highest crime rates in America. The part of Frenchtown from Alabama Street to West Tharpe was once designated a drug-trafficking corridor by the Department of Justice. On an ordinary day, police received an average of twenty reported crimes ranging from auto theft to strong-arm robbery. *Today was no ordinary day.*

The Suburban carrying Drew and Abbie crossed Alabama Street north on Old Bainbridge Road.

"What's happening, Ripley?" asked Drew into the comms. The front vehicle was slowing as hundreds of people were crowded around a building to their right. Drew informed Jonesy and Abbie.

"It's the county health department. Ripley said it's being looted."

"Do we have other options?" asked Jonesy. He looked back and forth across the hood of the truck. "I don't like being on this two-lane road. It's a natural choke point. We're surrounded on both sides by that stone fence. Can we back up?"

Drew turned to survey the options. He studied the GPS display. The side streets looked like a maze with no exit. You could drive on street after street and wind up where you started.

"Ripley, can we pass?" asked Drew. "Traffic is approaching from the south. We need to decide." Lightning filled the sky with momentary light.

"Drew!" shouted Abbie. "To the right. They're coming over the

35

hill straight for us!" Rocks and empty bottles were pelting the vehicles—reminding him of Kandahar City in the southern part of Afghanistan. *At least they're not shooting at us—yet.*

"Reverse, Jonesy!" ordered Drew. "Ripley, this way." The vehicle swerved in reverse to avoid the onslaught of over a dozen young men running towards the Suburban. For nearly two hundred feet, Jonesy adeptly avoided oncoming traffic until he could back into a middle school parking lot. Ripley was not as lucky, as he sideswiped a van, losing his passenger-side mirror.

"Straight ahead, go!" shouted Drew, pointing to the east. The truck vaulted forward across the rapidly approaching traffic. He glanced to the rear and saw the headlights of Ripley's vehicle, which was speeding to catch up.

"Left, now!" The truck once again snapped their heads back as they roared north on Gibbs Drive. Was it less than a mile to the interstate and *safety*? Traffic dissipated and they pulled up to a stop sign.

"Look at the mall," Abbie said, speaking for the first time in several minutes. Staring across U.S. Highway 27, Drew was more concerned with crossing six lanes of traffic than he was observing the mob scene at the Tallahassee Mall. The parking lot was packed with cars and patrons running into the mall empty-handed, but scurrying out with more than they could carry.

"Let the looting begin," said Drew. "But as your running mate's husband would say, you must—*feel their pain.*" Two men ran in front of their bumper with boxes containing laptop computers by Hewlett-Packard, holding them over their heads to protect themselves from the rain.

"I don't think those HPs are going to help them survive this, do you?" asked Jonesy.

"Nope."

"Look at the Cash America store!" exclaimed Abbie, pointing across the highway. A car was trying to drive through the front entrance to break in. Jonesy found an opening in traffic and shot across the median into the northbound lane. Ripley and his passengers were following close behind.

"Good work, Jonesy," said Drew. "I see the interstate up ahead. Looks like traffic is moving. Good news, for a change."

Drew looked on both sides of the highway as they approached the cloverleaf of Interstate 10. People were walking or running in all directions. An ABC liquor store's roof appeared to be on fire, but that did not deter looters from climbing through the broken plate-glass doors and carrying out bottles of alcohol. Stranded motorists stood angrily, hands on hips, waiting for the Shell gas station to resume operations. Even the shuttered Shoney's Restaurant, a victim of the economic downturn the country experienced, wasn't immune from the opportunists. One man carried out a microwave while another procured the electronic cash register. *Idiots.*

CHAPTER 9

September 3, 2016
10:53 p.m.
Eastbound Interstate 10
Near Lloyd, Florida

After the joyride through Frenchtown, the occupants of the Suburban were finally able to catch their breath. Each was quiet, trying to absorb the gravity of the situation, as the heavy rain pelted the windshield.

"I've gotta pee," announced Abbie.

"Me too," chimed in Jonesy. "The rain isn't helping."

"Well, sports fans, the crap has hit the proverbial fan, but first, we gotta pee," Drew said to a round of laughter. The tension in the truck immediately lessened, and you could feel the relief overtake their bodies.

"Ripley," barked Drew into the collar mic, "everybody breathing easier now up there? Over."

"Roger that," replied Ripley.

"Let's find an opportunity to pull over. Nature calls. No exits. Over."

"Roger."

Abbie once again unbuckled her seat belt and leaned forward to talk to the guys, drawing an admonishing glance from her protector. She shot back a *don't even* look, which was worth a thousand words. Men might think they were running things, but women had *the look* on their side. There wasn't a man on the planet who didn't recognize and respect *the look*.

"Okay, gentlemen. Seriously. Is this the twilight zone?" Abbie wanted to keep the mood light, but it was time to assess the situation. She looked out the side window at the numerous parked cars, some with hazard lights flashing. *Nobody is coming to help you, weary travelers.*

"Here's what we know," replied Drew. "The grid is down, but the extent of the collapse is just conjecture. I don't think it's localized."

"Solar flare or EMP?" queried Jonesy. "I mean, did you hear the transformer explode while we were inside Tucker?"

"I didn't hear it," said Abbie. "Was it before or after the lights went out?"

"Simultaneous," replied Drew. "I thought it was storm related. In fact, I still would except for the information via social media."

"Rumors spread like wildfire," added Jonesy. "Cell phones were lighting up throughout the arena. Within minutes, everyone thought the nation was under attack. How would anybody know that at this point?"

Drew shook his head. "They wouldn't, but speculation would run rampant. That's what people do."

"Why doesn't our satellite radio work?" asked Abbie. "The receiver would be pulling the signal from space."

"That's true, Abbie, but the satellites receive their programming from Earth," replied Drew. "If this outage is as catastrophic as it appears, then the Sirius/XM ground station in D.C. together with the supplemental repeaters on Earth would be without power. Thus, the static we experienced earlier."

"The AM station we picked up out of Thomasville, Georgia, had to be running on a generator strong enough to produce a decent signal," said Jonesy. "I'd guess fifty thousand watts."

"Not necessarily," said Drew. "The airwaves are deserted right now. A lower-wattage AM would not be diluted under the circumstances."

"A lot of good the station did," said Abbie. "All it did was repeat the NOAA weather warnings for Hurricane Danni. The owner of the station was asleep at the wheel."

"Losing the power grid is life-threatening to some, but can be endured for a limited time," said Drew. "But as we know in our business, losing comms feels crippling."

"Whether this was caused by a nuke or the sun, we've got a real problem on our hands," added Jonesy. "And by *we*, I mean the whole frickin' country."

The three remained silent and soaked in the magnitude of the situation. The staccato swipes of the wipers on the windshield appeared to lull them into a momentary trance. A flash of lightning to the south snapped Abbie back to attention.

"After my election in 2010, I was briefed on several national security matters," said Abbie. "Wisconsin Senator Ron Johnson, chair of the Homeland Security Committee, provided me with a copy of a 2008 EMP Commission Report. He said a grid-down collapse event is the greatest threat we face as Americans because not only would it cause immediate death and damage, but the rebuilding process would take many years." Abbie ran her fingers through her hair, trying to forget about her bursting bladder.

"But we don't know if an EMP caused this," said Jonesy. He slowed the truck to navigate through stalled vehicles on both sides of the interstate.

"That's true, but I think I see where Abbie is heading with this," replied Drew. "Whether an EMP, solar flare, or even an orchestrated cyber attack, the net effect on our nation is a collapsed power grid and chaos."

"You're right, Drew," said Abbie. "Regardless of the precipitating event, the damage to our critical infrastructure could be continental in scale. From coast-to-coast, our nation could be without power. Our utilities may be disabled for years. Senator Johnson stressed that a grid-down scenario represents a *high-consequence disaster*, as he put it, which is extremely debilitating. Within a year, ninety percent of Americans could die."

"From what we experienced in the last couple of hours, Senator Johnson may have underestimated the impact," said Jonesy. He slowed the wipers as they cleared the last hurricane feeder band.

"Listen, I always read that society would begin to fall apart in roughly seventy-two hours following a collapse event," opined Drew. "Hell, it was barely seventy-two seconds before the folks in that civic center began to freak out."

"The damage caused to the critical infrastructure in our wired world is only part of the problem," said Abbie. "The real challenge will be the way we treat each other. All of the governmental white papers I've read grossly underestimate the reaction of the human race after a collapse event such as this. As we witnessed, it's one thing for your power to go out in a storm. Even the most hotheaded among us will deem a storm-related outage as a mere inconvenience. But with the advent of social media, the majority of the population knew within minutes that our power could be gone for a long time."

"Hence the rapid deterioration of society," added Drew, finishing her thought.

"Societal collapse," said Jonesy.

"Again, regardless of the cause, if our nation has been thrust into darkness, God help us," said Abbie.

CHAPTER 10

September 3, 2016
11:29 p.m.
Eastbound Interstate 10
Near Monticello, Florida

As the two Suburbans slowed to enter a rest area, Drew was apprehensive. Granted, this was not Frenchtown in Tallahassee, but a new world that was forced upon them—a world with desperate people trying to understand, and survive.

He was trained on the importance of situational awareness. In Afghanistan, failing to maintain a heightened state of awareness would get you and your fellow soldiers killed. Situational awareness was not something practiced only by highly trained secret service agents or military personnel. It should be understood by everyone in this potentially dangerous society. Drew thought of it as *managed paranoia*. As far as he was concerned, a little bit of paranoia helped him develop a keen sense of situational awareness.

Clearly, it was time to be on *high alert*. This level of awareness, once mastered, enabled Drew to control the adrenaline rush needed to survive. It was the same type of rush a motorist might achieve when he saw an eighteen-wheeler rumbling through a red light towards him. Whether a motorist hit the brakes or mashed the gas might determine life or death. The adrenaline rush you received aided your reflexes and mental acuity.

Drew needed to keep his team on this level of readiness. He provided instructions for the two drivers, with a cautionary tone.

"Gentlemen, nothing is the same now. Based on our experience in Tallahassee and the magnitude of the situation, every person must be treated as a potential hostile threat. No exceptions. Understood?"

"Roger that," came Ripley's standard response. Jonesy nodded his head and appeared to grip the wheel a little tighter as the caravan slowed toward the rest area.

The rain abated, but the sixty-mile-an-hour winds were causing the Suburban to shake from time to time. Drew pointed to a truck parking spot to the left.

"Over there, Jonesy. Stay here and monitor my comms. Let me do a quick assessment." Drew exited the truck and walked over to the other vehicle to enlist Ripley's partner. As they crossed the parking lot of stranded and disheveled motorists, he wondered if they would make it to their destinations alive. There were no gas stations, no AAA wreckers to call, and no highway patrolmen coming to the rescue. *Has this dawned on the people of this country yet?*

After surveilling the buildings and finding nothing out of the ordinary other than the looted vending machines, he returned to the Suburbans. He approached Jonesy's window and opened up his mic to Ripley as well.

"Jonesy, stay with the vehicles. We'll take Captain and Rhona inside. Keep your comms open and report anything suspicious. In and out, nice and clean. Copy that also, Ripley?"

"Roger that. I'll send them over."

"Abbie, reach into my bag and grab a hat. Pull it down over your eyes a little. The last thing I need is for you to be recognized."

"Okay," she replied. Drew walked around to her door and opened it. A bathroom break for a vice presidential candidate was anything but normal on a good day. Today, at least thus far, was not so good.

After Abbie and Rhona had finished, they exited the ladies' room. A woman followed them with a young child dressed in a yellow rain slicker.

"Excuse me, can you please help us?" asked the young lady. She shielded her child from the wind-blown rain that was picking up again. "I'm out of gas and walked here with my little girl. The phones don't work, and I don't think the police are coming. Ever since they started breaking into the vending machines, we've been hiding."

"Where are you headed?" asked Rhona.

Drew cringed a little—conflicted. *We can't save the world. True, but what about karma?*

"Lake City."

Abbie pulled Drew close to her and whispered in his ear, "We can't leave her alone."

"Abbie, I understand. But we don't have time to help her. And it's too dangerous. The situation could get worse before it gets better."

"But, Drew," Abbie pleaded, "you see what has happened to people. This woman could get robbed, beaten or raped. What might happen to the little girl?" Abbie's voice trailed off as her words resonated in Drew's mind. He knew better than to make eye contact. That would seal it. Wasting time to contemplate a decision could be just as dangerous. The woman's eyes darted between Drew and Abbie.

After a moment, he looked at the young mother and daughter. *They didn't ask for this.* He decided to do a quick threat assessment by questioning the little girl, who was probably five years old. *Kids can't lie.*

While watching the body language of the woman in his periphery, he kneeled down to address the child.

"What's your name?"

"Roof," she replied. "But all my friends call me Roofie."

"Well, Ruthie." Drew laughed. "It's a terrible night to be out in the rain."

"Mommy and I saw my grandma in Abalama." The adults chuckled at her command of the English language in a four-year-old sort of way.

"And where do you live?"

"Wake City." She looked into Drew's eyes, and he studied her. Her smile showed her first missing tooth. *One last question.*

"Are you and your mom alone, Ruthie?"

"Yup. Papa wanted to stay home and watch footbaw." *Dad of the year.*

Drew stood up and patted the child on the top of her slicker-covered head. The rain was starting to come down in sheets.

"Okay, ma'am. We'll give you a ride to Lake City. Rhona, would you mind getting these young ladies settled in with you?"

"Not at all, Drew. Thank you," replied Rhona. "Come on, girls."

"Thank you so much," replied the young woman and gave Drew an unexpected hug. She looked into Abbie's face and mouthed *God bless you*.

The group made their way to the trucks.

"Look, Momma, a shiny bwack twuck like Papa's."

"Not quite, honey," the mom replied. "Ours is twenty years old. Are you with the government?"

"Rhona, get our friend Ruthie settled in with a seat belt, please," instructed Drew, ignoring her question. He turned to the young woman.

"Ma'am, I don't mean any disrespect. But I hope you understand what I am about to say is said in all sincerity. We are with the federal government, and by taking you to Lake City, we violate every protocol."

"I understand, sir. Truly, I do," she replied. She then turned and said, "Abbie, we love you in Lake City. We need someone like you that understands how to put the country on the right track again."

Abbie stepped past Drew, giving him the *side eye*, and gave the woman a hug.

"What's your name?"

"My name is Regina Gates. It's an honor to meet you."

"Regina, we'll do all we can to get you home safely in this mess. Okay?"

"God bless you, Abbie."

"Yes, of course," said Abbie, wiping the moisture from her eyes. "Thank you. Now, let's get out of this rain and back on the road."

Drew escorted Regina to Ripley's vehicle, and Ripley shrugged. Drew just nodded as he closed the door behind her. Abbie approached his side.

"You did a wonderful thing, *sir*," she said, adding a tone of sarcasm to *sir*.

"Okay, whatever. We can't save them all, Abbie."

"I understand. But we can save at least two."

CHAPTER 11

Sunday, September 4, 2016
12:40 a.m.
Eastbound Interstate 10
Near Live Oak, Florida

Jonesy continued to navigate the Suburban, with Ripley taking the lead. Abbie dozed off in the backseat, so the trio drove in silence for a while. Drew was trying to process things. There were so many scenarios and potential causes.

He glanced at Abbie, who was getting some meaningful but fitful sleep. He had feelings for her, but the relationship was taboo. Drew tried to remain professional and maintain his distance, but the nature of his job had resulted in a closeness between them. The playful banter and flirting increased, but the rigors of the campaign never gave them time alone together. In Tallahassee, he had become consumed with protecting her. At this moment, he knew with utter certainty that he would give his life to protect her—not because it was his job, but because he was falling in love with Abbie.

Jonesy was fidgeting and finally broke the silence. Both men couldn't stop their minds from racing.

"What the hell, Drew? What do you think has happened?"

"I don't know, man. It's like we said earlier, there are so many possibilities. I believe we can rule out a solar flare."

"Why?"

"With a solar flare, we would've had some warning. NASA and several other agencies, including the National Weather Service through their Space Weather Prediction Center, would have issued

47

alerts. From what I've read, SPWC would provide twelve hours warning, but up to forty-eight hours is typical. No, this has to be an attack of some kind."

"By whom?" asked Jonesy.

"Hell, pick one—Russia, China, North Korea, Iran, even terrorists like ISIS. This country hasn't exactly been making friends in the world over the last several decades. They all hate us. For that matter, they may have come together in a joint operation. They're all butt buddies."

"That's true. But if they nuked us, they would have to know we would hit back twice as hard. You know, the whole mutually assured destruction thing—MAD."

"I agree. Plus, realizing we know almost nothing in the way of facts, a lot of this is speculation. But the social media frenzy seemed to relate to the power going down, not a nuclear warhead detonation. It could have been a nuclear-delivered electromagnetic pulse."

"But that would take several bombs, wouldn't it?" asked Jonesy.

"I agree. A coordinated attack could take down the grid nationwide. But our defenses would be able to react to some of the incoming missiles. To me, that would prohibit a cross-country blackout."

"Okay, if an EMP, whether nuclear or solar, didn't collapse the grid, then what did?" asked Jonesy.

"Last Christmas, when I was visiting my folks, Pop gave me a book to read called *Cyber Warfare*. It was a detailed history of the use of cyber attacks by the bad guys we just mentioned, hacker activists like Anonymous, and our own Defense Department. Like Pop said, it was eye-opening."

"Yeah, look what hackers did in Vegas back in the spring. They took down the grid on the Las Vegas strip. People died in the mayhem," said Jonesy.

"I remember. There was one thing the author wrote that I've replayed in my head over and over again. He wrote—*No bombs. No bullets. No sword fights. Just a few keystrokes on the computer, and we're done.*"

"Sounds plausible, doesn't it, Drew?"

The sound of Ripley keying the mic in his earphone interrupted their conversation.

"Go ahead," said Drew. After listening for a moment, he reached for the handset in his pocket and adjusted the dials. "Let me put you on speaker. Okay, go ahead."

"We've caught a cell tower," started Ripley. "Rhona can give us an update."

Drew fumbled for his phone and held it up to observe the display. The signal strength meter gravitated between *no signal* and a single bar. Abbie stirred awake.

"We have cell service?" she asked in her half-awake state. "Is the power back?"

"Put her on speaker," said Drew. "Rhona, tell us what you know."

"Drew, I suddenly got cell reception as we passed the Live Oak exit. I didn't receive a call, and I wasn't able to call out. I continuously receive an all circuits are busy recording or a fast busy tone. Everyone in the country must be trying to use their cell phones as a means to get information."

"What do you have for us?" Drew asked.

"I received almost two dozen text messages from various sources. I guess text messages are less taxing on the obviously overburdened cellular network."

Drew was aware that Verizon and AT&T went to great lengths to upgrade their tower network with generators after the communications blackout triggered by Hurricane Sandy in 2012. As the storm battered the East Coast, flooding homes, destroying businesses, and taking lives, first responders felt helpless. Communications networks along the affected area were not functioning. As power outages became widespread in New York and Connecticut, cell towers relied on their backup power. As the demand in the region exploded, the backup generators were drained rapidly.

Telecommunications providers came under tremendous pressure to maintain complete service during any future disaster. As a result, Senator Charles Schumer of New York introduced legislation requiring telecom companies to beef up their systems and post-disaster capabilities. The companies banded together and successfully fought off the federal government mandates. Instead, they undertook to invest in more propane-fueled backup generators. They also had regional support facilities capable of erecting temporary cell towers if necessary.

All of this infrastructure upgrade was considered a positive step. However, the cellular companies did not expand their cellular traffic capacities to accommodate the potential onslaught of calls when millions of Americans sought to reach out to family or to gather information. The lines were jammed with attempts to call, which resulted in communications darkness for all.

Rhona continued. "The first messages were from Robby. He told me the plane would be grounded and to locate a safe place for Abbie. He was with Mrs. Clinton in New York for a fundraiser. The city was in utter chaos."

"Do the messages have timestamps?" asked Abbie.

"They reflect the time they came to my phone," replied Rhona. "I can only tell you the order in which they were sent."

"Anything else?" asked Abbie.

"Yes, a couple of things. Your father sent a text that just read *en route*. I guess he's on his way, Abbie."

Drew made eye contact with Abbie, and she smiled. *So far, so good.*

Rhona continued. "I have some news from my brother, who works at Randolph Air Force Base in San Antonio. Texas still has power. The rest of the continental U. S. is dark. The informal assessment is a massive, coordinated cyber attack on the grid."

Jonesy smiled and shook his head as he glanced at Drew.

Quiet settled into both vehicles as the occupants contemplated the magnitude of this possibility. Drew stared into the darkness and then suddenly realized it made sense.

"Have you noticed the amount of traffic headed westbound compared to the vehicles traveling in our direction?" he asked.

"You're right, Drew," replied Jonesy. "It's easily ten to one. Thousands of people have received the same information Rhona just related, and they're heading for Texas."

"If this power outage is long term, the entire nation will migrate there," said Abbie. "Rhona, has anyone heard from the President?"

"Robby didn't offer any information other than the President is still in Hawaii, and they have not been affected by the outage," she replied.

"Sir, do we continue as planned?" asked Ripley. As if on cue, a wind gust and its accompanying rain battered the Suburban. It was tempting to abandon this plan and adopt a new course for a military facility in unaffected Texas.

"Stand by, Ripley," said Drew. He turned to Abbie and muted his comms. "Abbie, I know it's tempting to turn around and head to Texas. It would be several hundred miles in heavier traffic. But we would be driving away from the hurricane instead of into it. At the other end, there would be any number of military facilities that could offer you protection. It is an option."

Abbie was deep in thought for a moment. "What do you think, Drew?"

"This is an unknown world now," replied Drew. "I do know your father is going to great lengths to travel here. He wants to protect his daughter. I don't think we should leave him hangin'."

"Okay. You know I will always trust your judgment. Let's proceed."

"Ripley, we'll stay the course," announced Drew. "Lake City is up ahead. We'll take care of your passengers and then head southeast." A Florida Highway Patrol cruiser sped past them on the entrance ramp.

"Roger that," said Ripley. "There's another rest area ahead. Is everybody good?"

Drew looked around and received a thumbs-up. "Proceed," replied Drew. The rain was coming down in gusty sheets. Jonesy had the wipers operating on their fastest cycle. The vehicles crept along at roughly thirty miles an hour as Drew saw the highway sign indicating Interstate 75 was just a mile ahead. He leaned back in the seat and took a deep breath. *They were coming to a crossroads.*

CHAPTER 12

September 4, 2016
1:27 a.m.
I-75–I-10 Interchange
Near Lake City, Florida

As the tandem Suburbans approached the intersection of Interstate 10 and the north-south lanes of Interstate 75, one of the most traveled highways in America, their view through the soaking rain was illuminated by headlights and brake lights shining in every direction. Ripley slowed the team as they approached to get a complete view of the traffic. Drew interrupted his assessment.

"What've we got, Ripley?"

"Sir, it reminds me of *Malfunction Junction* in Tampa on a Friday afternoon," he replied, adding, "during a hurricane, of course. It's difficult to see through this freakin' rain." While Ripley was sure every major city had its version of *Malfunction Junction*. In Tampa, the intersection of Interstate 4 and Interstate 275 was well-known to Floridians. Every day was a traffic nightmare at Tampa's *Malfunction Junction*.

"Traffic headed westbound has stopped as well," observed Drew. Ripley eased over towards the shoulder to get a better look. He could make out a tractor trailer that lay on its side on the grassy medium. Two palmetto trees prevented the fifty-three-foot rig from skidding down the hill into the westbound lane.

"Look out!" exclaimed Drew into his earphone. Ripley pulled into the passing lane just in time to avoid being hit by a car speeding past them on the left. *I almost lost the other mirror.*

Playing follow the leader, he saw several other cars pull out of

52

formation on both the right and left shoulders. Within minutes, they were blocked in on all sides as the two eastbound lanes quickly became a four-lane highway.

"Drew, I don't like this," said Ripley into the comms. "Traffic isn't moving in either direction. Something is wrong."

The winds began to pick up again, and lightning was now illuminating the sky. As the vehicles inched forward past the overturned rig, Ripley maneuvered to the inside shoulder along the guardrail. The other Suburban attempted to follow but was almost hit by a pickup that inserted itself between them.

"Come on, Jonesy, keep up," Ripley muttered to no one in particular.

"Doesn't matter, I've got you in sight," said Jonesy.

Ripley continued to inch forward when the sound of gunfire came from ahead of them.

"Were those gunshots?" asked Rhona.

"I think so, but it's hard to tell through the thunder," replied Ripley. Then he heard the unmistakable loud report of a shotgun, visible with its bright muzzle flash.

"Shots fired, shots fired ahead," screamed Ripley. He quickly looked in all directions. They were pinched against the guardrail. The only opening was behind them—where the semi had jackknifed.

Suddenly, the reverse lights on the minivan in front of them lit up before it crashed into their front bumper. Apparently panicked, other cars were now attempting to go in reverse. The van effectively pinched them into the pickup truck to their rear.

"Drew! We're wedged in, and we've got shots fired ahead!" screamed Ripley.

CHAPTER 13

September 4, 2016
1:32 a.m.
I-75–I-10 Interchange
Near Lake City, Florida

Drew's view was obstructed by the truck in front of them. Placing his communications unit on speaker, he replied to Ripley's call.

"Copy," replied Drew. "Jonesy, can you see around this truck in front of you?" Drew sat up in his seat, attempting to get a visual of Ripley and the lead vehicle.

"No, I can't," replied Jonesy. The blowing rain was continuous now as the feeder bands passed over more often.

"We need to get out of here," muttered Drew as he swung his attention in all directions. The only possible exit was through the guardrail torn open by the jackknifed rig. There was no guarantee that they could get through the water-saturated median to the westbound lane, and they would still face the obstacle of another guardrail blocking their access. *It was their only option.*

"Jonesy, I don't like this at all, but we don't have any options here," started Drew. He gestured as he continued. "We can still cut through the torn guardrail here and double back to the last exit. Make our way from there, right?"

"But Ripley is beyond the opening. He says he's stuck between this pickup and another vehicle."

"Right," replied Drew. "We need to get ourselves through the rail first with the goal of making it through the median. Then, we have to direct traffic and get the pickup out of the way. Ripley will have the opening he needs to follow."

"Got it," said Jonesy. He checked his secret-service-assigned weapon—a SIG Sauer P229 chambered in .357. "You'll take the wheel. Sir, I have to ask. What are the rules of engagement?"

"Well, it isn't passive," replied Drew. "Let's make this happen and hope it doesn't come to that. Just stay frosty oscar mike. Join them once you clear the guardrail. Double back to the last exit as our rendezvous point."

Drew unbuckled his seatbelt and checked his weapon. "Did you copy that, Ripley?"

"Roger," he replied. "Listen, there's not an inch between us and the vehicles fore and aft. By the way, the gunfire has ceased."

"Let's go, Jonesy!" As his driver exited the vehicle into the storm, Drew immediately climbed over to the driver's seat.

"Will this work?" Abbie asked apprehensively.

"It's all we've got, Abbie," replied Drew. "There's something wrong up ahead, and we need to move. Please lie down on the seat with your seat belt buckled. We have protection from small-arms fire, but not from vehicles being used as battering rams."

"Okay."

Drew put the Suburban into reverse and eased backward to the blare of horns behind him. He turned the truck left but was unable to clear the guardrail. He backed up further, nudging the left rear bumper of the car behind him, and then abruptly moved forward through the gap.

Jonesy, standing next to the pickup truck in front of them, waved the driver back, and the pickup slid into reverse. However, the irate driver behind Drew, still laying on the horn, immediately filled the gap left by the Suburban. Ripley's vehicle was still too far from the guardrail opening.

"This is a cluster—," shouted Drew, slapping the steering wheel. He suppressed his anger as shots rang out again, but this time they were close. The windshield of the pickup truck where Jonesy stood exploded into tiny pieces of glass. Jonesy hit the ground and crawled to safety behind the other Suburban.

"My God, Drew!" exclaimed Abbey. "What's happening? Why are people shooting?"

Drew ignored her question. "Jonesy is pinned down." Drew couldn't intervene to help him. He had to hold his position. His mind raced. A lightning flash helped shed light on the threat.

In the darkness, Drew could make out a group of men carrying both rifles and handguns walking toward each parked vehicle. As they approached, they would point their gun at the driver. Ripley provided more information on the threat over the open comms.

"Sir, it appears these thugs are demanding a ransom from each vehicle. Two teams are working their way down the highway, threatening vehicle occupants to turn over their valuables. The last shots fired were from a vehicle who attempted to take them out. It didn't work."

Drew thought for a moment. Protocol required him to extract Abbie immediately. But he didn't want to leave his team behind.

"Jonesy, you copy?" asked Drew.

Through the wind howling, Jonesy replied, "Roger. I believe the bullet that hit this pickup was a stray. I can take out the two in the middle lane if Ripley can hit the thug on the inside shoulder."

"I can do that," said Ripley. "They're approaching."

Drew thought for a brief moment. He looked into the rearview mirror at a reticent Abbie. Decision made.

"Okay, proceed. You do understand protocol. I need to extract Captain."

"No problem, sir, we've got this," replied Jonesy.

"It'll be our pleasure," chimed in Ripley. "Get our next Vice President to safety while we take care of business and get these young ladies to their destination."

"Thank you, gentlemen. Keep your comms open. It's been a pleasure. See you at the ranch!"

Drew threw the Suburban into drive and made his way through the crape myrtle trees past the crashed semi. He listened to the communications between Jonesy and Ripley as they methodically eliminated three members of the group attacking the helpless travelers.

As Drew and Abbie's truck reached the inside of the westbound guardrail, he heard his men shout that two more hostiles were approaching from the south. The sound of gunfire filled the speaker of the handheld unit. The members of the team were shouting instructions at each other. Clearly, there were several more hostiles. Through his side mirror, he could see a barrage of muzzle flashes in between the lightning strikes. *They're in a firefight. Dammit!*

"Drew, we have to help them—Rhona, the woman, and her little girl."

Once again, Drew was faced with an impossible decision. His choices could mean life or death regardless of the judgment he used.

"Abbie, you're my priority." Drew wheeled the Suburban back onto the pavement and headed westbound away from the melee.

CHAPTER 14

September 4, 2016
2:11 a.m.
Wellborn, Florida

Drew slowly approached the railroad crossing in the small town of Wellborn. The streets appeared deserted. He pulled into the parking lot of Bob's Butts BBQ and stopped. The wind was still blowing, but the rain had ceased, for the moment. The two needed to stretch their legs and regroup. *Wellborn seems safe enough.*

"Looks like the fire and rescue are closed up for the night," said Drew, pointing across the street at what was probably an all-volunteer department that only occasionally had to rescue cats from the moss-covered live oak trees dotting the landscape. "Let's stretch and get some water, okay, Abbie?"

"Okay," a meek Abbie replied. She was exhausted and distraught over the possible fate of Rhona and the innocent people they took on board. Since they turned back, she began to question the decision to help the young mother and her daughter, Ruthie. *Would they have been better off on their own instead of becoming embroiled in a gunfight?*

"Drew, did we do the right thing?"

"Abbie, I had to get you out of there. The team knows the drill. They're fine."

"No, I mean taking on the woman and her little girl. Did I unnecessarily put them in harm's way?"

Drew took a breath and moved forward to comfort Abbie. He was confident in the decisions they'd made so far. "Listen. Those two could have suffered a much worst fate, *unprotected.* I don't care how many hostiles the boys faced back there on that interstate. They would not let any harm come to Rhona or our guest passengers. Your compassion saved them from a certain fate, Abbie. Know that."

She looked up at him. She wanted him to hold her. Make it all go away. Just as he got close—he nervously backed away. There was still that wall of professional boundaries.

Drew popped open the back hatch of the Suburban and retrieved a couple of bottled waters from the cooler. He handed Abbie a towel that she used to wipe her face. She looked at her reflection in the truck's rear window. She was a hot mess, but she was alive.

"How much farther?" she asked.

"I wish we had a map. The GPS wants to take you on its preferred route. People rely upon these things too much. It's no wonder drivers aimlessly follow its directions off a cliff."

Abbie laughed.

She studied Drew. He was handsome but not in a movie-star kind of way. He was obviously well built and had a boyish charm about him. She appreciated his dry sense of humor. Most of all, he was very attentive towards her. He would perform small, unnecessary gestures of kindness that gave her the feeling he cared about her. *Did it take this crazy situation to allow her to see the obvious?*

"Let's get goin', Abbie," said Drew as he escorted her to the passenger side of the truck. She stopped at the rear door out of habit.

"Here you go," he said, opening the front door. "You're riding shotgun now."

"Oh, I got a promotion. Do I get a gun too?"

"Nope. The rules are simple. Eyes on the periphery. No excessive chatter. Keep your hands to yourself. Wear your seat belt at all times. Fair enough?"

"I'll take the job," she replied. As she climbed into the truck, she caught a glimpse of Drew looking at her—checking her out. *Now that we're alone, we'll see where this crazy ride leads us.*

CHAPTER 15

September 4, 2016
2:35 a.m.
SR 242
South of Lake City, Florida

Drew charted a route to the south and east of Lake City, avoiding every potential obstacle, town or major road crossing. What would usually take less than an hour on a sunny afternoon took double that in the throes of Hurricane Danni. Despite the torrential downpours, the ride was uneventful, but Drew was closely monitoring another very real problem—they were low on fuel. The delays, the side roads, and the fact they were only supposed to drive a few miles to the campaign event led to the probability of an empty fuel tank soon.

His thoughts alternated between the task at hand and his family back home in Tennessee. Drew grew up in a rural part of Tennessee known as the Upper Cumberland Plateau. His father, affectionately known as *Judge* by all who knew him, including Drew's mom, practiced law for many years in nearby Jamestown before he was later appointed to be a circuit judge. In Tennessee's rural counties, one circuit judge would preside over civil cases in several counties, so his father would travel a hundred miles a day to conduct the court's business.

His mom was a retired registered nurse from the local hospital in Jamestown. For thirty-five years, Janie Jackson worked in all aspects of the regional medical center, including eleven years as a surgery nurse. But her favorite position came at the end of her career when the hospital placed her in charge of the emergency room—*my ER*, as she called it. Nobody, including the physicians, challenged this designation.

Drew's brother and sister were freshmen at the University of Tennessee. Fraternal twins, the two were inseparable and best friends. Jasper, his eighteen-year-old brother, went to Tennessee on a football scholarship as a fullback. Six feet tall and made of solid muscle, he was a little undersized to play linebacker on defense and too small to play the offensive line. But Jack, as he preferred to be called, could open a hole and knock down anyone who stood in his way.

His sister, Alexandra, was the consummate farmer's daughter. She was a beautiful young woman—but more tomboy than a debutante. In Muddy Pond, where the family farm was located, hunting was the recreation of choice. Allie participated in every marksmanship course taught in the Fentress County school system. While the family supported Jack in his football endeavors, they also were proud of Allie for her shooting trophies.

"Hey, Drew. What are you thinking?"

"Sorry, my mind wandered. Did you say something?"

"Ignoring me already, I see."

"No, Abbie, I'm sorry. What did you say?"

"Nothing. I'm just messing with you. Relax, Drew. It'll be all right." She reached over and rubbed his shoulders, instantly relaxing him. "You've done great so far. We're going to be fine."

"Thanks. I mean, I know. I was just thinking about my family." Drew relaxed his grip on the wheel as the rain died down for the first time in an hour or so. Plus, Abbie's touch had a calming effect on him—even though she was violating the *keep your hands to yourself* rule.

"Are you worried about them?" asked Abbie.

"No, not really. My parents are prepared for things like this. Hell, Pop will live longer in the world with no power than he would have in an electricity-dependent life. I was thinking more about my younger brother and sister. Today was Jack's first home football game at Neyland Stadium in Knoxville."

"Wow. You never mentioned that before."

"My younger brother and sister are freshmen at Tennessee. They're twins. Jack made the team as a true freshman and probably saw some playing time against Appalachian State. He had a good first game against Virginia Tech last week. My sister, Allie, is his biggest fan. I'm sure she was at the game."

"Allie. Great name. We'd be friends. You know. Abbie. Allie. Get it?" The two laughed.

"Ha-ha. Maybe. Allie isn't a foo foo."

"What? Are you saying I'm a foo foo, mister? I have a gun. It's here somewhere. I'm sure of it!" Abbie teasingly started to take off her seat belt to search for the elusive gun just to aggravate Drew.

"Do not break any more rules or you will be relieved of your shotgun duties."

Drew knew Abbie was purposefully acting silly to loosen him up. Abbie was showing a side of her that he didn't get to enjoy often. In fact, this was the longest period the two had spent alone. *He liked it.* They both sat in silence for a moment. Drew could feel the tension between them.

"It's our anniversary, you know," said Abbie.

"Anniversary of what?"

"Our one-hundred-day anniversary. You started protecting me a hundred days ago."

"Really? Gawd," said Drew in his natural Southern drawl. "I thought it had been years. I was just thinking to myself—*is this detail ever going to end?*"

"Shut up, idiot! That's it. I'm finding that gun!"

"Abbie, stop. You are the worst protectee of all protectees."

"*Protectee* is not a word."

"Umm, yes, it is."

"Nope."

"You're breaking the rules of the shotgunner."

"What? No, I am not!"

"Yes, you are. Excessive talking."

Abbie petulantly sat back in her seat. Drew was enjoying this.

"*Shotgunner* is not a word either," said Abbie, folding her arms with a pout.

She may be right about that one.

CHAPTER 16

September 4, 2016
3:57 a.m.
County Road 241
Near Lulu, Florida

For miles, Drew looked for options. He hoped to see a gas can sitting in a carport or next to a tool shed. He watched for any other travelers or residents to lend a hand. But the drive along their circuitous route was mostly deserted. He had to tell Abbie.

"Abbie, we're only about forty miles from Camp Blanding, but I'm afraid we don't have enough fuel. I've routed us towards a small town on State Highway 100 called Lulu. I don't know if there'll be any help for us, but we have to try."

"When will we run out, Drew?"

"Very soon. I don't think we can make it to town, so we'll have to walk and ask for help."

"And if there isn't anyone to help us?"

"Then we walk straight down Highway 100 toward Lake Butler and hope for an alternative."

"That would suck."

"I couldn't have said it better." Drew chuckled.

Drew continued several more miles until he hit the intersection of County Road 241, where he turned left towards Lulu. Just as they passed the Speed Limit 45 sign, the truck sputtered and lost power. *End of the road.*

Abbie spoke up first. "Well, okay then. Let the adventure continue." Drew could tell Abbie was pretending to be in good spirits. This was not a good situation for them.

"Let me take a quick inventory of what would be most useful to carry with us," said Drew as the two exited the stalled vehicle.

His first concern was shelter in the event they had to walk the entire route. They were both in good condition, but in the midst of a hurricane and without alternate transportation, the trip would take at least eight hours. Drew was comfortable they could find respite from the storm, even if it was in a barn or an outbuilding.

Security was the next order of business. Drew carried his assigned weapon—the Sig Sauer P229. His personal weapon was a Glock 31, standard issue to his many friends in the Tennessee Highway Patrol. It used a common cartridge, the Sig .357. But he also kept in his bag a Glock 33 chambered in the same cartridge. The Glock 33 was a subcompact version. Its magazine held nine rounds. He strapped it in an ankle holster and covered it with his pant leg.

"Abbie, we've talked about this before. Ordinarily, there would be no circumstance that would require you to be armed. This is an exception to that rule."

"You know I'm trained on the P229. My father insisted upon it."

"I remember. I have a backup Sig for you. I have two paddle holsters, but they won't tuck into the waistband of your Juicy Couture tracksuit."

Abbie stood a little taller and somewhat indignant. "You'll have to give me a gun, Drew."

"Yes. I have a shoulder holster that I'll adjust to fit you." Drew reached into his bag and adjusted the straps on his shoulder rig. He turned toward her to get her outfitted. "I need you to stand tall and hold your arms out."

Drew slipped her right arm through one side of the straps and then her left. He reached around her to adjust the padding under her arms, accidentally grazing her breasts. Abbie shivered. With both hands, Drew carefully pulled Abbie's hair free from the shoulder straps, revealing her neck. She turned her head to expose her skin covered with goosebumps. Drew felt the attraction, and he knew Abbie wanted him to kiss her.

But he restrained himself. He pulled her arms down to her sides, and he leaned into her ear. "Abbie, I feel it too. Let's get out of this mess and we'll see where it takes us. Okay?"

Abbie exhaled and nodded. Then she turned toward him and touched his face. "I can't help how I feel, Drew. I'm falling in love with you. I have been for months."

"I know. Love you too. I—" Then an explosion ripped through the night. They both instantly turned towards Lulu. A streak of lightning momentarily lit up the sky to reveal black smoke drifting skyward.

Drew grabbed a few more things and stuffed them in his cargo pant pockets before he closed the Suburban and habitually locked it, tucking the keys away.

"Let's go."

CHAPTER 17

September 4, 2016
4:20 a.m.
County Road 241
Near Lulu, Florida

As Drew and Abbie jogged toward town, the frequent lightning strikes provided a view of the smoke that grew in volume and density. They had jogged almost two miles when they rounded the curve and saw fire dancing into the sky. The Lulu Baptist Church was engulfed in flames. Because of the intense heat and Drew's concern over what caused the fire, he led Abbie across the street under the oak tree canopy provided in the home's front yard.

"What should we do?" asked Abbie. The two crouched under a mature live oak, which shielded them from the rain coming from another feeder band. *Did this hurricane find a place to stop for the night?*

"I'm not sure, but something is out of place. I realize it's oh-dark-thirty, but that explosion could be heard for miles. Where is everybody? Why aren't the neighbors gathering around to see what's happened?"

"You're right, Drew. Somebody would come around, right?"

"Yeah." Drew looked around and grabbed Abbie by the hand. They ran across a gravel side road to another set of oaks and looked around. Suddenly, Abbie gasped.

"My god, Drew, look!" she exclaimed, pointing at a covered front porch in the midst of the trees. "Is that, is that a body?"

Drew immediately pulled his weapon. "Abbie, listen to me. Ready your weapon and follow close behind me. I want you to watch our backs. I've got the rest. If you see someone, slap me and we both go down to a crouch. Got it?"

"Yes." Abbie unsnapped the holster and pulled her weapon. "Okay, go."

The two made their way together toward the front porch. It was a quaint Florida farmhouse with white wood siding and a green metal roof. Baskets of ferns dangled between the columns and swung in the gusty winds. The empty white rocking chairs swayed from the squalls, or from the ghosts of past residents—including the dead elderly woman laying half in and half out of her front door.

"Abbie, you have to control yourself, okay?"

"What? Why?" Impulsively, she turned around to see what Drew was talking about. She gasped and began to shake. "Oh my god!"

The elderly woman, clad in a pink nightgown and light blue housecoat, had been beaten to death with a small sledgehammer. Her face was mangled, unrecognizable. The murderer had left the hammer embedded in her skull. Drew had seen death during his tours of duty in Afghanistan. What appeared before him was the most gruesome killing he had ever seen.

He turned to comfort Abbie, but she was vomiting over the white porch rail. She was crying hysterically as the emotions of the day and the convulsions of her retching overtook her. Drew took her gun and tucked it into his belt. He pulled her hair back behind her and wiped away her tears as she tried to regain her composure. After her stomach was emptied, her crying subsided, enabling her to speak.

"What is wrong with people? I mean, who could do this to an old lady?"

"I don't know," responded Drew. "We have to be careful, Abbie. I need you right now, okay?"

Abbie sniffled and nodded her head. She pulled her sleeves over her hands and wiped off her face and nose. She looked into Drew's eyes and once again nodded affirmatively.

"Okay."

"Abbie, here's your gun. I want you to wait here while I check the house. I imagine the killer is long gone based on the condition of the body, but I have to make sure. You watch the front and call for me if you see something—but quietly."

"Okay, hurry!"

Drew stepped over the body and quickly returned with a hand-knitted afghan he'd found folded on a sofa. He imagined she had used it to stay warm while watching her favorite television shows. It was difficult for him to keep his composure. *So senseless and unnecessary.*

Drew cleared the small two-bedroom, one-story home and found only evidence of looting. The bathroom medicine cabinet was torn off the wall, and the nightstand drawers were ransacked. *They were looking for drugs.*

Through the kitchen window, he saw a white sedan, maybe a Buick, parked under a carport roof. Fumbling through the kitchen using his UltraFire flashlight, he found the keys on a hook next to the pantry door. He returned to Abbie, who had stopped crying but was clearly very emotional.

"It's clear inside, Abbie. I think the murderer was a looter or looking for drugs, based upon the way the place was torn apart. There's a car out back, and I've got the keys. Here." Drew handed her a bottle of water out of the pantry. Abbie hesitated to take it at first. Once she did, she looked at it and then towards the now covered dead body. Drew knew what she was thinking. *Are we looters too?*

"Abbie, we have to make some tough choices now. The world has changed—at least our part of it. We have to survive. There is a difference between looting and murder—and *survival.*"

Abbie rolled the water through her hands. She looked at the body, then at the church burning across the road. The streets were still deserted. She looked up at Drew and opened the bottled water and took a drink.

"Let's hope the car has enough gas to get us out of here," said Abbie.

CHAPTER 18

September 4, 2016
5:10 a.m.
State Road 100
Lulu, Florida

Drew immediately looked at the fuel gauge and saw that it was full. The white Buick Enclave still had that new-car smell. Drew imagined that the family of the deceased woman insisted on her having reliable transportation. It also contained a Sirius XM radio with a navigation screen. He pulled out of the carport and turned right towards Lulu—*former population of one hundred forty-eight.*

As he turned south on Florida 100, he saw a group of men dressed in blue uniforms leaning against the front rails of the ransacked Lulu General Store. He slowed to get a better look, but when the men started running toward the car, Drew sped off toward the southeast. It was only ten miles to Lake Butler, but Drew had had enough of small-town Florida—during the apocalypse.

"I'm avoiding the town. After what I saw back there, give me some country back roads. Abbie, it will be daylight soon. I'd prefer to be moving under cover of darkness. I can go straight through the center of these towns to the camp's main gates, or we can work our way through back roads, which may help us avoid detection as we enter this Florida National Guard facility."

"I understand," she replied. "Let's try through town first. Do we have any southern bailout options?" Drew was glad to see Abbie was getting back to normal. She was a seasoned politician but also a valued member of the Senate Intelligence Committee. Her security clearance was just below that of the President. Her position required an analytical mind. He was glad she was able to help him think through their options.

"A few. We'll get our first view of the main drag in just a moment," replied Drew. The headlights illuminated the railroad tracks that ran parallel to the highway. Groups of men wandered along the tracks. Some wore coats to shield themselves from the rain.

"What are they doing out in the storm?"

"I don't know, but there's something else I find odd. Did you notice they're all similarly dressed to the guys in Lulu who chased the car?"

"Yeah. Maybe they're road or utility maintenance workers?" Drew wasn't sure, but he didn't intend to stop and ask.

He slowed the Buick as they began to see businesses on the outskirts of Lake Butler. On their left, at the S&S Food Store, people were streaming out of the building, carrying armfuls of beer and cigarettes. Up ahead, Drew spotted a car on fire in the middle of the road. There was no sign of first responders.

"I've seen enough." He stopped and threw it in reverse. Turning south down County Road 231, more looting was taking place. Another group of men was filling the back of an Aramark Uniform van with groceries from the IGA. The van's headlights exposed a body that lay lifeless in the parking lot nearby.

"They're all wearing the same type of blue uniforms," said Abbie. "I don't get it." A car sped past them in the other direction. Across the way, two pickup trucks were being loaded with building materials and lumber from Jackson Building Supply. The American flag was torn off the front entrance and lay under the tires of one of the trucks. *I guess that's how it is now.*

Drew hustled them out of town and started traversing the roads south of Lake Butler. He decided to avoid the northerly route through Raiford and Lawtey, opting instead to go on the other side of Starke.

"Based upon the navigation panel, Camp Blanding has several entrances. It appears the bulk of the base operations are located on the other side of this large round lake."

"Kingsley Lake," interjected Abbie.

"Right. We'll work our way up from the south, avoiding Starke. Once we get back on County Road 230, we should be able to find a checkpoint. I'll show the guards my Secret Service ID. Do you have any identification?"

"No, I never need it. Surely they'll recognize me." She laughed. "Maybe we should look for a campaign poster?"

"Very funny. We'll deal with it when we get there." Drew stopped and turned onto the highway. He approached an entry gate to the base and immediately saw it was not occupied by soldiers or military vehicles. Several men stood in front of the chain-link gate, smoking and talking. They hadn't noticed Drew's approach. The now howling wind and increased rainfall distracted them.

"These guys aren't military," said Abbie. "They look like they're waiting for something. And notice the uniforms again."

Drew cut the lights and slowly backed down the crushed-shell service road. Once back on the highway, he worked his way northward until they came upon another gated entrance.

"More of the same." Drew sighed. "Abbie, we've got to keep going, but we're also running out of darkness. I don't want to shoot our way through a situation. It's too dangerous."

"Keep going, Drew," said Abbie, running her finger across the GPS panel. "Try Lake Drive. It runs right into Kingsley Lake. Maybe we can walk to the base." The rain and wind picked up considerably courtesy of the approaching Danni—*the never-ending hurricane.*

They hit a dead end on the south side of Kingsley Lake at a small cluster of homes. It was dark enough for Drew and Abbie to make their way along the shore—if it was passable. Based upon the map, they were only a few thousand feet away from the base housing and another couple of thousand feet to a large open area that might be the airfield.

They donned ponchos and started through the yards. As they were passing in between the final two homes, they were blinded by a flashlight.

"Stop right there!" shouted a younger man's voice from behind a fishing boat on a trailer.

Drew dropped to one knee and pulled Abbie down with him. They were temporarily in the darkness again until another flashlight illuminated their position from the right. The first man shouted again.

"Stop right there and put your hands in the air where I can see 'em!"

Drew heard the distinctive sound of a shell being racked into a pump-action shotgun—a sound that would scare away the bravest of burglars.

"Don't talk," he whispered to Abbie. "This is just a scared homeowner."

Drew stood with his hands in the air and Abbie followed his lead.

"Sir, we don't mean you any harm. My name is Andrew Jackson, and I'm with the United States Secret Service. I have my identification if you will allow me to reach into my pocket." Drew began to reach under his poncho but stopped suddenly when he heard the sound of another shotgun chambering a shell.

"That's probably a load of crap, Grandpa," said a younger voice to their right. Then directing his attention at Drew and Abbie, the young man shouted, "You're trespassing!"

"I'm sorry that we've come on your property. We need to get to Camp Blanding. We'll just turn around and leave, okay?"

"Don't move. Drop your ID on the ground and move away slowly. The police are on the way." *No, they're not, but somebody else is. I'm just not sure who.* Drew dropped his ID, and he pushed Abbie backward a few steps. He kept his body between her and the guns pointed at them.

He whispered to Abbie, "This will be fine."

An older man walked around the fishing boat with the flashlight in Drew's eyes. The younger man came from his right. They approached tentatively. *Please don't make me have to kill you both today.*

The man studied Drew's identification and then compared the picture to his illuminated face. He seemed to relax as he tucked the ID inside his shirt pocket.

"Why are you sneaking around here during a hurricane? Why not drive up to Blanding's front gate?" he asked.

"Something's wrong," Drew explained. "We approached two gates to the south of here, and both were surrounded by civilians dressed in blue uniforms. We've seen similarly dressed men between here and Lulu."

"Who's with you?" asked the young man, raising his rifle once again. Drew cringed as Abbie spoke up.

"My name is Senator Abigail Morgan."

A woman's voice came from behind them, and Drew spun around to see her armed silhouette standing in the rain.

"Abbie? Let me see." She flashed the light in Abbie's face and immediately lowered her rifle.

"For heaven's sake, Thomas, this is Abbie Morgan. She's going to be the next Vice President. Put your guns down, boys." The woman approached Abbie, but Drew moved to stand between them.

"It's okay, Drew," said Abbie, gently touching his right hand before he drew the weapon hidden in the small of his back. "Hello, ma'am. It's a pleasure to meet you." Abbie approached the woman and extended her hand to shake but was greeted with a hug instead.

"Oh my, this is so exciting," exclaimed Rhetta Vance. "Abbie Morgan right here in my yard. Honey, what are you doing out here in this fretful weather? Come inside and let's get you dried off and see if I can find some dry clothes. You're much smaller than I am, but I could hem something up for you." As if greeting an old friend, she took Abbie by the arm and escorted her towards the front porch as she continued to babble. Abbie turned and smiled at Drew, who looked to the sky, not only for guidance but to assess the coming daylight.

CHAPTER 19

"They sound like escaped inmates," said Thomas Vance, grandfather and retired chief of Probation and Parole Field Services for the Florida Department of Corrections. He and his wife, Rhetta, lived a quiet life overlooking Kingsley Lake. "They must have broken out of confinement when the power went out. We've had no information whatsoever. My grandson and I decided to stay up and keep watch in case anyone tried to steal from us. When the sun came up, I planned to check on my neighbors."

Abbie finished her glass of Tropicana Orange Juice and stood up in the family's living room.

"Thomas, these inmates are on a rampage," said Drew. "I believe they may have murdered the entire town of Lulu. They are wreaking havoc in Lake Butler. Now, I think they're preparing an assault on the base with a possible target being the National Guard Armory."

"You're right, Drew, and in a way, it was fortunate we met under these unusual circumstances. I sense you need to go, and I need to sound the alarm—the best way I know how. The eye of the storm is heading our way, so we both should get started."

"Yes, sir," said Drew. "Thank you for not shooting us."

"Of course. It was never my intention," replied Mr. Vance. "We figured to scare you off is all. My grandson will help you get started."

"Drew, I'll take you to the beginning of the trail through the woods. If you follow it, you'll come out right onto Avenue A. Follow

75

the street along the lake and then take the third right, which is Hollywood Street. Hollywood Street takes you straight to the airfield and the fuel depot. You can't miss it."

"Thank you again," said Drew. "Abbie, we need to go." Everyone exchanged hugs, and Abbie promised to call when this was *over*. Like most Americans, this family couldn't fathom that their electricity might be off for months or even years. *Under the circumstances, you can't hit them with that revelation.*

It was dawn when the two cleared the woods and walked onto Avenue A. Drew cautiously led Abbie into the clearing. Camp Blanding was an active military facility. They were home free, as they say. But there was no sense in getting shot after the night they'd just experienced together.

"Are you ready?"

"I think so," replied Abbie as she adjusted her shoulder holster. "I think we should hold hands as we walk. You know. Lend the appearance that we're just a typical couple out for a stroll."

Drew laughed. "Sure. I've got an exposed sidearm, and you're wearing a shoulder holster packing a P229. Don't mind us; we're *just a typical couple.*"

"Well, maybe not typical. But you can still hold my hand while we walk." Abbie reached for his hand, and they continued up Avenue A and rounded the turn to Hollywood Street.

"I've met your father once before," started Drew. "I don't think he liked me."

"Why do you say that?"

"When I was introduced to him, he didn't say a word."

"Oh, that's just how he is. Trust me, as I've said before, you wouldn't be my number one if he didn't *like you*." She gripped Drew's hand tighter and led him toward the clearing. He was her *number one*. It was raining steadily now, and as they cleared the pine-lined street, the salty wind and rain peppered their faces.

"I see his helicopter on the other side of the buildings," observed Drew. "The tanker truck just completed refueling. See it pulling away?"

"Yes! Come on, Drew!" Like a schoolgirl with her new boyfriend, she pulled his arm and ran up Hollywood Street into the driving rain. Within moments, they walked onto the grassy airfield—sloshing through the wet turf. Abbie slowed as she saw a group of men running on the other side towards her father's helicopter.

"Abbie!" exclaimed Drew as he pulled her to a stop. "Wait, look. Over there. The inmates are storming the chopper. The pilot must see them too. He's started his engines to leave." Panic set into Abbie.

"Does he see us? Father. Daddy! Over here!" Abbie was jumping up and down, waving her arms, trying to get her father's attention.

"Keep running, Abbie. I'll distract them!" Drew shoved her forward.

Abbie ran ahead as Drew began firing at the approaching inmates. She glanced to her left as Drew shot and killed one of them. She heard three more shots that apparently missed the mark. But the diversion was working. They were now running toward Drew. He fired two more rounds, and then his weapon jammed.

"Come on, Drew! Run!" shouted Abbie. She stopped and turned back towards him.

Her father climbed out of the helicopter and grabbed her arm.

"We must go, Abigail," said Morgan. He began dragging her inside when Drew got overrun by the first three escaped inmates. He was fighting back with the butt of his gun. The other escaped prisoners joined in and tried to hold him down.

Drew slipped out of their grasp and managed to get onto his feet. Shortly after regaining his balance, he moved towards the helicopter again.

"Run, Drew! We have to help him!" Abbie tried to pull away from her father's grasp. Morgan held her back. Abbie thought she saw Drew's bloody face repeatedly mouthing the words *love you*.

A strong gust of wind shook the Sikorsky.

"Sir, the weather is becoming too severe for flight," said the pilot. "We have a limited opportunity, sir. We must take off."

Once again, Drew was running toward her, but they tackled him again. He was only twenty yards away. Abbie's tear-soaked faced was pressed against the window. She was yelling, "Love you, love you."

"Take off," Morgan said dryly as he pulled the door closed.

"No, Father, please! They'll kill him!"

As they lifted off, Abbie, still sobbing, pressed her face against the glass and said, "I love you too."

Then, through her tears, she turned to her father and said, "How could you leave him?"

"Abbie, you're my priority."

Abbie stared at her father in stunned silence, not because he left Drew behind, but out of a sense of déjà vu. As the helicopter lifted off, she stared out into the howling wind-blown rain at Drew's motionless body, and she understood.

PART TWO

Call of Duty

CHAPTER 20

Saturday, September 3, 2016
9:11 p.m.
100 Beacon
Boston, Massachusetts

The city of Boston was dependent upon six electricity substations operated by Eversource, formerly known as NStar. These substations were responsible for the delivery of electricity to nearly seven hundred thousand residents. In 2012, a fire at one of the substations located in West Boston on Scotia Street cut power to twenty-two thousand customers.

Investigators believed the mysterious fire at the facility might have been caused by a failed connection between a power line and a transformer. The connection sparked and ignited mineral oil that was used as a cooling agent in transmission lines. The flammable mineral oil fueled the fire, which found its way into the transformers at the Scotia Street substation. The transformers caught fire, imploded, and then melted down everything adjacent to them, including structural steel.

The fire was believed to have traveled ten miles toward the east along transmission lines to the South Charles Street substation, near Boston Common. This facility was also shut down, causing a cascade of power outages throughout Boston. By the next day, much of the electrical grid was offline until other substations were able to pick up the slack.

Electricity was delivered to the substations from the city's main power plant located at Kendall Square in Cambridge. The Kendall Station was a natural gas-fired power plant that produced the vast majority of electricity in the metro Boston area. It relied upon a thirty-mile network of pipeline running beneath Cambridge and Boston.

As one city official proudly announced when Kendall Station came online:

It has become the beating heart and arteries of our system. We couldn't operate the city without it.

Kendall Station was about to have a heart attack.

*****

Sarge sat quietly for a moment, contemplating Julia's question. The township of Cambridge twinkled in the distance, and he followed the navigational lights of a boat traveling up the Charles River toward the yacht club.

He knew she wanted to get married, as did he. Nothing was preventing them from having a loving relationship for the rest of their lives. Of course, children would become part of the equation. He loved *her*, not the prospect of having children with her. But he enjoyed her company so much, why would they want to inject another person, *or two*, into their lives. *Weren't relationships complicated enough without the additional hurdles created by raising kids?*

"Julia, I love you," started Sarge. He caught his breath as he sat upright in his chair. The evening was beautiful, despite the unrest throughout the city. This conversation was long overdue. For now, they were in their world. He needed to tell her how he felt.

The first explosion rocked their building as the Scotia Street substation erupted into flames just one mile to their southwest. Julia spilled her wine, jumping out of her chair. Sarge got to his feet as the Mystic substation exploded into flames to their northeast in Everett. A dark hole appeared where the power grid collapsed. Within thirty seconds, similar sudden and violent detonations occurred in all directions.

Sarge and Julia instinctively ducked with each explosion. Methodically, Boston was thrust into darkness. As each substation became overloaded, power was rapidly transferred by predetermined computer protocols. The cascading overload of the transformers throughout the city resembled mortar rounds reaching their targets. The substation explosions sounded like bombs detonating.

"Sarge! Are we under attack?"

"I don't know. Are you okay?"

"Yes, but what the hell?"

"I don't know, but let's get off this roof. Stay down and head for the stairwell."

The lack of moonlight hindered Sarge and Julia's ability to find their way to the rooftop entry door. Sarge's first instinct was to get to safety. He had never experienced an adrenaline rush like this. Now he knew what Steven experienced when in a war zone. The unknown made his mind race. They reached the door and found darkness in the stairwell except for the faint glow of emergency lighting on each of the floors below.

"Julia, I have no idea what's happening. But we don't need to panic. We've prepared for something like this."

"Like what? What is *this*?" asked Julia.

"We'll find out as soon as we can. First, we have to secure the top three floors. Follow me downstairs and then get us some different clothes and temporary lighting. I'm going to make my way through the stairwell and put into place the reinforced door security bars."

"Safety first, young man!" shouted Julia. Sarge laughed and was proud of Julia. She might have been apprehensive for a moment, but then she caught herself.

"Let's take care of business first, and then we'll figure out what happened. Okay?"

"Yes. Weapons too?" she asked.

"I'm afraid so. Not the heavy stuff. Just sidearms until we can conduct a better assessment."

"Let's go!" Julia pushed past him and bolted down the first flight of stairs, which led into the Great Hall near the pantry. She pressed the electronic keypad to gain entry. As she did so, Sarge patted himself on the back for insisting that the three floors he occupied at

100 Beacon be off the grid. There were many collapse scenarios anticipated by Sarge and the rest of the Loyal Nine, but all contemplated a grid-down scenario. *Like this one?*

Sarge quickly descended the remainder of the three flights of stairs to the security door installed to prevent access to the roof by the other residents. When the Boston Brahmin led by John Morgan acquired 100 Beacon, they spared no expense in creating an inner-city fortress designed as a haven in the event of social unrest, or worse.

Sarge was first approached in 2009 about the concept of preparedness when Morgan was considering the purchase of 100 Beacon. The building was in need of renovation, but one of the conditions of the Board of Zoning Appeals was that it be architecturally restored in a manner consistent with its original construction—dating back nearly one hundred years. Morgan retained ownership of the top three floors. He immediately began putting together a team capable of protecting him and his fellow Boston Brahmin, in anticipation of a collapse event. He wanted Sarge to oversee the renovations and occupy the top-floor penthouse. Morgan had a vision, and now Sarge was implementing years of planning.

With the assistance of the local fire marshal and the building inspector, a private stairwell was allowed connecting the three floors occupied by Sarge—the eighth floor and the two penthouse floors above it. When Morgan advised Sarge to spare no expense, the three levels of 100 Beacon containing twelve thousand square feet was the first indication that he'd meant it.

The top floor, known as Penthouse I, consisted of Sarge's master suite, the guest room suite occupied by his brother Steven, a study, and the Great Hall—a massive living and dining area overlooking the Charles River. Penthouse II, located on the ninth floor, had a similar floor plan except there were more bedrooms. This level was designed as a housing unit for long-term guests—*under circumstances just like this one*. The eighth floor was the most important part of the entire 100 Beacon project. All aspects of a comprehensive preparedness plan had been addressed—nutrition, security, medical, communications, and alternative energy.

Sarge reached the eighth floor and the steel security door connecting their three levels to the remainder of the building. This door had reinforced locks and a biometric keypad on both sides to grant entry. Sarge confirmed that the keypad was functional. He glanced up at the security cameras to confirm their operation. The flashing red light provided his answer.

The steel door was virtually impenetrable. Only several direct hits from a rocket-propelled grenade could breach the door frame, but the weapon's operator would die trying in the close confines of the stairwell. An external door to the building's fire escape was located here as well. The fire marshal refused to allow a reinforced steel door for this purpose. So, as an extra precaution, steel bars were available to Sarge to block entry from the outside. Every castle had a weak spot. This fire exit was their soft underbelly.

CHAPTER 21

September 3, 2016
9:22 p.m.
100 Beacon
Boston, Massachusetts

Boston was entirely dark except for fires burning throughout the city. Sarge returned to the penthouse and found Julia lighting candles in the Great Hall. The emergency lights of first responders could be seen scurrying back and forth on Storrow Drive and across the Longfellow Bridge to their north. There was no discernible pattern or priority for them. They were only reacting.

"There are some clothes for you on the kitchen island," said Julia as she lit the last candle. "Was everything good downstairs?"

"No problem. I did hear some faint voices in the stairwell below, but that was it." Sarge slipped out of his dress pants and polo shirt into khaki cargo pants and a black long-sleeve tee shirt Julia laid out for him. Forgetting the circumstances for a moment, he grabbed a bottled water out of the refrigerator. This simple act reminded him that decisions had to be made about the generator.

"Some of these fires appear to be out of control," said Julia. "If there's no electricity, the city's fire departments won't be able to keep up." Sarge joined her at the window and hugged her around the waist. She took his water and finished it off.

"Did you pull out some of the communications gear?" he asked.

"Only your satellite phone. If this is EMP related, we should leave the other equipment in the Faraday cages for a while in the event there is another strike. But I'm beginning to doubt it was an electromagnetic pulse."

"Tell me what you're thinking."

"After the hack on the Vegas power grid in February, I became very interested in what the potential threats are to the grid. As we discussed in the hotel that night, a solar flare provides us at least a modicum of warning. Usually, NOAA or NASA would detect an incoming coronal mass ejection a day in advance. No country has ever experienced a catastrophic nuclear-delivered EMP, so it's hard to say what might happen. But the cell phones are operable, although the circuits are overloaded. Vehicles are operating. Our alarm and entry system is off the grid, but the small circuits that make up the systems might be fried by an EMP."

"Are you thinking cyber attack?" asked Sarge.

"Yes. But to what extent—I don't know."

"Based on what we saw from the roof, Boston's power grid has collapsed. Every substation and transformer for miles exploded or is on fire. What we don't know is whether it's localized or part of a larger attack. Either way, there's work to be done."

"Have you tried to connect to the Internet on the satphone?"

"Not yet. The standby battery life is one hundred hours. It's down to an hour talk time now, so it needs to be charged. We have some calls to make first." Julia walked into the kitchen to retrieve the Iridium handheld IsatPhone. It rang as she picked it up, startling her.

"Little jumpy, are ya?" asked Sarge in his best Mainah accent. He took the phone from her as it rang again. He leaned in and gave her a quick kiss. "Grab the broadband satellite so we can figure this thing out."

Julia gave him a thumbs-up as she headed for the next floor down and the Faraday cages.

"Yes," Sarge said into the receiver.

"Of course, Mr. Morgan, I was expecting your call." Sarge took instruction from his benefactor without interrupting. He fumbled through the kitchen drawer, looking for pen and paper. "May I put you on speaker while I write this down? Okay, sir. I'm ready."

"Henry, they're waiting for you to contact them," said Morgan. "I do not believe the cellular service will be operating much longer, so you will have to communicate with them soon to make the arrangements. I don't know whether my associates kept their batteries charged on the satellite phones Mr. Quinn provided. You will know soon enough."

Great. "Yes, sir," said Sarge.

"These are my friends, Henry, and I trust you with their lives," said Morgan as he provided the names of the Boston Brahmin executive council. "Cabot. Lowell. Lodge. Bradlee. Endicott. Winthrop. Peabody. Tudor." Sarge scribbled the names on a lined notepad. He knew where some of them lived. Picking them up, and in what order, would require some thought.

"Okay, sir, I've got it. Do I keep them here?"

"Henry, this power outage is widespread and quite likely long-lasting. You will need to have them taken to Prescott Peninsula. A military escort will be available to you. Let me reiterate, I am entrusting you with the lives of my oldest and dearest friends. I know I can count on you."

"Of course, sir. Travel safe and bring home your daughter, sir."

"Thank you, Henry." Morgan disconnected the call.

Sarge placed the phone on the counter. He picked up the notepad and looked at the names—the Boston Brahmin executive council. Sarge walked into his study to retrieve his address book from the safe. He took a moment to examine the collection of Thomas Cole reproductions given to him as a gift by the Loyal Nine. The collection, entitled The *Course of Empire*, was a five-part series of paintings created in the 1830s. In the paintings, Cole depicted the rise and fall of empires—from its savage, uninhabited state to destruction and then desolation. These paintings represented Sarge's core beliefs about the future of America. His lectures reflected this central theme:

All Empires Collapse Eventually

Morgan's words weighed heavily on his mind—*widespread, long-lasting.* Sarge believed he was groomed for this moment. After the death of his parents, John Morgan, as his godfather, became a big part of his life. His interest in the raising of Sarge and his brother, Steven, went beyond his role as their godfather. He had a plan for their lives. For the past seven years, somehow Sarge knew this moment would come. *So did John Morgan.*

Julia interrupted his thoughts. "I assume that was the boss?"

"Yes, indeed. We have our marching orders. But we need to sit down for a moment."

Julia set the Hughes broadband antenna and the MacBook on the island. "That sounds ominous."

"Yes. As usual, he was aloof and brief. In the face of collapse, he will always remain stoic."

"Collapse?" asked Julia.

"Honey, the words he used were *widespread* and *long-lasting.*"

"How does he know?" she asked.

"He's John Morgan."

CHAPTER 22

September 3, 2016
9:47 p.m.
100 Beacon
Boston, Massachusetts

Julia set up the broadband satellite connection. When she and Donald Quinn researched the options available from Inmarsat, she looked for a system that made sense in an urban environment. Donald chose a system ideal for remote operations, like Prescott Peninsula. She chose the BGAN system that was designed for a temporary office environment. Plus, it met military and government requirements for encryption. *You never knew who would be listening.*

"Julia, I can't find the Endicotts' address. Did I send them a Christmas card last year?"

"I think so, but I don't have that address book with me. Let me see what I can find." Most Americans were frantic, seeking information about the power outage. Julia knew the nation was screwed. It was time to get used to this new way of living after *the end of the world as we know it.*

She found the address and scribbled on Sarge's notepad. He had been studying a map and was formulating a plan to retrieve the Boston Brahmin. As the satellite Internet system booted, she turned her attention to Sarge.

"We have eight families to pick up," said Julia. "We can't get them all at once." She sat down next to Sarge on the couch. Ordinarily, the six flat-screens would be distributing the news from all points of view. Tonight, they hung on the wall dormant.

"I'm going to start making calls, but I have a general plan. I want to start with your aunt and uncle, followed by the Winthrops—here." Sarge pointed to the home of Dr. and Mrs. Arthur Peabody in Brookline. Estelle Peabody was Julia's father's sister. Dr. Peabody was a plastic surgeon in private practice. He was the youngest of the Boston Brahmin at age fifty-five. Sarge then circled an area to the southwest called Ledgebrook, in Newton. Ledgebrook was an upscale condominium complex where the best friends of his parents, Mr. and Mrs. Paul Winthrop, resided. Now in their late seventies, they were longtime friends of the Sargent family and Sarge's namesake.

"How many do you think we can pick up tomorrow?" she asked.

"We need to discuss logistics. I don't like leaving 100 Beacon unattended. I think this first trip should be made as early as possible in the morning before the entire city realizes we're screwed. After that, you need to stay here."

"You shouldn't go out alone, right?"

"I agree. I think Art might be up for it. He's in great physical shape, and I've seen him at the range. He can handle a weapon. What do you think?"

"I think Aunt Stella is going to say hell no, that's what I think." Julia threw her pen on the map. She didn't want her uncle in harm's way either. It wasn't fair to him or her aunt.

"Julia, I understand where you're coming from. But I have to be brutally honest. I don't know what it will be like on the streets. Tomorrow morning may be okay, but what about the afternoon when word starts to spread? Or Monday morning when the entire city could be crazy?" Sarge looked her in the eye and held both of her hands. "We can't both be out there if something goes south." There. Sarge said it out loud. *The reality.* Picking up the Boston Brahmin was not just a matter of a Sunday drive down to Brookline to pick up the old folks for brunch. Their part of the world had become very dangerous—*rapidly.*

"If Uncle Art is capable enough to ride with you on the pickups, then he should be able to handle things here while we're gone," protested Julia halfheartedly.

Sarge squeezed her hands a little tighter. "Honey, if something happens to me, they'll need you here. You know everything that we've done, and how our planning has to be followed."

Julia started to well up with tears. Her emotions had nothing to do with the collapse, but everything to do with the thought of losing Sarge. "I love you, Sarge."

"I love you too. Listen. Nothing is going to happen to either one of us. We just have to be smart. Okay?"

She nodded as he wiped away the tears.

"Let me make the calls while you find out what has happened." Sarge turned his attention back to his map and notes, and Julia returned to the kitchen island. The MacBook awaited her commands.

Accessing the Internet via satellite was not that different from using a modem at home. Julia retrieved a small rectangular antenna and attached it by cable to her MacBook. The satellite sent and received a signal from an orbiting geostationary satellite about twenty thousand miles above the equator. This satellite communicated with various network operations centers around the world. Julia laughed to herself. Contrary to the popular belief of egocentric Americans, the world did not stop just because your personal universe was awry.

Any obstacle, such as a mountain or a building, would interfere with a satellite signal. Before she received delivery of the unit and its backup, she utilized a Look Angle Calculator to determine if her plan was feasible. An online tool, the calculator allowed you to insert your address anywhere in the world and the closest longitudinal satellite to determine your line-of-sight. The southern line-of-sight from the top floor of 100 Beacon was not obstructed by the buildings across the street. If necessary, she could move to the rooftop, but so far, her connectivity was excellent.

Once received, Julia was amazed at the satellite system's capability. This ability to connect to the Internet became the centerpiece of her Digital Carrier Pigeon communications system.

She found the Inmarsat home screen and got started. The power outage itself would affect individual websites and their servers. She might not be able to access BostonHerald.com, but a foreign news source like the BBC should be functioning. She started there. The home-page headline said it all: *Most of Continental U.S. in Dark.*

The report was admittedly based upon sketchy details. Julia read the article:

Based upon sporadic cell phone communications, the BBC can report that the entire lower forty-eight states, except for Texas, are without power. At approximately 9:11 p.m. Eastern time, the United States experienced a massive cascading blackout of its western and eastern interconnected grid. Apparently, the Texas grid, which is separate from the rest of the country, is still fully operational. There was no immediate known cause, but speculation ranges from an electromagnetic pulse weapon to a massive cyber attack. No terrorist group has claimed responsibility. Reports and video are streaming into the BBC newsroom and are currently being analyzed for authenticity. At this point, no one at 10 Downing Street is prepared to comment.

Julia tried CNN International to no avail. The Reuters website contained a story similar to what was released on the BBC. The USA.gov and FEMA.gov websites were operating, but there were no announcements or warnings. It was simply too early to gain any credible information. The fact that the majority of the power grid was collapsed was all they needed to know at this point. If they waited on the government to give them advice, it would be too late. *We can always take the Boston Brahmin home if the power comes back.*

"Okay, that was my last call. I couldn't reach the Tudors or Endicotts. I'll try again later or in the morning. Truthfully, they're probably asleep already and don't even know about it. What did you find out?" Sarge walked over to Julia and put his arm around her waist as he studied the laptop's screen. "I see our government is still pushing Benefits, Grants, and Loans."

Julia laughed. "Sorry, America, the government freebie spigot is closed indefinitely because the Treasury could no longer pay its bills." She turned towards Sarge.

"The BBC is the only reporting I could find. According to their initial reports, only the utility grids of Texas, Hawaii, and Alaska are unattected. There is no known cause, and no terrorist group has taken credit. We're in the dark—pardon the pun." She stood up and walked to the pantry, grabbing a box of Triscuits. She and Sarge both took a handful.

"So, former Professor Sargent, what's the plan?" She munched on the crackers and smiled at him, tilting her head to one side playfully. He walked towards her and grabbed some more Triscuits.

"This is going to sound crazy, but there's nothing to do right now except make calls to the rest of the Loyal Nine. Steven and Katie are in D.C. Brad's at Fort Devens. The Quinns are at Prescott Peninsula with J.J. and Sabs."

"What about the generators?"

"We don't need the generators yet," replied Sarge. "Tomorrow, we'll run them for a while to charge batteries and chill the refrigeration units. I want to wait until there's sufficient road noise to drown out the hum of the units."

"The weather is very mild for Labor Day weekend. The AC is out of the question. Of course, we have to maintain light discipline at night." Julia poured water out of the tap into their bottles, which reminded her of the gravity-fed rooftop water tank. "Will you switch the tank tonight or in the morning?"

"Already done. I turned the valves on the way up the stairwell."

"You're on top of it, I see." Julia shrugged. "The apocalypse is boring so far."

"There are three things we can do before the excitement of the apocalypse picks up tomorrow."

"Okay, what?" Julia set the water and Triscuits on the counter, eager to help.

"It might be a while, but we should take a good hot shower and get a solid night's rest." Sarge came toward her with that *man look*.

"Makes sense. And what is the third thing?" *She already knew.*

"We should probably take advantage of this last opportunity *alone*, if you know what I mean?"

"You're so full of it, Henry Sargent." She led him toward the master suite. *No need to turn out the lights as we go.*

Chapter 23

Sunday, September 4, 2016
6:17 a.m.
100 Beacon
Boston, Massachusetts

Sarge was up before sunrise, as always. Julia was sleeping peacefully, and he resisted the urge to give her a wake-up call. Today was going to be an interesting day. He made arrangements with the Winthrops and Peabodys to be ready between seven and eight this morning. The concept of America in a state of collapse was going to be difficult for these families to grasp. They were all wealthy and used to a posh lifestyle. Money or comfort had never been an issue for them. Their world was about to become much smaller, less social, and less complicated. Sarge hoped that would not hinder his dangerous task this week—keeping them safe.

Out of habit, he approached his Keurig machine for his morning fix of a Gevalia Mocha Latte. That wasn't an option yet. He almost reached for his plan B, a bottled Starbucks Frappuccino out of the refrigerator, and he caught himself. *Don't let the cold air out.* He stared into the living area in just his pajama bottoms. It was still dark outside. Pitch black. No lights whatsoever except for the flashing red aircraft warning lights atop the skyscrapers. They twinkled like red Christmas lights—there to warn low-flying aircraft that no longer flew.

The reality was setting in for Sarge. This was not a drill, as Donald liked to call them. This was not a minor inconvenience until Eversource Energy got their act together. Morgan's words rang in his head: *widespread and long-lasting.* We now lived in the 1800s.

"Sarge, is everything all right?" asked Julia from the bedroom. Sarge walked back that way to get dressed.

"Yeah, it's fine. I'm just getting my bearings. I'm trying to get used to the *new normal*."

"I know what you mean," said Julia. "When I woke up and you weren't here, the first thing I did was look at the clock to see what time it was. It's weird, isn't it?"

"It is," he replied. "It was kind of nice to wake up naturally. You know, not rousted out of bed by a screaming alarm clock."

Julia crawled back under the covers. "It's still dark outside. There is nothing *natural* about this at all." Now that she was awake, he was tempted to join her, but today was day one of a different world.

"Stay away from me, temptress. I need to get ready."

"Boo. Party pooper." She rolled over. Sarge fumbled his way in the dark to his clothes from last night. Laundry was going to happen less often as well.

As he dressed, he thought about weapons and the perils of going into public. Would a concealed-carry weapon in a paddle holster be sufficient? Should he take a backup strapped to his ankle? Should he wear a full kit and tote an AR-15 everywhere he went? He knew going onto the streets unarmed could get him killed. But carrying an AR down the stairwell to his car this morning might scare the bejesus out of the neighbors and draw unnecessary attention to himself. He decided it was too early for the heavy firepower.

Sarge made his way in the dark and found the hidden compartment behind a wainscot panel. When he popped it open, the inside light illuminated the biometric safe, which contained his sidearm options. He grabbed his favorite Heckler & Koch HK45C. He left the Gemtech suppressor in the vault. If he was forced to use his weapon at this stage of the collapse, he wanted it to send a loud and clear message. He placed the HK45C in an ankle holster and strapped it to his leg. He grabbed his 5.11 tactical belt with his Galcon holster. He inserted an HK45 full-size tactical model and strapped it to his waist. Sarge's long black tee shirt covered the weapon, but not the bulge. Seasoned law enforcement or military personnel would be able to recognize the telltale signs that he was carrying. Most citizens would not. But Sarge knew he would never leave 100 Beacon without these two weapons—at a minimum. He slipped an extra loaded magazine into each cargo pocket of his pants, and he was good to go.

Before he closed the safe, he picked up Steven's Glock G38 and his thoughts turned to his brother. He and Katie had a long trip home under normal circumstances. What kind of hurdles would they have to leap to make it in one piece? If anybody could make it, his brother Rambo and his girlfriend Rambette were the ones.

Sarge closed up the safe after retrieving Julia's sidearm, a matching HK45C. All of the Loyal Nine were issued sidearms in .45 caliber. Donald insisted on interchangeable makes, models, and calibers for all weapons. Sarge liked the HKs, which were lightweight, suppressor ready, and provided the lightest recoil. The low recoil helped the women shoot better and kept everyone on target at the range. Also, the ambidextrous controls on the weapons helped the two lefties in the group.

"Julia, I've gotta get going." Sarge headed back to the bedroom, where she stood inside the door naked.

"You are so sexy when you are all *gunned up*," she said seductively. He walked up and admired her beauty.

"Bad form, missy. How am I supposed to concentrate on the task at hand when I have this vision of loveliness clouding my brain?"

"This is what you have to come home to, sir. It should be an incentive not to get your ass shot off."

Sarge closed his eyes and enjoyed the moment as he held her. "I do love you," he whispered.

She pressed against him. "And I love you, soldier. Come back to me safely—direct orders from headquarters."

"Roger. I love you." They kissed, and Sarge headed for the outside and the new normal.

CHAPTER 24

September 4, 2016
7:11 a.m.
The streets of Boston, Massachusetts

Sarge bounded down the eleven flights of stairs to the basement garage where his vehicles were parked. At this hour, he didn't encounter any neighbors in the stairwell. *Good. Stay home.*

While it was tempting to drive his Mercedes G-Wagen, he knew the prudent option would be to take the slightly less conspicuous 1968 Toyota OJ40. Most of the Loyal Nine had a bug-out vehicle that was EMP-resistant. The research on the effect an electromagnetic pulse might have on a vehicle was spotty at best. Most of the articles found on the web were based on speculation. In an abundance of caution, Sarge purchased the Brazilian-made Bandeirante model because it had a reliable Mercedes-Benz diesel engine and a lack of electronic-dependent parts. If they were ever forced into the country, farm diesel or comparable biofuels was an option. His OJ40 was the long, hardtop model often used in Africa for sightseeing in the bush. For today, it would make the perfect post-apocalyptic limousine for the Boston Brahmin.

Sarge checked the three security lenses that allowed views of appropriately designated Back Street to the north, and the east side of his building. He unlatched the safety bar and pulled down on the chain, rolling the door overhead. With his hand on his weapon, he quickly walked out onto the inlaid brick driveway to check for threats. It was remarkably quiet except for the sparse traffic on Storrow. *Maybe this will go smoothly after all.*

Sarge pulled out and closed the door behind him. Immediately, he realized he made a mistake by leaving the keys in the ignition and the engine running. Innocent habits or mistakes from before could cause real problems now. He drove around the building and turned southwest onto Beacon. There were a couple of his neighbors standing on the front sidewalk, talking—undoubtedly exchanging theories and opinions. None appeared to have weapons. One appeared to be in his pajamas and robe. Before they could flag him to chitchat, Sarge sped down Beacon. The streets were mostly deserted except for the occasional pedestrians. As he drove the six miles to Chestnut Hill and his first pickup, he wondered how long it would take to spread the word that the power was going to be off indefinitely. *At what point will curiosity turn to aggravation, then to panic, and finally to desperation.*

Businesses and residences appeared to be intact until he approached the Harvard Street intersection. The entrance to Trader Joe's had been demolished by a large box truck. The truck appeared to have backed into the entry to break in but then got stuck. The truck was too tall to fit under the arched brick entryway and got wedged. A Boston police department unit was on the scene.

Sarge thought about how the local grocery stores would deal with their inventories. Without power, they would be unable to conduct sales transactions. Once it became general knowledge that the power was out virtually nationwide, would the stores give the food away? Perhaps donate it to the police for distribution? More importantly, would the good citizens of Boston, or anywhere in America, for that matter, wait on the local grocers to make a decision? Perhaps they would simply help themselves.

He continued down Beacon Street past the Chestnut Hill Reservoir toward Boston College. His students immediately came to mind. Fall classes were supposed to begin on Tuesday, although his lectures started a day later. Every year during Labor Day weekend, students would be returning from their hometowns all over the world. Some might already be here. After ten years, he still felt excited for a new semester. While the subject matter stayed the same, current events would shift, yielding a new twist to each lecture. God, he loved teaching. *He would miss it.*

After turning onto Hammond, he noticed a CVS Pharmacy being guarded by a private security team. No surprise there. He always thought the first business to be looted after a collapse event would be the drug store. The addicts would be looking for drugs, and the preppers would be looking for antibiotics. None of the security guards were armed. Sarge was sure that whoever hired them insisted they not scare the residents or patrons. He doubted they would feel the same way tomorrow, if they even showed up.

Sarge finally reached the Beaver Country Day school that Julia said was across from the entrance to the Peabodys' home. He resisted the urge to drive the wrong way on the one-way street, opting instead to follow *the rules.* When did the rule of law get thrown out the window? There was a lot to contemplate, but for now, Sarge was ready for his first pickup.

Art Peabody was waiting for him alone in the driveway. He was wearing khakis, a black polo shirt, and tennis shoes. *Should he call him Uncle Art? Maybe it was too early for that.* Sarge cranked down the window and smiled.

"Hi, Dr. Peabody, I see you're ready." Sarge pulled to a stop and shut off the engine. Dr. Peabody opened the door for him.

"Henry Sargent. It has been a long time, but not so long that you shouldn't remember to call me Art." He extended his soft surgeon's hand, and the men shook heartily. He seemed to be in good spirits. From around the hedgerow came Julia's aunt Stella. She was wearing golf attire.

"Hello, Mrs. Peabody," greeted Sarge. He attempted to shake her hand but was treated to a hug instead.

"Now listen," she started. "You will call me Stella, just as Art and I will call you Sarge. We are practically *family*, you know." Sarge had to think through the Sargent family tree quickly to see if the Peabodys, Hawthornes, and Sargents ever crossed paths.

"She's right, Sarge," interjected Dr. Peabody. "Our Julia is very fond of you. You are practically *family*." Sarge got it. Family—used in the *practically-our-son-in-law* sense of the word. Sarge tried not to seem uncomfortable. Maybe *Uncle Art* was appropriate after all.

"Thank you both, very much. Have you packed a few things?" Sarge didn't see any luggage or bags.

"Well, we weren't sure how long we'd be when you called last night, Sarge," said Mrs. Peabody. She looked down at the ground, appearing to gather courage for the statement. "But then Art received a few random text messages from colleagues around the country who believe this may take months or even years to resolve."

"Information was spotty last night, Mrs.—Stella," said Sarge, catching himself. "Julia will know a lot more when we get back to 100 Beacon. If necessary, we might be able to come back and get more things for you."

"Sarge, thank you," said Dr. Peabody. "But we are under no illusions here. John has told us repeatedly that you have prepared for this scenario, and we trust you to have our best interests at heart. We will follow your instructions."

"Thank you, Art," replied Sarge. Sarge steered them back toward the entrance. "Please, lead the way."

They each had two Louis Vuitton duffels that Sarge loaded through the back hatch of his truck. Dr. Peabody went in to retrieve one more item. He closed the front door and locked the bolt lock. *Was this habit, or hoping for the best?*

"Whatcha got there, Art?" asked Sarge. He was carrying a gun case.

"We might need these," he replied. "I have two Browning AB3 hunting rifles in .308. We each have one, plus compact nines in our bags."

"Stella, do you like to hunt?" asked Sarge. He was impressed.

"I prefer target practice," she replied. "I was born on a farm, you know."

Dr. Peabody laughed. "Farm, my ass, Stella. The Hawthorne Vineyards hardly qualified as a farm. Over a thousand acres, Sarge." Dr. Peabody gave his wife a hug and a squeeze. "Don't let her modesty fool you. If necessary, we'll put her on the roof of your building. Trust me. She doesn't miss."

"Good to know," said Sarge. "Well, let's go, troops. We need to pick up the Winthrops."

CHAPTER 25

September 4, 2016
8:08 a.m.
Newton, Massachusetts

Sarge hoped all the stops would go this smoothly. He had not visited the Winthrops since Thanksgiving last year. He was sure he would catch an earful from Mrs. Winthrop. She had been his mother's best friend. In fact, the Winthrops and Sargents were inseparable—frequently traveling together and sharing other *common interests*. Descendants of John Winthrop, one of the leading figures in the founding of the Massachusetts Bay Colony, their family became synonymous with the state's politics and philanthropy. The two families became close when Sarge's grandfather was governor of Massachusetts and his lieutenant governor was R. C. Winthrop. The families remained close friends and became a valuable political force on behalf of the Boston Brahmin. Sarge's parents would have been glad their safety was placed in his hands.

"Here we are," said Sarge as he pulled into the circle driveway of the Winthrops' home that was modest by Boston Brahmin standards. Julia's aunt and uncle exited the truck to assist with the bags. The Winthrops were in their late seventies, and Millicent Winthrop had been in ill health. Her husband, Paul, expressed these health concerns to Sarge, who assured him her medical problems would not be an issue.

After some pleasantries were exchanged, Sarge filled the truck to capacity. Like Art Peabody, Paul returned with one last addition to be loaded—Winnie the Frenchie. The Winthrops brought along their French bulldog. Sarge had not contemplated pets as part of the plan, and he chastised himself for not taking this into consideration. Pets were an integral part of most families, as important as children to some. Winnie the Frenchie would have everyday needs like shelter, food, water, and medical attention.

"I hope she's okay, Sarge?" asked Mr. Winthrop as he easily scooped up the twenty pounder. "Winnie is a part of our family, and Millie gets very depressed without her. Winnie will not be a bother, I promise."

Sarge could not object, especially under the circumstances. But he had not planned for the addition of pets in their preparedness plans. Several things came to mind, including how to dispose of a dog's waste.

"Well, my concern is that it's unsafe to walk pets now," started Sarge. "We will be confined to the building."

Mr. Winthrop, anticipating the objection, interrupted Sarge. "We have pet piddle pads, Sarge. Winnie is house trained too. She conducts her business on the piddle pad. We seal it up using the leak-proof backing and into the garbage it goes."

Garbage. How could he forget? How would they dispose of their trash? The waste chute at 100 Beacon would quickly overflow from the lack of city services. Winnie the Frenchie's piddle pads would be the least of their concerns.

"So, are we good to go, Sarge?" asked Mr. Winthrop, snapping Sarge's attention back to the task at hand.

"Of course," said Sarge. He glanced at his watch. It was after nine now, and the city of Boston would be awake in earnest, *for better or worse.*

CHAPTER 26

September 4, 2016
9:15 a.m.
100 Beacon
Boston, Massachusetts

Sarge took the same route back to 100 Beacon but was amazed at the difference in activity in just two hours. The rumored details of the grid collapse must have been spreading, because large groups of people were gathering on streets and at the front of closed businesses. People were shocked and in a state of panic. A large contingent pushed their way towards the front door of the CVS Pharmacy.

"Look, everyone," said Dr. Peabody, pointing at the dozen or so customers who demanded access to the CVS building. "They just knocked one of the guards down, and they're trying to break in. Should we help him? He looks injured."

"This is going to get worse," said Sarge as he continued past the store. "As people gather information, whether accurate or misinformed, their shock will turn to fear. The elderly, including some of our friends, will not have sufficient medications to last more than a month or two. As this becomes reality, then panic will set in. Looting and violence will increase, resulting in a state of mayhem. I suspect what we just observed at CVS is tame compared to what the coming days and weeks will produce."

Sarge worked his way toward Storrow. "Look at all of the cars leaving town on the Mass Turnpike!" exclaimed Mr. Winthrop. "Where are they going?"

"They're fleeing the city already," replied Sarge. "As each day passes, this urban environment will become far more dangerous. We have to move quickly to gather our friends and make arrangements to move you guys to a safer place."

"Prescott?" asked Mrs. Peabody. Two police cars roared past them towards the city. Very few cars were traveling in this direction.

"Yes," replied Sarge. "As you know, Mr. Morgan has undertaken an incredible project with our assistance. You will meet my friends, Donald and Susan Quinn, together with Dr. J.J. Warren."

"Everything has been arranged, dear," said Dr. Peabody to his wife. Sarge tried not to show a reaction to this statement, but it struck him as odd. *Arranged?*

Sarge slowed the truck as the exit for 100 Beacon drew near. Next to the garage entrance, there was a group of young men looking through the dumpster. Sarge wasn't comfortable entering the garage at this time but did not like the exposure of unloading his passengers at the front entrance of 100 Beacon either. He could have waited for the dumpster divers to leave, but he had another pickup to make today. As the afternoon progressed, these excursions into the city would grow perilous.

He decided to circle the block to assess the front-door option. He eased up to the stop sign at Beacon Street. Three calm-looking residents were standing at the wrought-iron fence. The lobby entrance might be more crowded, but for now, his neighbors' twenty questions posed less of a threat than the dumpster divers to the rear.

Sarge pulled up to the curb and parked under the *Evacuation Route* sign. He doubted parking enforcement would be issuing tickets for a long time.

"Everybody, before we get out, I need you to listen up. The less said to my neighbors, or anybody for that matter, the better. No one needs to know about our plans or intentions. If you're asked any questions, please do not answer. I am giving you carte blanche to be rude. From this point forward, remember the phrase from World War II—*loose lips sink ships.*"

"Okay, Henry." Mrs. Winthrop spoke up. "We trust you." Sarge looked in the back and smiled at her. For a moment, he saw his mom in her smile.

People were curious by nature. Some, in fact, felt they had an absolute right to know what you were doing. At times, when a person's curious nature was not accommodated, they grew hostile at the perceived insult. The fact that your activities were none of their business was lost on them. *They had a right to know.*

Sarge stepped out of the car and opened the door for the Winthrops. Art Peabody followed suit and assisted his wife out of the backseat. As Sarge rounded the vehicle, he was immediately approached by the male resident whom he recognized as a local attorney.

"You're Professor Sargent, the occupant of the top floor, are you not?" cross-examined his neighbor.

"Yes."

"Do you know what the hell is going on?"

"No, I don't," replied Sarge. Laying luggage on the sidewalk at the inquisitor's feet, he added, "Excuse me."

"Well now, you've obviously been around town. What have you seen?"

"Sir, I'm sorry, but I didn't see anything out of the ordinary," started Sarge, standing up and looking the attorney directly in the eyes. "I would like to help my friends upstairs, if you don't mind allowing us a little room to do so." Sarge didn't want to alienate the man, and he wasn't happy with the crowd of five nosy neighbors that had gathered around. He just wanted to get off this sidewalk. He decided to give a little information to move this along.

"Well, excuse us for intruding," said the man with disdain. "Like the rest of your *neighbors*, we are trying to ascertain a few facts."

"I am so sorry," said Sarge. "This is a stressful time for all of us as we cope with this situation. I probably know about as much as you do, and most of my information is based on rumor and conjecture. I believe the power grid is down across most of the nation, except for maybe Texas. I have no idea for how long. At this point, I'm trying to help some of my elderly friends by making them a little more comfortable."

"That's understandable, Professor," said the attorney. "I'm sure if you learn anything, you will come downstairs to inform the rest of us."

"Of course. We'll be on our way." Sarge led the Peabodys and Winthrops inside the lobby to the stairwell. It was a long walk up the eleven flights to the penthouse, requiring several rest stops. Sarge thought about the conversation on the sidewalk. As the realities set in for his neighbors, their curiosity would turn to demands. He would have to prepare for the consequences of their malevolence.

CHAPTER 27

September 4, 2016
12:15 p.m.
100 Beacon
Boston, Massachusetts

Sarge studied the laptop as Julia served their guests lunch. She focused on eating perishable food items first. Everyone understood and was delighted at the array of fruits and vegetables Julia displayed. As they talked around the dining table, this felt more like a Sunday family get-together than their first postapocalyptic meal. Sarge joined them with a look of concern on his face. Mrs. Winthrop noticed it first.

"Is everything okay, Henry?" she asked.

"There's nothing new," he replied. "It will take some time to gather details from the foreign news sources. I am sure their correspondents in the States have difficulty reporting and protecting themselves at the same time. Some cities are reporting that violence and looting are out of control already. New York, Chicago, LA, and Seattle are descending into anarchy."

Julia studied Sarge and knew that he was holding something back. Thus far, he had remained calm during this process, but she sensed he was tense after reviewing the news.

"Is there any reporting on the situation here in Boston?" asked Mr. Winthrop.

"Fortunately, at least thus far, we haven't seen any reports emanating from Boston," replied Sarge. "I don't think we're immune from the violence. It's just not widespread yet." Sarge only ate a few apple and orange wedges. He was bothered by something.

"Well." Julia spoke up, breaking the tension. "Who wants some sorbet?"

"What a fabulous treat, Julia," said Mr. Winthrop. His heavy frame shook as he laughed. "Let me help you."

"Oh no, you are our guests," said Julia. "Sarge, would you mind?" He was staring out towards Cambridge.

"Sure." Sarge gathered some dishes as the Winthrops and Peabodys engaged in small talk. Julia helped him set the dishes in the sink. Hand-washing the dishes would focus on eliminating bacteria with a minimal amount of water. Julia and Sarge agreed that using dishware was preferable to paper plates and cups as some had suggested. Trash disposal in an urban area was more difficult than the country.

"Sarge, what's wrong?"

Sarge glanced over his shoulder toward the dining table and then leaned into Julia's ear to whisper, "I was on the English-speaking website for the German newspaper *Die Zeit*. Chancellor Merkel has called an emergency meeting of the United Nations Security Council in Geneva. Several NATO members are pointing their fingers at Russia for attacking the United States. They're concerned about a sudden increase in Russian military activity in North America."

"Like what?" Julia asked.

"For months, Russian submarines have maintained a presence off our Gulf and Atlantic coastlines. It's now being reported Russian ships armed with unmanned submersibles have been seen operating in a major corridor of undersea transmission cables between Washington and Europe. NATO analysts believe the cables are vulnerable to compromise to further isolate America from communicating with the rest of the world."

"The Russians taking an interest in our cables is not a new thing," said Julia. "This potential was raised by Washington a few years ago."

"That's true, but we didn't do anything about it. Just like we didn't do anything about protecting our power grid from a cyber attack."

"What does it all mean?" asked Julia.

"Well, there's more. The Russians have established a major

military presence at the abandoned NATO facility near the Arctic Circle. This base gives the Russians a clear shot to our Atlantic Seaboard."

"They're preparing for war. Would they kick us while we're down?" asked Julia.

"The Russians may be the reason we're down. This is their MO."

"What do you mean?"

"If the collapse of our grid is the result of a cyber attack, there are several potential guilty parties. The Russians, Chinese, North Koreans, and Iranians constantly initiate cyber intrusions on the private and public sector in America. The Chinese use the cyber realm for espionage—military technology in particular. The North Korean and Iranian cyber capabilities are less sophisticated, but they would love nothing more than to cut off the evil Americans at their knees. But the Russians are different."

"How?"

"In the past, the Russians used their cyber capabilities as a precursor to war."

"Like Ukraine?" asked Julia.

"Ukraine is one example, although their cyber activities were not showcased like in previous conflicts," replied Sarge.

Julia finished wiping down the dishes with a moistened bleach towelette. She leaned against the sink and listened as Sarge continued.

"A better example was the Russian invasion of Georgia in 2008. In preparation for the Russia-Georgia border war, Russian hackers covertly penetrated the Internet infrastructure of Georgia to deploy an array of cyber attacks, logic bombs, and other cyber tools. Once the hot war began, the cyber weapons disabled the Tbilisi government and paralyzed Georgia's financial system. The resulting uncertainty lead to a de facto international banking quarantine, as international lenders and other payments processors feared infection from the cyber attack."

"Was this the first use of cyber attacks?"

"Oh no. Just a year before, in 2007, entities believed to have been associated with the Russian government or its allies launched a cyber attack against the nation of Estonia. The attack was undertaken as a result of a dispute sparked by the removal of a World War II–era Soviet soldier from a public park. The attacks crippled Estonia's digital infrastructure, paralyzed government and media sites, and shut down the former Soviet Republic's largest bank. While a hot war did not result, the Estonian virtual invasion proved to Putin that a cyber attack was a valuable first-strike weapon."

"Do you think the Russians did this?" asked Julia.

Sarge took in a deep breath. "The Russians are moving their naval vessels out of the Arctic base towards our eastern seaboard. Also, reports have the Russia Red Banner Pacific Fleet departing Vladivostok for the Aleutian Islands in Alaska. Despite our purchase of Alaska from the Russians in the 1860s, Putin has eyed Alaska as an oil-rich resource."

"He might be making a move against Alaska," said Julia.

"Or worse. He might be making a move on us. I believe this is why they have called the emergency meeting in Geneva. The world is pointing the finger of blame at the Russians. Putin might be preparing for war."

CHAPTER 28

September 4, 2016
2:24 p.m.
The Lowell and Cabot Estates
Wellesley, Massachusetts

Sarge studied the map as he planned his next route. It was time to
pick up the Cabots and Lowells. Mr. Morgan insisted on their
retrieval first, but Sarge chose to protect the members of the Boston
Brahmin closest to him and Julia. Sarge knew there was no formal
hierarchy amongst the Boston Brahmin. Wealth or lineage did not
determine leadership. The ability to wield power and influence was
the determining factor—*and respect*. Without question, John Morgan
was in charge.

In an 1860 article in the *Atlantic Monthly*, physician and author
Oliver Wendell Holmes Sr., father of the infamous United States
Supreme Court Justice, originated the term as a means of identifying
Boston's upper class. Members of the Boston Brahmin formed the
core of America's East Coast aristocracy. Descendants of the earliest
English colonists who came to America on the Mayflower, the
Founding Fathers, were represented within the group. Most of the
Boston Brahmin families could trace their ancestry back to the
original seventeenth-century American ruling class of
Massachusetts—including governors, magistrates, Harvard presidents
and the clergy.

At first, readers of the *Atlantic Monthly* became confused at the
comparison of America's gentry to the social caste system in India.
Brahmin, in the Hindu tradition, referred to one of four classes of
people who supposedly had gained a higher knowledge of the Hindu

religion. When asked about the use of the term, Holmes simply replied that the Brahmin were the harmless, inoffensive, and untitled aristocracy of America. After that, the term became used in literary circles of New England and stuck with the descendants of the Founding Fathers.

Bostonians and the rest of the world were unaware the Boston Brahmin existed as a loosely held organization, complete with an executive committee—and an agenda. While John Morgan was unanimously recognized as the head, Lawrence Lowell, and Walter Cabot were clearly next in the hierarchy.

The names Lowell and Cabot were learned by every school-age child in Massachusetts when the history of the American Revolution was taught to them. The Lowells and Cabots were also widely considered New England's first families.

Lowell was the son of the former president of Harvard and a direct descendant of John Lowell, a federal judge in the first United States Continental Congress. As far back as the sixteenth century, the Lowells and Winthrops were allies and friends. When Governor John Winthrop was named the governor of the Massachusetts Bay Colony, he immediately called upon the Lowell family to help settle the New England region.

As part of the present-day contingent of the Boston Brahmin, Lawrence Lowell and Walter Cabot were John Morgan's closest confidants. They were privy to *everything*.

"Turn here on Winding River," said Dr. Peabody. "The Lowells live at the end of the cul-de-sac on the Charles River." Sarge pulled up to the security gate that was closed. Dr. Peabody jumped out and entered the code to gain entry. Because the system was solar powered, it remained operable despite the power outage.

"Thank you for coming with me, Art. As we saw on the way over here, the further we go into this catastrophe, the more dangerous it is to be on the streets."

"It's not a problem at all, Sarge. I've trained with my handgun extensively, although I didn't want to remind Mrs. Peabody of that point. I don't think she considered the potential for use of weapons while we're picking up our friends."

Sarge exited the truck and replied, "I want to get everyone gathered as soon as possible, Art. I don't like the fact that some of the families will have to wait until tomorrow."

"Has Julia reached Henry Endicott yet?"

"Not yet. I know that he was instructed on the use of the satellite phone and the protocols to follow in the event of a situation like this one. We'll keep trying, but I feel compelled to help those we've contacted first."

Lawrence Lowell greeted them at the door. "Hello, Art! Greetings, Henry! It's a beautiful day to *bug out*, as they say." The men laughed at the elderly Lowell, whose portly belly shook at the reference to bugging out. Most of America's citizens were probably experiencing panic and fear, Lawrence Lowell was embracing the apocalypse as a new adventure.

"Hello, Mrs. Lowell," said Sarge as Constance Lowell emerged from the magnificent stone arched entry.

"Thank you for coming, Henry," she said. It did not appear that Mrs. Lowell was quite as enthusiastic as her jovial husband. "Lawrence, I suppose you will need help with my bags."

Lowell opened both entry doors to reveal six suitcases, two hanging bags, and a hatbox.

"Oh crap," Sarge muttered to Dr. Peabody. He wasn't sure if he could get all of this in the truck.

"Connie may have packed a little too much," started Lowell apologetically. "I tried to explain to her that we could return to get more clothes later."

Clueless. "Mrs. Lowell, I'm afraid we don't have room for all of your bags. We have to pick up the Cabots, and they will have bags of their own."

"You see, Lawrence," Mrs. Lowell said. "We should just drive our car. Why don't you be a dear and drive the Bentley around? Then we won't have to *inconvenience* this young man." Sarge bristled at the reference but then brushed it off. Mrs. Lowell was elderly and had been New England gentry her entire life. This was just her—*way.*

"Mr. Lowell, it's not an inconvenience, but we have limited space—and time," said Sarge. "Also, sir, driving a Bentley around Boston right now is a terrible idea."

Mr. Lowell pondered for a moment, and then he turned to his wife. "Constance, pick the two most important pieces of luggage, and we'll hold the suit bags in our laps. I don't believe you'll need any hats in the near future."

With a pout, she tapped two suitcases and grabbed up her suit bags. She never spoke a word after that. Sarge hoped that she would come around after reality set in. Otherwise, she was going to make things difficult for everyone with her attitude.

It took only a few minutes to reach the entry of the Cabot Estate. As Sarge approached, he was surprised to see two armed men approaching from his left. He was about to hit reverse out of the private drive when they raised their hands and shouted for him to wait. Sarge pulled his weapon and laid it in his lap. He rolled down his window. He didn't like being in this vulnerable position.

"Professor Sargent, we're with Aegis. We've worked with your brother, Steven." Sarge analyzed their posture and the expressions on their faces. They were not a threat to him. He holstered his weapon.

"I wasn't expecting security. When I spoke with Mr. Cabot last night, he didn't mention having a team present." Sarge's eyes darted to the rearview mirror to catch Lowell's attention. "Mr. Lowell, did you have security as well?"

"I did," replied Lowell. "They were sent home this morning just before your arrival. They have families too, Henry."

Sarge turned his attention back to the Aegis security personnel. "How many members of the team are on the premises?"

"There are two more of us at the house."

"Okay, thank you for approaching us with caution, and the explanation. Open the gate, please." The security team operated a remote-access fob and opened the solar-powered security gate. As Sarge drove down the half-mile-long driveway toward the main house, he thought about the dispatch of security personnel to the Lowell and Cabot residences. *Does Aegis keep staff available twenty-four seven for emergency security details?* Why wasn't he informed?

"Mr. Lowell, did you have four security members as well?"

"Yes, Henry." *Well, they could have brought you to 100 Beacon.* Sarge was puzzled by this. Something was nagging at him.

As he entered the circle drive, the other members of the Aegis team approached the truck. They opened the door for Sarge as Walter Cabot greeted them. After a few friendly words exchanged between the passengers, they were soon on their way.

CHAPTER 29

September 4, 2016
4:06 p.m.
100 Beacon
Boston, Massachusetts

Sarge brought up the last of the luggage. The trek up and down eleven flights of stairs would take its toll as food became rationed. It was important to maintain their nutrition levels, but calorie intake would suffer. The Quinns had spent a considerable amount of time researching nutritional supplements to complement the food stored in their *prepper pantry*.

In addition to vitamin supplements, one of the most useful items was high-calorie protein powders. The shelf life was typically a couple of years, but the potency levels would maintain much longer. Susan had stocked their pantry with vanilla-flavored powder. Even past its sell-by date, the intensity of the vanilla flavoring would start to fade. But its value as a supplement could still be used by cooking it with oatmeal, pancakes, and muffins. In an urban environment where the ability to hunt was nonexistent, Sarge considered these drink supplements an excellent source of protein and energy.

The ambient traffic noise, although sparse, allowed the generator to run. The twenty-two-kilowatt Generac unit, which powered the three floors occupied by the Loyal Nine, was only a temporary solution to their power needs. Their urban off-grid system was designed to run via the powerful generator, which was charged by being hard-wired to the grid. In the event of an EMP or extraordinary power surge, the GE-designed protection devices would act as a shield to the Generac—absorbing the surge. The electronics and appliances servicing 100 Beacon would never be vulnerable to the surge in power.

Sarge planned to use the Generac for a few hours a day until the solar array could be installed. He had counted on Steven or Donald to help with the task, but Donald was at Prescott Peninsula, and Steven was heading home. He also needed to install the HughesNet Gen 5 satellite Internet system to provide more information options. The Gen 5 was a more complex system than the portable unit Julia was relying upon, and with faster speeds. A similar system was being installed at Prescott Peninsula. Around the country, like-minded *friends* would be installing their version of the Digital Carrier Pigeon to keep open lines of communication and to share information.

"Sir, I believe you've earned this," said Julia as she handed Sarge his beloved Gevalia Mocha Latte. He closed his eyes and took in the aroma.

"Wow, this is heaven. Are you an angel?"

"Sort of, but not always, sir," she replied, giving him a much-needed hug.

"Are our guests settling in?" Sarge asked. The Winthrops and the Peabodys decided to share a room on the ninth floor—known as Penthouse II. They allowed the Cabots and Lowells to share the master suite.

"They are indeed. Mrs. Lowell has been a little fussy, but the other ladies decided to let her stew in her own madness. I've been very impressed with Aunt Stella. It appears she has been practicing shooting with my uncle, and they both have been watching disaster films of late. They have the mindset to survive."

"Good," said Sarge as he finished his latte. "My last stops for the day are the Lodges, Tudors, and Samuel Bradlee. They all live near each other on Beacon Hill. I don't think I'll take Art on this trip. That will allow me to chauffeur them all at once—assuming no surprise items of luggage or *pets*." Winnie the Frenchie ran through the Great Hall with a plastic water bottle in her mouth.

"I just called all three of them, and they understand. They will be waiting for you. Can you make it back before dark?"

"Easily," replied Sarge. "But I have to say, as the day progresses, the amount of activity in the streets increases. I've also noticed a rise in unsavory characters. I believe this evening will be a rough one for some."

"Then you better get going and stay safe."

"A couple of more things. Did you get in touch with the Endicotts?"

"No," replied Julia. "I assume they're at their condo at the former Fairmont Battery Wharf Hotel. Remember, they purchased the penthouse unit next to Patricia Cornwell."

"Yeah, that's right. I don't mind getting them, but I don't want to gallivant all over Boston if they're not home. Doesn't General Endicott travel a lot with his new bride?"

"I've heard she is new," Julia said sarcastically. "She's younger than all but one of his children. You know all of these ladies were good friends with Jane Anne, his first wife. I'm not sure the latest and greatest Mrs. Endicott will get along with this crew."

Sarge laughed. The world had collapsed out there and would in here as well when they showed up.

CHAPTER 30

Sunday, September 4, 2016
7:55 p.m.
100 Beacon
Boston, Massachusetts

Julia made Mrs. Lowell a cup of hot tea. Mrs. Lowell was having difficulty adjusting to her new life. Julia assumed her husband had shielded her from the threats their nation faced. Like so many husbands, Lowell, most likely in an attempt to protect his wife from stress or worry, avoided the subject. She was in a state of shock.

After Sarge's return with the last of the Boston Brahmin, except for the Endicotts, who were still out of contact, they decided to gather the group together and discuss the events of the last twenty-four hours. Julia spent the day scouring the Internet for news reports. Fluent in Chinese, Julia spent some time on the official website of the State Council of the People's Republic of China. Premier Li stressed that China was not involved in the attack on the United States power grid and pledged to build the EHV, extra-high voltage, transformers and replace parts necessary for damaged units as quickly as possible. However, the time frame for replacing the massive transformers was estimated to be one to three years, and the premier stressed payment must be made in gold or equivalent—*not the almighty dollar*.

The U.S. interconnected grid had three main components: *generation*—creation of electricity; *transmission*—the cross-regional transportation of electricity; and *distribution*—connecting the electricity to the end user. America had eighty thousand miles of EHV transmission lines making up the backbone of the power grid that enabled the long-haul transport of electricity.

Ninety percent of consumed energy passed through a high-voltage transformer at some point. As these transformers failed in large numbers, a cascading effect rippled throughout the entire western and eastern interconnected grid. Reports indicated these EHV transformers were damaged beyond repair, except in Texas, which was not connected to the eastern and western grids.

EHV transformers were huge, weighing hundreds of tons, making them difficult to transport—in some cases requiring specialized railcars, which were also in short supply. Before the cyber attack on Saturday night, the EHV transformers installed in the U.S. were approaching or exceeding the end of their forty-year design lifetimes—increasing their vulnerability to failure.

The vulnerability of the critical infrastructure was a frequent topic in the *Boston Herald* newsroom and among the Loyal Nine. It was agreed that a grid-down scenario was the worst possible scenario for America. While many would die from the lack of power to medical devices, most would die from disease, starvation, and violence.

After the last pickup of the day, Sarge began to show concern about the conditions outside 100 Beacon. As the day progressed, unrest escalated. Bostonians began to learn through the limited cell phone service that the grid was down nationwide. Julia suspected many were in denial as to whether this event was going to be long-term and catastrophic in nature. Her online research reported unrest across the nation. A brief trip to the rooftop earlier in the day revealed fires burning out of control toward Dorchester, Roxbury, and Mattapan. The sounds of sirens from first responders filled the air—together with black smoke.

She closed the laptop and whispered to Sarge, "Should we tell them everything we know? I don't think the husbands have kept their wives informed as to the severity of the situation."

"Have there been any news reports directly affecting Boston?" asked Sarge.

"No—other than what we've observed from the rooftop or your outings," she replied.

"I think it would be a mistake to sugarcoat the situation. Let's be factual, but not over the top. A few people in this room need a wake-up call, but there are a couple of the ladies that concern me. Especially Mrs. Lowell. She seems genuinely upset by what's happening—more so than the others."

"What do you think is troubling her, besides the obvious?" asked Julia.

"I don't know," replied Sarge. "Try to engage her in conversation tomorrow. Maybe enlist your aunt's assistance. She might be in denial, but I sense something else. Anger maybe."

Julia recalled a book she'd read on grief counseling. If Mrs. Lowell was grieving over the circumstances or a loss unknown to the rest of the group, she and Sarge would have to choose their words carefully.

"Let's get started." Julia walked into the Great Hall and offered everyone something to drink. Candles were burning throughout the space. Sarge stood in front of the televisions.

"I wish we were gathered here under more pleasant circumstances," said Sarge. "We all have questions and concerns. Julia has spent the better part of the day gathering information and staying in contact with our friends at Prescott Peninsula. Before I let her relay the details to you, I would like to take a moment and outline some logistics."

"Where are the Endicotts?" asked Mr. Lowell.

"I'm sure *she* insisted on the south of France?" sniped Mrs. Cabot, dragging out the pronunciation of France with a considerable *aaahhh*. Some of the ladies nodded and snickered.

"We've been trying to reach them continuously, to no avail," replied Sarge. "I'm sure Mr. Endicott was instructed in the procedures to follow. He also knows about 100 Beacon. He is either traveling or perhaps failed to keep his satellite phone unit charged. I will assess the situation tomorrow morning."

"I'll go with you, Sarge," offered Dr. Peabody. Uncle Art had become a valuable ally to Sarge as the day progressed. Julia and Sarge were able to have frank discussions and assessments with him without fear of raising a panic.

"Thank you, Art," said Sarge. "I know there is a lot of uncertainty surrounding this event. There are long-term questions, but the actions we take in the short term will determine our safety." Julia brought Sarge a bar stool to sit on. She thought he might revert into *Professor Sargent* if he continued to stand in front of his new *class*.

"Thank you, darling," he said to her. Aunt Stella beamed. She was for *Team Julia and Sarge*.

"After the power went off, we immediately prepared 100 Beacon. As you know, John Morgan tasked us with this responsibility many years ago. We hoped a collapse event of this magnitude would never occur, but we prepared nonetheless. All of us equated this plan to insurance. Many of you have insured your homes against fire, tornado, and earthquakes, yet never experienced a loss. Our plans involving 100 Beacon, Prescott Peninsula, and the protection of you were another form of insurance."

"Thank you, Henry," said Mr. Lodge. Julia patted Lodge on the shoulder and mouthed *thanks*.

"We have established a protocol for a catastrophic event," continued Sarge. "Before we picked you up today, Julia and I assessed the situation, conducted a threat analysis to our building, and then established communications last night with a predetermined contact list. These initial steps were deemed critical to secure 100 Beacon in the event human threats developed rapidly."

"What kind of *human threats*?" asked Mrs. Winthrop.

"Desperate people are capable of doing desperate things," replied Sarge. "Most Americans only have a few days of food and water in their cupboards. They live paycheck to paycheck. Those families on America's vast social welfare network will be panicked as they learn their government benefits no longer exist. The majority of humanity will become a very real threat to those of us who have prepared in advance."

"Simply put," interrupted Dr. Peabody, "they will do whatever is necessary to take what we have." Most in the room nodded in agreement. Mrs. Lowell remained stoic, staring out the window.

"Very true, Art," said Sarge. He continued. "Our primary purpose of today's activities was to gather together our group—all of you, and the Endicotts, of course. I have been in contact with General Bradlee's nephew, whom we call Brad, at Fort Devens. Many of you know that Brad is the battalion commander at Devens and will be instrumental in protecting all of us in the coming weeks."

"Weeks?" asked Mrs. Lowell, snapping out of her trance.

"I'm sorry, Mrs. Lowell, I shouldn't have been loose with my estimates," sugarcoated Sarge. Julia shot him a glance. *You've already buckled under pressure, mister.* "We do not have sufficient information to make that accurate of an assessment yet. Julia will expand on that in a moment. At this point, Brad is making arrangements to move you to the safety of the Prescott Peninsula. There are active-duty soldiers from Brad's unit on site and he will assign more, I'm told."

"When will this happen?" asked Mr. Winthrop.

"In the next few days," said Sarge. "In the meantime, while I want everyone to be comfortable, we must also remain vigilant. We must be prepared to react to any threats from outside, and we must undertake certain operational security measures to minimize our exposure to others."

"OPSEC," added General Bradlee.

"Yes, sir," said Sarge. "That's a military term for operational security. OPSEC is a discipline and a mindset. Our goal is to survive and avoid conflict with others until we can safely deliver you to Prescott Peninsula. We need everyone to stay within the confines of the two penthouse floors and stay off the roof unless assigned there."

"Are you going to assign jobs to us?" asked Mr. Cabot. "If so, I would like to be in charge of the wine cellar." The room burst out laughing, easing the tension. Even Mrs. Lowell managed a smile.

"I would be happy to assist you, Cabot." General Bradlee laughed, the unofficial social coordinator of the Boston Brahmin.

"No foxes in the henhouse, gentlemen," Mrs. Cabot chimed in.

"We need everybody's help in these critical first days," said Sarge, after allowing the playful banter to subside. "I want to establish a watch team. Some of you are early risers, others may be night owls. We will create shifts to maintain a two-man rooftop observation post. Also, we need to set up a meal schedule commensurate with our generator operating. The generator will be limited to four hours per day, most likely in the afternoons when the outside activity masks the noise. I'll let Julia coordinate showers, meal prep, etc."

"We'd be glad to do our part, Henry," said Mrs. Lodge. "Please tell us what you've learned, Julia. I, for one, am very nervous about this. I trust that you and Sarge will take the utmost care, but we're facing a greater danger than an extended power outage."

Very astute woman.

Julia walked around the couch and traded places with Sarge. "As the day progressed, I was able to learn more from American news networks," replied Julia. "We have confirmed that the power grid has been taken down by some sort of cyber attack. The collapsed grid does not include Texas, Alaska, or Hawaii—where the President was on vacation."

"How did they get a reprieve?" asked Mr. Winthrop.

"Texas and Alaska have their own separate power grids," replied Julia. "For an unknown reason, their grids were not attacked or the attack failed. Hawaii relies on imports of oil and coal for their power, although they also have an extensive solar and wind power program. It was fortuitous that the President was in Hawaii at the time."

"Indeed," snorted Lowell.

"Has anyone claimed responsibility?" asked Mr. Lodge.

"Not officially, although ISIS immediately praised the attack," replied Julia. "The Chinese have officially denied involvement and actively denounced the attack. The North Korean response has been ridicule of America and its way of life. The official Iranian statement was similar."

"What about the Russians?" asked General Bradlee. "They have been very active on the border of our territorial waters of late."

"They have?" asked Mrs. Winthrop.

Sarge interjected. "This is concerning, of course. Remember, some of this is conjecture. But the Russians have used cyber intrusions in the past in preparation for military action. We don't know this to be the case, but the possibility is there." The room grew silent for a moment. Sarge continued. "I don't want to alarm anyone, but there is no benefit to hiding the facts."

"Sarge is right," added Julia. "From all accounts, the cyber attack caused extensive damage to transformers and substations across the country. Some estimates claim damage in the trillions to the infrastructure alone, not to mention the loss to our economy."

"Somebody will become very wealthy replacing that equipment," interrupted Mr. Lowell, glancing at Mr. Cabot.

"It's not just economic loss," said Julia. She needed to dissuade some fears. "There will be a loss of lives. This is why we've gone to great lengths to prepare. We've made every attempt to insulate ourselves from the health and famine issues as well as the societal collapse that is likely."

"We've seen society collapse all year," added Mrs. Lodge. "I can only imagine what it will be like soon."

"We see the signs already," said Sarge. "Shock is being replaced with a feeling of dread today. Hysteria is not that far behind."

"And then mayhem," said Mr. Cabot.

"Precisely," added Mr. Lowell. "This country has been on the brink for quite some time. Is there any doubt it will fall apart quickly?" Again silence overtook the room. Julia looked at Sarge, seeking guidance. *Should I say more, or should we break out the pinochle cards?*

Sarge answered for her. "The next several days will provide us more answers. At some point, the President will have to address the nation in some fashion. What he says may set the tone for how people react. An uplifting message of hope will calm fears. Any other tone might exacerbate problems." Again, silence.

CHAPTER 31

Monday, September 5, 2016
8:55 a.m.
100 Beacon
Boston, Massachusetts

It was appropriate on this Labor Day 2016 to assign duties to all of their guests. The wives were all tasked with monitoring the communications system Julia designed—the Digital Carrier Pigeon.

Julia retrieved a handheld scanner, a ham radio, a CB radio, a portable world band radio, and another satellite phone from the Faraday cages on the eighth floor.

The Bearcat scanner was chosen because of its portability and ease of use. With TrunkTracker technology, it was the first handheld unit that required no programming. The user-friendly digital scanner required the user to input their local zip code, and the unit immediately broadcast communications used by aircraft, public safety, weather spotters, and the military. It was the best way to monitor local activities.

The BaoFeng dual band two-way radio was perfect for use while the Yaesu base unit and its antenna were being set up. Ham radios were used throughout the world, and Julia cultivated an extensive list of contacts. Her fellow *hammers* would share information with each other regarding military and geopolitical activities, as well as assist in a future recovery effort. The BaoFeng could monitor ham networks while also being used as a means of communication between the penthouse and the rooftop observation team.

The Midland portable CB unit had always been a favorite of truckers and travelers. In addition to its forty citizen band channels, the Midland had ten NOAA channels. Sarge would carry one in his car in the event he had to leave the building. A CB unit had a longer range than a typical two-way radio.

The Sony portable world band radio was a capable backup to the satellite Internet system. With the lack of AM and FM broadcasting from the states due to the power outage, worldwide broadcasts could be heard during the daytime. The BBC was one of the most prominent shortwave broadcasters available on world band radio.

Finally, Sarge and Julia would each carry their satellite phones. Each of the Loyal Nine had one, except for Abbie, who was always protected by secret service. Both Steven and Katie had their satphones with them, but they'd failed to check in last night as promised. It was too early to panic, Sarge said to Julia last night. *Those two can take care of themselves.*

Sarge returned from the rooftop where, with the assistance of his new right arm, Dr. Peabody, he connected the HughesNet satellite dish and the ham radio antenna.

"You should be good to go," said Sarge. "I'll work on the DirecTV hookup this afternoon. Art and I want to go to Battery Wharf and look for the Endicotts."

"But they haven't called and could be anywhere," said Julia.

"We talked about that, but we feel it's our obligation to look," said Sarge. "Mr. Morgan would expect that of me." Julia knew Sarge was right, and there was no sense in arguing. This morning appeared to be quiet in their Back Bay neighborhood, so she reluctantly acquiesced.

"I understand. Let's try again to raise them on the satphone," said Julia. "Why don't you round up your sidekick and gear."

"I've got the truck in the garage. I'm going to take an AR-15 with us. Art claims he's comfortable with one. I don't want to find out today." Sarge gave her a peck on the cheek.

"Listen, before you go, I'll let the ladies know the plan. They can monitor the scanner and CB radio for activity between here and the Battery Wharf area. If there's any sign of trouble, we'll raise you on the two-way." She handed him two of the BaoFeng portable units.

"At least this time, you can carry some comms with you."

"I need to think about this for a moment," said Sarge. "There are a few ways to get there, each with its risks. Granted, it's only a few miles, but Battery Wharf is on the opposite of downtown. Ordinarily, the quickest way would be to take Storrow along the river and connect over to Commercial Street."

"Are you concerned with traffic?"

"Not necessarily. I've watched the outflow of vehicles all morning. People are fleeing the city."

"I don't blame them," said Julia. "Then why not go against the flow?"

"Mass General is on the way, and I'm afraid there'll be a mass of humanity there, pardon the pun."

"Ha-ha, I get it. But you're right. You could easily get bogged down. What's your other option?"

"I could approach from the south by taking Boylston and picking up Atlantic Avenue."

"Okay," said Julia cautiously. She could see where Sarge was heading with this. "Chinatown."

"On any other day, Art and I would stop at Hei La Moon's and enjoy a plate of dim sum," said Sarge. "I'm not sure about Chinatown during the apocalypse."

Julia could picture it. Fried dough stuffed with shrimp and then wrapped with rice noodles.

"Last but not least, drive straight through the concrete jungle?" asked Julia.

"I could take the direct route through the heart of our fair city. We could get bogged down. I have no idea what to expect today. Yesterday was different because we were traversing the suburbs. Even then, the signs were there. As time passes, it will become more dangerous."

Julia took Sarge in her arms to provide them both a much-needed hug. Common, everyday decisions took on more import now—life or death significance. "Get ready and I'll try them one last time. I'll tell the ladies our plan. They can tell me if they've heard any chatter on the police scanner."

"I love you," said Sarge as he tore himself away. "We'll hurry back, I promise." Julia didn't want to let go, but she didn't want Sarge to know she was worried about him. The last thing he needed on his mind was her emotions weighing on his shoulders.

"I love you more," she said as he headed for the stairwell.

CHAPTER 32

Monday, September 5, 2016
11:25 a.m.
100 Beacon
Boston, Massachusetts

Sarge knew this pickup wasn't going to be routine. He wasn't sure if the Endicotts were home. But he also knew John Morgan had placed the lives of his fellow Boston Brahmin in the Loyal Nine's hands. *It was Sarge's duty.* Traffic was light on Beacon as he passed the Massachusetts State House. The gold-leaf dome glistened in the morning sun. In its two-hundred-and-twenty-year history, the *hub of the solar system*, as Oliver Wendell Holmes called it, contained the offices of some of the most influential politicians in history, including John Hancock, Samuel Adams, and Calvin Coolidge.

Sarge recalled the day his grandfather left office as governor. The large main doors entering the main hall of the building were only opened when the President or foreign heads of state visited and when the outgoing governor exited the building on their last day of office. This ceremony was known as the *Lone Walk* and had been a tradition for hundreds of years. It was an emotional day for Sarge as a young boy. On that day, he realized the importance of our republic form of government and its seamless transfer of power. *Will Americans forget how lucky we are to have a peaceful transition of power from the outgoing government to the new one?*

"We're going in," Sarge said as he passed Park Street. Empty cars littered the urban landscape, but there was no evidence of accidents. He weaved his way through the maze of one-way streets towards Boston City Hall. As he turned onto Court Street, traffic suddenly stopped. There were thousands of people crowded in the plaza surrounding the building. They were pushing and shoving to force their way toward the entrance.

"What the hell?" exclaimed Dr. Peabody. "And where are the cars associated with all of these people?"

"From what I can see, they're transients," replied Sarge. "Look over there. Is that a FEMA truck?" A single tractor trailer rig was parked near the front steps of city hall. Sarge could not see what they were handing out, but he suspected one truckload wasn't going to satisfy this crowd.

"This has the potential for disaster," said Sarge. "I'm gonna try to do a U-turn in front of the Boston Transit station. We need to avoid this powder keg in the making." As he made the turn, the shouts from the crowd exploded like Gillette stadium full of Patriots fans decrying a bad call by the referee. Apparently, FEMA had already run out of freebies.

"Clear on my side, Sarge," said Dr. Peabody. "Let's get out of here."

It took them another twenty minutes to make their way to the Battery Wharf hotel. Julia's voice came over the two-way.

"Sarge, do you read me? Over."

"Go ahead."

"There appears to be a disturbance of some kind at city hall. You might want to avoid that."

"Yeah, we know. We were almost in the middle of it. Have you heard of anything else?"

"No," replied Julia. "I've tried calling the Endicotts continuously since you left. My guess is their satphone is dead."

Of course it is.

"Okay, we'll keep you posted. Out." Sarge made his way up Commercial Street and approached the Battery Wharf entrance slowly.

"They have the entry blocked," said Dr. Peabody. "I think it's intentional based upon the way the vehicles are angled. You won't be able to turn down Battery Street or Battery Wharf." Sarge surveyed his options. After finding an opening, he pulled into an alley across Commercial.

"I have no problem walking, but carrying *those* is not such a good idea," said Sarge, nodding toward the backseat and the AR-15s. They both looked around for a moment to see if there was any obvious danger. Dr. Peabody spoke first.

"At the moment, the threats are raising hell at city hall. Let's cover the guns and try to exit the vehicle when nobody is paying attention."

"Agreed. At least for today, the sight of a moving vehicle is not out of the ordinary. If the Boston Wharf security team thought to block the two entrances to their property, it's entirely possible they're armed at the entrance." They waited for a moment and looked to see if anyone was watching their movements. Finally, Sarge was ready.

"Okay, let's go," Sarge said. "Just two guys taking a stroll down the Harborwalk for lunch at Aragosta's."

"A meatball ciabatta for me, and the rigatoni for my friend." *Those days are over, for years.*

As they approached the entry, absent were the traditional bellmen for the Fairmont, now replaced by guys in dark suits with matching sunglasses.

Sarge whispered, "I'll state our business and have them do the work for us. I doubt they'll let us inside, especially without surrendering our weapons. That'll never happen."

Sarge and Dr. Peabody approached the men, who spoke first.

"Nobody is allowed entry unless they are a verified guest or resident," said a husky Asian man.

"No problem. My name is Professor Henry Sargent, and my friend is Dr. Arthur Peabody. We're here to check—"

"I know," interrupted the other guard. Two additional security personnel appeared from their immediate left and right. *Was it something I said?*

"You know what?" asked Sarge.

"I know who Dr. Peabody is," he replied. "He did my wife's boobs. Sir, her name is Bobbie McDermott. You might not remember."

"I'm sorry, Mr. McDermott, but I don't remember," said Dr. Peabody. "But it is nice to see you again. How is your wife?"

"Divorced," he replied coldly. "She ran off with another dude and took her boobs with her." *This just keeps getting better and better.*

"Oh, well, I'm sorry about that," said Dr. Peabody.

"That's not your fault, Doc. She turned out to be a golddigger."

The big guy spoke again. "How can we help you, gentlemen?"

Sarge took a deep breath. Picking up the Endicotts was supposed to be in and out. No problems. "We came to check on our friends, the Endicotts. They live in one of the penthouses—next to Patricia Cornwell and her husband."

"You mean her girlfriend?"

"What?" asked Sarge.

"Patricia Cornwell, the author. She's married to her girlfriend."

"Okay. Well, would you mind telling the Endicotts that we're here? Tell them we're here to pick them up."

Big guy gave instructions to one of his team, who immediately went inside. After an awkward ten minutes of relative silence, a bellman came out with a cart of luggage and the Endicotts in tow.

"Hello, Sarge," said Henry Endicott. The Endicott family fortune was based on the most advanced, modern weaponry available on Earth. *Would they defend America when we are at our most vulnerable?*

"Hello, Mr. Endicott," greeted Sarge with a handshake. "We have been very worried about the two of you."

"That's my fault," said Emily Endicott, his newest wife. "My job was to keep the phone charged, and I forgot. Please forgive the error." She was dressed for dinner at an upscale restaurant—a stunning dress, heels, and a full complement of jewelry. *Young and pretty. Those ladies will not like this.*

"Art, how are you?" Endicott shook Dr. Peabody's hand. "Gentlemen, this is my wife, Emily. Emily, meet Professor Henry Sargent and Dr. Art Peabody."

"You can call me Sarge."

He looked at his watch and debated whether to have her change clothes. They had been gone nearly two hours. He decided against the delay and asked the bellman to accompany them to the truck. Once their bags were loaded into the back of the Toyota, Endicott tipped the bellman a hundred-dollar bill, much to the young man's delight.

After the bellman left, Endicott laughed and said, "The American dollar is worthless now. Why not give him a big tip?"

"Where are we going?" asked Mrs. Endicott.

"We're taking you guys to my place on Beacon Street, where you'll be safe for a while," replied Sarge. "You'll probably head over to Prescott Peninsula in a few days."

"Where?" she asked.

"I'll explain later, dear. Don't you worry your pretty little head about it, okay?" *Great.*

Julia knew to maintain radio silence while Sarge was out of the building unless it was an absolute emergency. She knew the squawk of the two-way could put Sarge in peril if he were in a compromised position. He contacted her first.

"Julia, do you copy?"

"Five by five. Sitrep," she replied.

"How about you with the lingo?"

"This handsome general is teaching me a thing or two."

That was funny, but don't say stuff like that over the radio. "I bet. Our friends are safe, and we're heading back. Any advice?" asked Sarge.

"Avoid the center of the city. That situation has become worse. Also, as you suspected, a riot broke out at Mass General. The staties have closed all roads in the area. The southern route is your best option."

"Thank you. We'll make our way and advise of any difficulty. Out."

Sarge started them south toward the John Fitzgerald Expressway. He glanced to his left at the former location of Sargent's Wharf, founded by his ancestor Daniel Sargent. Today, it was a parking lot.

"Sarge, I see Smith & Wesson made your AR," said Endicott. "Why didn't you choose the Colt SOCOM?"

"That's a good question, sir," replied Sarge. "The Colt is used by most special ops teams worldwide. The S&W is a little lighter. Why do you ask?"

"My company owns Colt Manufacturing in West Hartford, Connecticut. I had plans to move the facility to Alabama."

Dr. Peabody pointed at the traffic jam entering southbound I-93. "You might want to stay to the right on the surface road."

"I didn't know you owned that gun company, Henry," said Mrs. Endicott. "After that horrible school shooting, shouldn't you do away with that one?"

Sarge glanced at her in the rearview mirror. *Was she serious?* Endicott Industries built weapons systems that could level entire cities—obliterating all its inhabitants. Sarge was momentarily distracted by the conversation and entered the tunnel before he could turn.

"I was afraid of this!" he exclaimed.

"What?" questioned Mr. Endicott.

"I didn't want to go through the tunnel," replied Sarge. Traffic began to slow as they approached the exit of the tunnel. Cars were at a standstill as they attempted to merge on the Mass Turnpike. Sarge inched his way through the tunnel until he emerged near the China Gate Plaza. He cut across the famed Chinese checkerboard that was created by a mosaic of bricks in the pavement. Sarge navigated through several parked cars that blocked the gate and quickly shot through.

Boston instantly changed. The streets of Chinatown, once filled with tourists, were now deserted, and ominous-looking men stood in front of every storefront. Dr. Peabody broke the tension in the truck.

"They're standing guard over the businesses. They don't look like business owners." Sarge tried to keep a steady speed without drawing unnecessary attention. *He could feel the eyes upon them.*

"Maybe we should turn on one of these other roads," said Mrs. Endicott. Sarge ignored her. He could see far enough down the side streets to realize they were obstructed with manned blockades. He could see the Kensington building just two blocks ahead. As he approached Knapp Street, several men moved to block the street in front of him. There was now a white van immediately on his bumper. Sarge was not going to stop, but he also hesitated to run over the men, who were probably armed.

Sarge had studied escape and evade techniques and covered the concept extensively with Steven. Of course, stealth was your greatest ally. That was why Sarge chose the Toyota OJ40 instead of the G-Wagen. Speed was only used for emergencies, and in an urban environment, the benefit of speed could be quickly reduced. There was more to employing evasion techniques than putting distance between you and your pursuers.

Staying calm was key. Sarge had to outmaneuver these guys without endangering his passengers. He was faced with a blockade on every street and a vehicle to his rear. He slowed to a crawl.

"Hold on, everybody. I don't think we're welcome here." Mr. Endicott handed Dr. Peabody the AR-15. "Art, use your handgun and make sure your arm is outside of the window if you have to fire it. Otherwise, we'll all concuss. Get down in the backseat, please."

He immediately stopped the truck, catching the van behind him off guard. They screeched to a halt. Sarge then lunged at the men in the road in front, who began to pull weapons. Just as he reached Knapp Street, he whipped it to the left and roared toward the men, who were now running toward him. They didn't expect Sarge's truck to come at them so fast and jumped behind a concrete construction barrier at Stuart Street. Sarge drove onto the narrow sidewalk and plowed through the stop sign. He barely missed the men at the wall. Careening onto the four lanes of Kneeland Street, he barely averted a head-on collision with another white panel van that must have been dispatched from the other roadblock. This van slammed on the brakes, throwing tire smoke into the air and attracting attention from onlookers.

Sarge roared ahead with both vans in pursuit. They gained ground on him as he turned onto Charles Street. He was going to use the OJ40 for its intended purpose—off-road travel. He was going to lose them in Boston Common. Cars were stopped at the four-way intersection of Boylston Street, politely taking turns through the intersection. Sarge passed them all on the wrong side of the road and shot the gap between two cars. One of the pursuing vans was not so lucky, jumping the curb and blowing out its front tires. The other van continued its pursuit.

Obviously aggravated, they began shooting at Sarge as he turned through the stone columns onto the sidewalks of Boston Common. He was in familiar territory now. Not only did Sarge frequently jog on Boston Common, but he was only a couple of hundred feet from where he'd protected the woman and baby from an assault back in the spring. Sarge cut across the grass and under the tree-canopied sidewalks. The van was fishtailing in the sod, and Sarge surged ahead.

"Time to go where they can't," said Sarge. He carefully but quickly drove across a bridge barely wide enough to allow his OJ40 passage. It worked. As they cleared the other side of the lake, the van ripped into the wrought-iron guardrail with its front fenders, causing it to screech to a halt. Sarge came out on Arlington and headed west on Commonwealth in case they gave chase. He didn't want to lead them to his front door.

Feeling comfortable he had successfully evaded the van, he turned towards the Charles River and the back of 100 Beacon. He was sweating and wiped his hands on his shirt. He immediately rolled down his window and gasped for air. He was certain he'd held his breath during the chase. Mrs. Endicott was crying.

"What happened to your head?" asked Dr. Peabody.

"I hit my head on the window handle," she replied. "The knob fell off back there." She handed her husband a black plastic knob.

"Hold pressure on it, and we'll get you taken care of upstairs," said Dr. Peabody. Sarge pulled to the back of 100 Beacon, where several residents were talking. There was a tremendous commotion in the direction of Massachusetts General Hospital, but that was not Sarge's concern. These people would see the young woman bleeding, and demands for answers would be forthcoming.

He jumped out of the truck and quickly opened the door. They approached him and peppered him with questions. Sarge ignored them and hustled into the garage. All of these trips in and out of 100

Beacon were drawing unnecessary attention. Sarge knew this had to be the last one until Brad's transportation arrived.

CHAPTER 33

Tuesday, September 6, 2016
5:26 p.m.
100 Beacon
Boston, Massachusetts

The unfortunate injury to Mrs. Endicott's scalp was minor. The favorable result of the treatment of the wound was a bonding between her and the established women of the Boston Brahmin. The entire incident shook Sarge. He discussed the events several times with Julia. He was concerned that he'd overreacted. He wondered if he could have diffused the situation by talking to the men. He couldn't take that chance. America was now a society without the rule of law. There were no police to call for assistance. The world had become much smaller, and groups were moving quickly to establish their turf. Chinatown was no exception.

Tuesday was an easier day for Sarge. Only one incident occurred when some of the neighbors were knocking on the steel security door. They shouted questions, and after one last round of fist pounding out of frustration, they left. Sarge would have to deal with the neighbors sooner or later. Julia decided to finish off the fruits and vegetables in the refrigerator, but several of the ladies offered to prepare dinner for everyone that night.

Sarge and Julia were enjoying a rare quiet moment together. There was nothing new in the news except for some horrific events being reported from various locations across the country. General Bradlee took the lead in news gathering and said he would provide a report at tonight's meeting. They had not heard from Steven and Katie since

Sunday, and although he wouldn't admit it, Sarge was concerned for his brother.

"Dinner is served, Julia," said Aunt Stella. "Are you guys doing all right?"

"Yes, Aunt Stella, thank you," replied Julia. "I think fatigue is setting in right now. Sarge needs to rest from all of his heroics."

"I'm all right," Sarge interjected. "Just a lot to think about right now. Let's eat, ladies!" The three joined the others, and Sarge took his seat at the end of the long dining room table made up of a variety of furniture pieces to accommodate the seventeen diners. Lowell and Cabot were on security duty on the roof, and Julia assured their wives that she'd saved some for them.

The group made small talk through dinner, and one of the topics of conversation was the economic and social condition of America before the collapse event. Even though this was Sarge's favorite lecture topic at Harvard, he was oddly quiet. He seemed concerned about his brother, but Julia thought he was more concerned about his reaction to the threats in Chinatown. She would talk to him further when they settled in for the night. First, she would take those old soldiers on the rooftop some dinner.

The Lowell and Cabot families had been friends for centuries, and the gentlemen on the roof had been best friends since they were young boys. Julia also knew they were John Morgan's most trusted confidants. As she arrived on the rooftop with their plates of food, she found them deep in conversation. It was not her intention to eavesdrop, but she inadvertently overheard a portion of their conversation.

"When we met at 73 Tremont, I knew something was afoot," said Lowell. Lowell and Cabot were staring across the Charles River at several homes on fire. "His words were *a reckoning is upon us.*"

"I remember, Lawrence," said Cabot. "I distinctly remember him adding that a *reset is imminent.*"

"Yes, Walter. I realize the Russians and Chinese have been rattling their sabers of late, but how could John or the President envision something of this magnitude?"

"It does make one wonder. Is this the cataclysmic conflict Samuel spoke of that day?" asked Cabot.

"It might be," replied Lowell. "Walter, I have always trusted John to handle our affairs and position us to maximize our financial and political stature. But there is one more thing he said that bothers me. John said *It's coming. We won't know from where or from whom, but we'll certainly know when.*"

"His words were either prophetic or contrived. Either way, we live in a new world, and I'm anxious to speak with John soon."

Julia didn't know whether to run or hide. *Did John Morgan know this was coming? Even worse, did he have a hand in it? My God!* Suddenly, Julia became frightened with the prospect that the benefactors of the Loyal Nine, especially John Morgan, had advanced knowledge of the collapse. She quickly retreated to the rooftop door and pretended to appear for the first time by slamming it closed. Both men were startled by the noise.

"Hello, night shift!" Julia pretended to be chipper as usual. "I have some dinner for you." Both men approached Julia and relieved her of the plates. Their expressions reflected the seriousness of the conversation from moments ago.

"Thank you, Julia," said Cabot. "I must say the service in this establishment is impeccable. However, a nice bottle of Domaine Meo-Camuzet would lift our spirits considerably. Wouldn't you agree, Lawrence?"

"Indeed!"

"Sorry, gentlemen, you're on duty." Julia laughed. "Alcohol is off-limits to the active-duty troops."

The men grumbled but accepted their dinner without imbibing. Julia exchanged a few more words and quickly retreated to the penthouse. She had to tell Sarge what she'd heard.

CHAPTER 34

Tuesday, September 6, 2016
7:15 p.m.
100 Beacon
Boston, Massachusetts

"I need to talk to you, Sarge," said Julia. "I overheard something on the roof."

"Okay, but I need to tell you something first," he started. "Brad called while you were upstairs. He's sending men to pick up everyone tomorrow morning. I haven't announced it yet because General Bradlee was in the process of updating everyone on today's news."

"Yes, but you—" started Julia before General Bradlee interrupted her.

"Julia," said Bradlee, "this might be of interest to you." Julia and Sarge joined the group.

"Yes, General?" queried Julia.

"As we know, the President is in Hawaii on vacation. Fortunately, the island has full power, and he is maintaining executive office functions at his newly purchased mansion on the big island. He has announced a news conference for tomorrow night to address the nation."

"I thought it would have come sooner," said Julia.

"Apparently, he's waiting on some other personnel to join him," replied Bradlee. "Rumors are swirling that the Vice President has been killed." Several people in the room gasped.

"How awful," said Mrs. Lowell, whose sister went to Villanova with the Vice President's wife and were still close friends.

"How did it happen?" asked Dr. Peabody.

144

"It was a freak accident and a result of the power outage," replied Bradlee. "The Vice President was experiencing chest pains while traveling on Saturday night. They were unable to get through traffic to the hospital, and he died of a sudden heart attack."

"Was he in Washington?" asked Dr. Peabody. "How could he not get to a hospital?"

"No," replied Bradlee. "He was making a campaign appearance in western Pennsylvania on behalf of Mrs. Clinton when it occurred. People were evacuating Pittsburgh, taking up both north and southbound lanes of traffic on the interstate."

"I didn't know the Vice President had heart issues," said Julia. "In fact, when he contemplated his run for the presidency last year, he was supposedly given a clean bill of health."

"At his age, these things can come on quickly and unexpectedly," replied Dr. Peabody. The room grew quiet, undoubtedly contemplating the lack of medical treatment ordinarily available to all of them. Julia decided to change the subject, although she wanted to talk with Sarge.

"Has there been any indication that power is being restored?"

"No," replied Bradlee. "It's been seventy-two hours, and apparently the transformers aren't the only problem. The computer systems the utilities relied on for monitoring and controlling the flow of electricity must be replaced. Obtaining the hardware is not the problem as much as the logistics of delivery. Once operational, they will still be useless without the replacement transformers."

"Thanks, General Bradlee," said Sarge. "I have some good news, I think, for everyone. I spoke with your nephew after dinner. He is making arrangements to pick you up and take you to Prescott Peninsula tomorrow morning. The city is becoming more dangerous by the day, and we run a risk by delaying your trip."

"I kinda like it here," said Mrs. Endicott. Her face was still bandaged, but it was healing. She turned to her husband. "Henry, can't we just stay?" Sarge knew she would prefer to remain in the more friendly confines of 100 Beacon rather than cohabitate with the *Real Housewives* of the Boston Brahmin.

"Dear, I don't know," started Endicott.

Sarge chose to be the villain. "I'm sorry, Emily, but that's not possible. The city will become a very dangerous place. In fact, Julia and I will need to make a decision once my brother returns. We may come to Prescott Peninsula to join you. In the meantime, you will be more comfortable there, and General Bradlee's nephew has assembled an excellent squad of Marines to protect you."

"See, dear, it's for the best," said Endicott. Mrs. Endicott started to pout, which ordinarily worked on her nearly-twice-her-age husband, but Sarge wouldn't bite.

"He's correct," said Sarge. "Why don't you guys start packing and get a good night's sleep. Brad plans on being here at seven in the morning." The Boston Brahmin and their wives began to shuffle toward the stairwell to the next floor. Sarge caught General Bradlee's attention before he could leave.

"General, could I have a moment?" asked Sarge.

"Of course, Sarge."

"Brad said I should ask you about Operation Vigilant Eagle. Do you know what he's referring to?" asked Sarge.

"Yes. It was originally intended to be a joint U.S.-Russian counterterrorism operation near the Arctic. The goal was to simulate the hijacking of a commercial jetliner and develop cooperation between the two nations in dealing with the potential terrorist threat."

"Okay, why would that be relevant to what's happening now?"

"My nephew and I were particularly interested in a domestic aspect of Vigilant Eagle that was not reported on in the media. As part of the FBI's involvement in the operation, the administration required a domestic terror component."

"Like what?" asked Sarge.

"The FBI was tasked with identifying white supremacists and sovereign citizen extremist groups. Through executive order, the President declared that persons associated with extreme left-wing or right-wing extremist groups were to be considered homegrown terrorists and treated with the same scrutiny as al-Qaeda or ISIS."

"I've never heard of this."

"That's by design, Sarge. The concern Brad and I had dealt with those placed on the watch list. The vast majority of the groups named were right-leaning politically—the Tea Party, libertarians, sovereign citizens, antiabortion activists. Even vets."

"Why would vets be on a terrorist watch list?"

"As our veterans returned from active duty overseas, the Veteran's Administration encouraged them to claim they suffered posttraumatic stress disorder. If a vet displayed any angry or irritable mood, they were diagnosed as having oppositional defiant disorder. Under the President's executive order, our brave military veterans who returned home with either PTSD or ODD are now being monitored. Something as simple as posting an angry Facebook or Twitter rant could land them in a mental institution or, at a minimum, require them to surrender any weapons they may own. What was once hailed as an opportunity to secure more post-service military benefits has now become an opportunity to take away one's constitutional freedoms."

Sarge thought about the importance of this domestic terrorist list. The President, for purely political reasons, could create an enemies list based on certain criteria. All of the criteria might apply to those who didn't share his political ideology. *How far will this President go in a time of crisis?* Then Sarge remembered the infamous words of the President's Chief of Staff when the administration first took office— *never let a good crisis go to waste.*

CHAPTER 35

Wednesday, September 7, 2016
7:00 a.m.
100 Beacon
Boston, Massachusetts

Sarge and Julia were on the rooftop, standing morning watch, when they saw two Humvees and two M35s, commonly known as a Deuce and a Half, exit off Storrow toward 100 Beacon.

"Looks like Brad's men have arrived," said Julia. "I'll go downstairs and tell everyone to get ready."

"Let's get everyone out the door and we'll talk more about what we learned yesterday. We also need to talk about Steven and Katie. But first things first."

"Sounds like a plan," Julia said as she and Sarge briskly walked down the stairs. Julia peeled off to the ninth floor, and Sarge went all the way to the security door on the eighth floor. Throughout the day yesterday, there were knocks on the steel door from the neighbors. On day four, desperation would be taking hold of the unprepared. Sarge needed to greet the military personnel and make sure things went smoothly. Sarge wanted to avoid a confrontation.

As he exited the stairwell, several residents were gathered near the now obsolete elevator. They attempted to get his attention, but he ignored them and went straight outside. He was glad to see a familiar face in Master Gunnery Sergeant Frank Falcone. MGySgt Falcone had been under Brad's command for many years and would be an integral part of the future of the Loyal Nine. For now, Gunny Falcone was assigned the task of security at Prescott Peninsula. Sarge was glad to see Brad sent his best man to deliver the Boston Brahmin and their families to the safety of Prescott Peninsula.

"Hello, Sarge," greeted Gunny Falcone heartily. The two men shook hands as Sarge surveyed the vehicles and the men, who were quickly exiting.

"It's great to see you again, Gunny," replied Sarge. The two men competed in an informal training competition at Camp Edwards in June. Steven and Sarge, as a team, were the only nonmilitary personnel present and did very well against their more experienced counterparts. Brad and his men from Fort Devens were impressed with Sarge by the end of the weekend. Sarge was thrilled to have Gunny Falcone in charge of the safety of his precious cargo.

"Sarge, Brad filled me in. I have ten men with me. I hope we can make this quick. The southern part of the city is in chaos. Traffic heading westbound on the Mass Turnpike looks like a parking lot as the day progresses. I plan on taking the northerly route through Lexington and Concord along Route 2." Sarge saw they were already drawing a crowd at this early hour. The neighbors stood on the front steps of the entrance to 100 Beacon, and several other people were approaching the military trucks from all directions.

"We're going to attract a lot of attention this morning, so we need to make this fast," said Sarge. "Can you spare some of your men to help carry our guests and their bags down the stairs?"

"Absolutely," replied Falcone as he instructed four of his men to follow Sarge. As they approached the entrance, the neighbors hit him with questions.

"*Why is the army here?*"

"*Who are you? Are you in the military?*"

"*Did they bring us food and water?*"

Sarge elected to defer to buy some time. "I'll be glad to answer all of your questions, but first I must comply with the orders of these gentlemen. Now, if you will stand to the side and let them do their jobs, we can discuss it all in a moment."

Without waiting for an answer, Sarge pushed his way through the contingent and led the Marines up the stairs. Halfway up, he was greeted by the blustering barrister from a few days ago.

"What's going on here?" he said.

"Sir, I need you to stand aside so these gentlemen can do their jobs," demanded Sarge.

"Why is the military in my building?"

Your building? "Excuse us, sir. If you would like to meet me in the lobby in a few minutes, I'd be glad to address your questions. But for now, move aside!" Sarge bulled his way past the man and a woman who had now joined him. On the eighth floor, he opened the security door and was pleased to see Julia had everyone in line ready to go. She also had a sense of urgency during this process.

The Marines escorted the Boston Brahmin down the stairs while Sarge and Julia helped them gather their things.

Sarge turned to Julia and whispered, "I may have some trouble downstairs after they leave. We're drawing a crowd."

"I thought we might. I hoped to avoid that because it's so early. What can I do to help?"

"Wait here. I'm afraid the neighbors are going to become a problem for us. But there's also a crowd gathering around the trucks. I'm comfortable Brad's men will get going, but I'm sure I'll face the wrath of some angry people when the trucks pull off without leaving supplies."

"Okay. You have your sidearms. Do you want to take an AR too?"

"No. Just listen to the voices. If you hear me yell *enough*, then start screaming like you saw a ghost. That should give me enough distraction to take off up the stairs without them." Julia kissed him on the cheek and told him to be careful.

Sarge bounced down the stairs to catch up with the entourage. When he entered the entryway of the building, there were a dozen people waiting for him. He took the proactive approach.

"I know you have several questions, and if you let me assist these soldiers in doing their jobs, I'll tell you what I know. But please, don't interfere with them!"

Sarge turned and quickly ran out the front door before they could protest. Gunny Falcone had his hands full, explaining to the locals that this was not a food and water giveaway. The people surrounding the M35s looked haggard. By day four, most Americans had exhausted their pantry's food and water supply. These people were relying upon the government to deliver what they needed. Today was not the day. Sarge hoped their exhausted bodies did not rise to some form of violence.

"Gunny, do you foresee any problems here?" asked Sarge.

"Not really. My men have been inundated with questions but have remained silent per my orders. They are very aware of the threats desperate people pose to their safety. Brad and I picked the best, like-minded soldiers in our battalion." The crowd pressed forward as the Boston Brahmin exited the building. Their curiosity prompted more questions about whom the elderly people were and why they were being taken away in military trucks. While Sarge was able to avoid giving them a response, he expected his neighbors blocking the front entrance would demand similar answers. The last of the passengers headed for Prescott Peninsula were settled in, and Gunny Falcone's men gave him the thumbs-up, indicating they were ready to leave.

"Thank you, Gunny," said Sarge. "I imagine I'll see you at 1PP shortly. My brother still hasn't arrived from D.C. When he gets here, we'll decide our next step." Falcone looked past Sarge to the awaiting residents.

"Do you need some help with them?" he asked, nodding towards the entry.

"No, I'll talk my way through it. I'm good at that."

"I'm sure," said Falcone. "Listen, Sarge, day by day, the situation deteriorates rapidly. The reports we hear at HQ is that the major cities are burning out of control. You may not have experienced it on Beacon Street, but the gang activity is growing. In East Boston, the MS-13 Hispanic gang has taken control of the entire area surrounding Logan International. Chinatown's Asian population has rallied around the White Devil, who was recently released from prison. Dorchester, Roxbury, and Mattapan have been on fire since before the power went down. They've consolidated the gangs behind a gangbanger calling himself J-Rock."

"Trust me, I learned my lesson driving through Chinatown the other day," said Sarge.

"No, Sarge, it's worse than that. The gangs are expanding and moving into other parts of the city as an armed force—like an army. When they hit Beacon Street, it won't be a few of them in a used Cadillac. They'll come as a unified, well-armed force."

Sarge soaked this in for a moment as the crowds began to surround the trucks. "You need to go, Gunny. Thank you for the advice and for taking care of these folks. I'll see you soon; I'm sure." Sarge slapped Falcone on the shoulder and headed back to the entrance. In that short time, he planned his approach with the neighbors. *Fear is a great motivator.*

As the convoy pulled away, the onlookers turned their attention towards Sarge and 100 Beacon. He turned towards his neighbors and told them all to get back in the building. He pulled the wrought-iron steel gates closed behind them.

"Quick, does anybody have a key to these doors?" he shouted, attempting to raise a sense of alarm.

"I do," came a voice from the rear. "But these doors always stay open during the daytime."

"Not anymore," said Sarge. "Get up here and lock these doors now unless you want all of these people in our lobby!" A portly man made his way to the front and secured the single-bolt lock. Sarge patted him on the back and then led the neighbors away from the front door. He positioned himself at the stairwell in case he decided to make a quick exit.

"Who are you?"

"My name is Henry Sargent, and I'm a professor at Harvard. Listen, I would love to answer all of your questions, but there's no time for that at the moment."

"Why not? What's wrong?" asked an elderly woman with genuine fear in her voice.

"Everybody, the military told me armed gangs are moving into our neighborhood," said Sarge. He intended to divert their attention away from him and the top three floors to the more pressing threat—the people outside. He was also going to use this as an opportunity to learn about the thirteen neighbors who stood in front of him. "How many more residents live in the building in addition to us?"

While the group spoke amongst themselves, Sarge took mental notes of ages, physical capabilities, and attitudes. *Who was an ally, and who was a potential threat?*

"There are few more—namely spouses and a couple of elderly parents."

"Good. You need to band together as a group and create a watch schedule. The front door and the fire exit need to be under constant guard. When I say constant, I mean day and night, no exceptions."

"What do you mean by a guard?" asked the lawyer—*a potential threat*.

"Exactly what it sounds like," replied Sarge. "How many of you own guns?" *This is very important.*

Three people raised their hands. Sarge took an inventory. There were two revolvers, a shotgun for skeet shooting, and a Korean-era M1 Garand. Sarge diffused the situation by giving everyone a task and making them feel part of the security effort. He encouraged them to help one another until the situation resolved itself.

Sarge did not offer to share information learned from Julia's Digital Carrier Pigeon network nor did he offer to share supplies or weapons. Either one of those things would have put his home and friends at risk. Sarge's position on sharing the results of their preparedness strategy with others might seem callous and heartless, but it ensured his and Julia's survival—*his priority*. Both before and after the collapse event, the extent of their preps was nobody's business but their own.

PART THREE

Road Trip

CHAPTER 36

Saturday, September 3, 2016
9:07 p.m.
51ˢᵗ State Tavern
Washington, D.C.

Katie brought them another round of beers as the Mets fans in the 51ˢᵗ State Tavern erupted following a Curtis Granderson home run over the home team Nationals. Known as a hangout for New York sports fans, the twelve-year-old haunt was a typical sports bar featuring flat-screen televisions, a pool table, and *guy food*—buffalo wings, burgers, and cold beer. Situated in the West End near Foggy Bottom, Katie and some of her co-workers would slip away for drinks with the purposeful intent of avoiding their colleagues who preferred the traditional politico hangouts like the Capitol Lounge and Bullfeathers.

"I thought we came up here to get away from this," moaned Steven to a grinning Katie. "The stadium is only two blocks from your townhouse. We could have stayed at your place and dealt with mouthy *fans*."

"Shut up, you big baby," said Katie as she gave him a hug. "It feels good to get out—*on a date*. We don't get to do this often. Besides, this is one of my favorite spots. You're just pissed 'cause I'm kickin' your ass on the pool table!"

"Whatever. How do you know I'm not letting you win?"

"By the look on your face when I do win," replied Katie. They clinked their Samuel Adams and took a long drink of the lager. Steven racked the pool balls and grabbed his stick.

"Let's go, rematch time," said Steven. Gesturing with his stick, he indicated it was Katie's turn to break.

Katie took her position and was ready to shoot when the power surged—brightening the room. Then the 51st State Tavern, and the rest of D.C., suddenly went black. The fans groaned, hurling a few curse words and a chorus of boos at the perceived inconvenience.

Katie found her way to Steven and said, "You did that on purpose so I wouldn't beat you again, didn't you?"

"Hell no. But maybe I should take advantage of you in the dark!" Steven groped in the dark and tried to grab an elusive Katie.

"Free beer!" shouted a man in the pitch-black bar, turning the jeers to cheers. For a minute, the patrons waited patiently, searching their cell phone browsers for ESPN.

Then the phones started ringing. Replacing the muffled conversations were the sounds of different ringtones, pitches, and volumes filling the air. Text messages illuminated smartphone screens while everyone fumbled in the darkness for their most beloved handheld devices.

Within moments of the lights turning off, the excitement level of the bar turned up to a fever pitch. Not even a Granderson home run could elevate the enthusiasm of the crowd as much as the news coming across their screens.

"The power's out everywhere!" shouted one man.

"You mean in D.C.?"

"No, the whole country!" replied another.

"I have my sister on the phone in Kentucky," shouted a woman. "Their power is out too!"

The restaurant manager brought out a flashlight to get everyone's attention.

"Folks, I'm sorry the emergency lighting isn't working," he said. "I'm sure this is just temporary. Please keep your seats and we'll see if there's a solution."

"No way, let's get out of here," screamed an inebriated Mets fan. The manager moved to block the door.

"Let me repeat," he began with an authoritative voice. "This is probably temporary. Be calm, please, but if you must leave, I'll need you to settle your tab first."

The displaced New Yorkers would have none of that. Many were angry at losing the televisions. Some were genuinely frightened at the melee that was brewing inside the 51st Street Tavern. Others saw this as an opportunity to leave with free wings and beer in their belly. Regardless of motive, the final guests of the last night of business for the 51st Street Tavern hit the doors en masse, knocking the manager to the floor and carrying their adult beverages with them.

"Katie, stay against the wall with me until this clears out," said Steven, pulling her toward him. "We don't want to get caught in the stampede."

Katie was looking at her iPhone and scrolled through a couple of text messages. Katie knew from reports following the San Francisco Bay earthquake in '07, cell phone usage skyrocketed following a major emergency. Verizon said that within minutes of the 6.6 magnitude earthquake, cell traffic in Santa Clara County increased tenfold. Loved ones were either checking on the safety of family or friends or were simply excited to talk about the drama. Most cell users received *circuits are busy* or fast busy signals. The inability to communicate with others elevated the public's anxiety following the quake, which increased demand for first responders and communications networks.

One of the solutions wireless network providers suggested was the use of text messaging during an emergency situation because the text messages required less bandwidth than a phone call. The use of text helped keep bandwidth available for emergency responders during a disaster.

"Steven, I have a text blast from the NSA," said Katie. "This is serious."

Steven leaned in and whispered, "Okay, let's make our way outside and assess the situation. Stay close behind me." Steven led Katie through the darkness toward the exit. They emerged in the cool night air and made their way under a tree canopy to the right of the entrance.

"I think the game's over," said Katie.

"What?" asked Steven.

Katie pointed at the pool cue Steven had carried outside with him.

Steven continued. "Oh, this," he said. "Well, I'm not carrying a weapon because your fair city is a gun-free zone. Besides my knife, a pool stick is better than nothing." Instinctively, Steven felt his pants pocket to confirm his Cold Steel Recon Tactical Knife was in his pocket.

They stood for a moment and took in the chaos on Pennsylvania Avenue where it intersected with L Street. People poured out of the buildings in search of answers. Typically heavy traffic came to a standstill at the intersection because the traffic signals were inoperative. Fire alarms were screeching from the direction of The Melrose Hotel.

"Steven, we've been attacked," said Katie. She was scrolling through the messages on her smartphone again to make sure she read them correctly.

"They know this already?" asked Steven.

"Yes. Information travels much faster over secure government networks, especially at the time of a disaster. The NSA suspects cyber terror. The grid has collapsed across the country, according to the text."

"We're screwed."

"Yeah, all of us, in fact. They want me to come to the White House."

"Okay, straight ahead eight blocks," said Steven, pointing down Pennsylvania Avenue with the pool cue. They jumped back to avoid a Vespa scooter roaring by them on the sidewalk. "Dammit!"

"Here's the problem," said Katie. She was serious. "If I go in, you can't come with me. You don't have clearance, and I suspect the White House is on serious lockdown."

"Okay. So I'll wait outside or head back to your place and get the car," said Steven.

"Once I'm there, I won't be able to leave. I'll be stuck for days, Steven."

Steven thought about this for a moment. He didn't want to be apart from Katie—*especially under these circumstances*. He also didn't think Washington would be the safest place to be if a cyber attack was being used as a first strike.

"Katie, I don't want to be selfish. But I have to point out a couple of things. If this was a cyber attack, and the collapsed grid is nationwide, life has changed for this nation in a bad way. Just as important, there are some countries, namely the Russians, who use cyber warfare to gain military advantage before an invasion. Estonia, Georgia, and Ukraine come to mind. Either way, we need to stay together—*because I love you*."

Katie let the words soak in. She loved Steven too and did not want to separate. Their corner of the world had become extremely dangerous.

"I don't want to be in Washington, D.C., when the bombs start flyin'," she said.

"Me either," said Steven. "Let's get outta here."

"For sure."

With the decision made, Steven and Katie made their way down Pennsylvania Avenue through Washington Circle, which resembled a NASCAR track crammed with a thousand cars. K Street, the world headquarters of lobbyists and special interests, was full of cars in both directions. The blaring of car horns was deafening. The shrill sirens of the Capitol Police reverberated off the buildings.

Thus far, there were no violent outbursts or signs of unrest where they were located. Katie was glad they reached their decision to leave the city without delay because calm could soon turn into bedlam. As they passed the buildings that housed the International Monetary Fund and the World Bank, her phone rang. Ironically, it was John Morgan.

"Hey, you're getting a call."

"It's Mr. Morgan," said Katie. "Hello."

Katie listened to Morgan's instructions. She was to contact General Mason Sears's chief of staff and advise him to expect a call for the general shortly. Katie never questioned the tasks given to her by Morgan. She was paid handsomely and given the additional opportunity to be a part of the Loyal Nine. *What's the harm in facilitating a phone call when the country was collapsing around them?*

They turned south down Eighteenth Street toward the Washington Monument. After she had hung up the phone, Steven quizzed her about the call.

"What's on the big guy's mind besides TEOTWAWKI?" asked Steven. Katie hesitated to make sure her answer wouldn't be deemed classified by the *Big Guy*. She considered for a moment and thought the information was harmless enough.

"Hang on," she replied, holding one finger in the air as she attempted to get a call through. "Figures, circuits are busy." She wrote a text, and it went through.

"He only wanted me to contact General Sears's chief of staff to expect an incoming phone call from Mr. Morgan. Sears is the chairman of the Joint Chiefs. I suppose Mr. Morgan gets his information from the top of the informational food chain."

"I guess so," said Steven. He grabbed her hand as they crossed Constitution Avenue onto the west side of the National Mall. Typically, the Tidal Basin reflected the lights of the King and Roosevelt Memorials. Tonight, the absence of the moon gave the water an eerie darkness. "Let's work our way along the water down Maine Avenue. I don't think it will be a good idea to walk through the inner-city streets. Once we pass the Gangplank Marina, we'll make our way towards Nationals Park and your place."

Katie replayed the phone call through her mind. Morgan had numerous other sources of intelligence, including the President's staff. *Why General Sears?* As they crossed under Interstate 395, they were greeted by thousands of newly created pedestrians courtesy of the Metro system's shutdown. The premature ending of the Nationals game dispersed fans to the west towards Arlington, Virginia, and the south towards Maryland. A mass of humanity, partially in shock and fear, made their way out of the city. But probably the oddest part of the entire hike towards her home was the lack of air traffic at Reagan National. Planes were grounded, the

Metro was stuck in place, and confused people walked in all directions. Washington, D.C., was devoid of mass transit. *My, how things have changed already!*

CHAPTER 37

Saturday, September 3, 2016
11:49 p.m.
27 O Street Southwest
Washington, D.C.

Between the delays for traffic and travelers, together with the extra precautions they took walking across the heart of D.C., it took over two hours to traverse the five miles from 51st State Tavern. Steven and Katie quickly moved through her townhouse to gather up some essentials for the trip. Her Toyota Highlander was spacious inside and could carry a lot of gear. Steven wished she had more gas in it. The gauge read around two-thirds of a tank. They would have to find more along the way.

"Will you try to call Sarge while I load the truck?" asked Steven.

"Yes. I wish the satphone had a better charge. If I can't reach them now, I'll charge the phone in the truck and try again a little later." She handed Steven another duffle packed with clothes.

"Where are the medical supplies that Donald put together?"

"I keep them in the back of the truck," replied Katie. "I never remove certain bug-out essentials like the medical bag, a basic clothes duffle, and an *everything-else-I-wish-I-had* bag."

"What the hell is that?"

"You'll see it," she replied. "It probably weighs fifty pounds."

"If you had to walk, how would you carry it?"

"I wouldn't take all of its contents, only the ones most useful under the particular circumstances."

"Everything you wish you had?" asked Steven.

"Exactly. For example, I have things to create temporary shelters

164

like paracord, mylar blankets, and a tarp. I have ways to procure and purify water like a LifeStraw, Aqua Iodine Tablets, and a small vial of bleach. There is a variety of fire starters like flint, waterproof matches, and wet fire tinder."

"Whoa, you've been watching that show called *Alone* where they throw those poor suckers to the wolves in Canada."

"That, plus Google is my friend." She laughed. "I read a lot of survival fiction and imagined myself in the shoes of the characters. I learned from that and picked up the things I thought I might need if I found myself in a pickle out there. Some of this stuff may keep us alive."

"Well, I'm impressed. But this should take care of all our needs," said Steven, patting one of Katie's 9mm handguns in a paddle holster.

"No doubt, our weapons will go a long way to protecting ourselves and what we've got in the truck." She moved closer to Steven for a hug. "But a 9 millimeter can't keep you warm at night, mister." Steven resisted the urge to postpone the trip until tomorrow in favor of a roll in the sack with Katie.

"Listen, you better get away from me, or you'll be in big trouble," said Steven.

"Fine," said Katie with a pronounced pout. He reached down for his duffle and zipped it up.

"Do you think we should get some sleep and head out in the morning fresh?" he asked, starting to have second thoughts.

"I've got a feeling that leaving D.C. is a good idea. This town can be volatile, and there are plenty of riot-control personnel to clamp down hard on all the citizens of the District."

"Agreed," he said. "I'm gonna pack the truck and then grab some food out of your kitchen for the road."

"Let me find a map and try these calls again. Then we'll leave."

"Road trip!" shouted Steven as he walked to the front door.

"Yeah, road trip!" replied Katie.

CHAPTER 38

Sunday, September 4, 2016
1:35 a.m.
14ᵗʰ Street Bridge
Washington, D.C.

Steven settled in behind the wheel of the Highlander while Katie attempted to use its navigation system. The traffic and weather apps were inoperable, but the preloaded maps and navigation were available. As they made their way toward the Fourteenth Street Bridge heading west toward the Pentagon, Katie thought about her staff and friends who might remain in the metro D.C. area out of a sense of loyalty to their jobs and the government. She had a brief sense of guilt for not fulfilling her duties, but her priority was survival and Steven. There were plenty of bureaucrats in Washington who would love to have her job.

"I guess it's obvious," started Steven. "We'll avoid the cities at all costs. I have no desire to drive anywhere near Baltimore, Philly, Trenton, or New York before, during, or after the apocalypse."

"According to this navigation app, it's four hundred and fifty miles to Boston as a straight shot," said Katie. "If we take a northerly route, finding our way as we go, it will be over five hundred miles." She picked up the map book and started thumbing through the pages to find the state of Maryland.

"Up ahead!" shouted Steven.

"What?" Katie looked up from the map. Traffic was at a crawl heading across the Potomac River. "Is everybody leaving the city?"

"Do you blame them?" asked Steven.

As they passed L'Enfant Plaza, the traffic began to move a little more often.

"Nobody is headed into the city." As the Jefferson Memorial came into view on the south side of the Tidal Basin, so did the military vehicles blocking the eastbound lanes of Interstate 395 and the Fourteenth Street Bridge. "Look, they've blocked access to inbound traffic."

Several military transports and Humvees blocked the road, and cars leaving the city were stopped and given a cursory inspection before being allowed to pass. As Steven approached the checkpoint, he rolled down his window.

"Good morning, Airman," Steven said to the National Guardsman.

"Good morning, sir," he replied. "I must advise you that the city is closed to incoming traffic. Once you leave, you will not be allowed back into Washington until further notice."

"We understand, Airman," said Steven. He pointed at the guardsman's uniform. "You're with the Mississippi Guard. Aren't you a long way from home?"

"Yes, sir," he replied. "We were deployed two weeks ago as part of a special security detail. We've been instructed to cordon off the city. Please keep moving, sir."

Steven rolled up his window and gladly continued across the Potomac. He sat quietly for a moment to digest what he just observed.

"I've never seen the military or the government move this quickly," he said, breaking the silence. "They've closed off the city in less than five hours."

"And they used National Guardsmen from Mississippi, who were in place two weeks in advance."

Steven pulled off onto the George Washington Memorial Parkway and headed northbound along the river. "Do you know of any reason Washington was in need of heightened security?"

"No, I would have been informed. Maybe the troop deployment was routine. They did expand the Jade Helm exercise into FEMA

Region Three this summer. Their stated purpose was to avoid the 2015 debacle in Texas and across Region Nine, where armed citizens monitored their activities. I guess in this region, people might welcome a strong military presence in the event of unrest."

Steven thought for a moment about the public uproar during last year's exercise. As he followed the news, he tried to differentiate between fact and conspiracy. Some aspects of Jade Helm always bothered him. "Have you noticed that the Jade Helm exercise has continued to expand every year?" asked Steven.

"It makes you wonder if they're planning for something," replied Katie. "Nothing has ever crossed my desk that would indicate the government hopes to implement martial law, but most of what I do is international in scope."

People were fleeing the city, naturally. But no one, including a lawful resident, was being allowed back into the city. A National Guard detachment was a thousand miles from home, deployed just in time to secure Washington at the time of a catastrophic collapse of the nation's power grid. *Very interesting.* It would take them days to travel to Boston, during which time there would be a lot to ponder.

CHAPTER 39

Sunday, September 4, 2016
4:22 a.m.
York, PA

Steven and Katie swapped driving after passing Frederick, Maryland. Upon crossing into Pennsylvania near Gettysburg, they turned northeast towards York. They had less than half a tank of fuel and decided to turn off onto some rural roads to look for gasoline and sleep for a few hours. The small York Airport helped on both issues.

"Turn here," said Steven, pointing to the entrance to the York Airport on the right. "They might have some ninety octane fuel stored for the Cessnas or their groundskeeping personnel." Katie cut the lights and made her way carefully along Airport Road. They reached the last building that had lawn-mowing equipment outside of it.

"I bet there's gas in there," said Katie. She pulled the truck to a stop.

"I bet you're right, but do you want to climb the fence with the razor wire?"

"No, smartass," she replied jokingly. "But I do have bolt cutters in the back."

"Really?"

"Yes, and other essential burglary tools, including a lock-picking set and a four-way sillcock key." Katie laughed because she'd walked right into Steven's warped sense of humor.

"A sillycock key? I can assure you, it's not silly at all!"

"You are so predictable. Get your mind out of the gutter. A sillcock key is used to open and close various types of water spigots when the handles have been removed. A lot of people remove the handles to keep thieves from stealing their water."

"Thieves like you." Steven laughed.

"Well, there's a fine line between survival and looting when after a collapse. But this is another example of where my bolt cutters and sillcock key trumps your nine millimeter."

"No argument there."

"So, Clyde Barrow, are you gonna do the B and E honors, or do you want a girl to show you how?" asked Katie.

"I'll do it, Bonnie. You keep the Edsel running."

A few moments later, Steven came jogging out of the building with a five-gallon can of gasoline and a machete. He quickly poured the roughly four gallons of gas into the Highlander and jumped in.

"How many gallons did you score?" Katie turned the truck around and headed back for the highway.

"Maybe four gallons—another eighty miles."

"What's the machete for?"

"Zombies."

CHAPTER 40

Sunday, September 4, 2016
12:35 p.m.
Allentown, PA

Katie and Steven took the opportunity to sleep in the car for several hours before continuing east towards Allentown. The gasoline they acquired would advance them closer to the Connecticut state line, where they planned on taking backroads to avoid Hartford. Once off of the major interstate system, they hoped to encounter less traffic and locate another can of fuel to move them that much closer to Boston.

"Mother Nature doesn't stop calling just because the world came to an end," said Steven as he returned from his morning constitutional.

"It feels weird, doesn't it?" asked Katie rhetorically. "Waking up in the car, in BFE Pennsylvania, was an additional reminder that our lives have changed forever."

He replaced the toilet paper in Katie's version of a bug-out bag and rummaged around in the back of the Highlander to find them something to eat before they hit the road. He slammed the hatch shut and jumped in the driver's seat. "It could be worse."

"How so?"

"You could've woken up with a hangover next to a naked Mets fan!"

Katie gave him a well-deserved slug. "Let's go, pain-in-the-neck. If we hustle, we can make the four hundred miles or so to Boston by tonight."

Steven wheeled the Highlander onto Route 30 and set his sights on Allentown. In this new world, he couldn't focus beyond one hundred miles at a time. Lancaster and Reading were the next two towns on the map. As America learned about the extent of the collapse, travel would become more precarious.

"Seriously, the concept of a country with no power is just now settling into my brain," started Steven. "You want to believe that the utility companies can send out their repair crews and make it better."

"We saw the transformers on fire. Some of the substations were still smoldering as we drove through northern Maryland. If this has happened all over the country, there aren't enough parts to put our Humpty Dumpty power grid back together again."

Steven laughed. "Yeah, it may take a year or more to repair the entire grid. I wonder who gets first dibs on restoration."

"There's no doubt that someone will make a fortune deciding that," replied Katie. "We are a nation totally dependent on electricity and advanced communications. This collapse of the grid is going to be brutal on the country."

"Especially on those who haven't prepared," added Steven. He looked around the countryside and realized they were approaching Lancaster County—home of the second-largest Amish population in the world.

There were nearly three hundred thousand Amish in America, the majority of which resided in Pennsylvania, Indiana, and Ohio. This area, known as the Pennsylvania Dutch countryside, was revered for its relaxed, slower-paced lifestyle. Most Americans had limited knowledge of the Amish religion but were very much aware of the Amish limited use of electricity.

Amish did not use electricity due to their religious belief that too much reliance on worldly influences tied them too closely to the secular world. However, the Amish approach to power was somewhat complicated. Almost all Amish forwent power from the public grid, but the use of batteries, liquid propane, and diesel generators, for example, had become accepted. Many states required the Amish to illuminate their horse-drawn buggies that dotted the landscape of the Amish communities. In Pennsylvania, battery-operated lights were deemed acceptable. But in Nebraska, the much more conservative Amish used kerosene lamps hung on the side of the carriage.

Steven slowed as he passed a black Amish buggy carrying two men. The wooden wheels bounced on every crack in the road, but they carried on at somewhere between five and eight miles per hour. The large quarter horse seemed to nod his head as Steven passed—*show off.*

"These guys don't give a rat's ass about electricity," remarked Steven.

"They are entirely self-reliant. I've studied the Amish, as well as the Mennonites and the Latter Day Saints—LDS. Each of these religions practices self-reliance and preparedness. I've never been religious, but now I have to wonder if they had it right all along."

As they passed the rows of corn, Steven wondered if the average American was capable of going back to this nation's roots. They'd been thrust into the nineteenth century and were now on the same level as the Amish. *Can a typical family adapt to growing their food, hunting their meat, or healing their sick without the aid of doctors or pharmacies?*

"US 222 takes us straight to Allentown," said Katie, looking at the map book. "Take the right fork up ahead."

As they drove along without incident, Steven checked the fuel gauge from time to time. They would run out of gas on the other side of Allentown. At some point, they would have to turn north to avoid New York City, and gas would become a priority again. Fuel was a problem, but it was manageable. Steven was glad the human element hadn't reared its ugly head—*yet.*

"If the satphone is charged, try to touch base with Sarge and Julia."

"I will. The cell phone is totally worthless at this point. Sirius/XM is the same story."

Katie placed the call and got through to Julia. They both expressed surprise at the relative calm on both ends. Julia confirmed the status of the nationwide power outage, adding the caveat about the Texas grid being untouched by the attack. Katie assured them not to worry, but that it would most likely be Monday night when they arrived in Boston. Katie promised to call at the same time Monday morning to give them an update.

"Everything cool?" asked Steven.

"Oh yeah. Julia is getting 100 Beacon ready for guests."

"Oh, of course—our friends and *benefactors*," Steven added sarcastically.

"They've been good to us, Steven. It's our job to protect them."

"I know. But as I've said before, Mr. Morgan sent me on some dubious missions. I always question his motives, but somehow the results work out."

"That's why you're a soldier, G.I. Joe."

"Very funny, Katie. We've learned in the military that the generals, and the politicians who pull their strings, are aware of the bigger picture. We're supposed to focus on our jobs. But I still get curious about the intent."

Katie ran her fingers through his hair, which needed to be cut. "We've analyzed the aftermath of your missions for the last year or so. Haven't we always concluded that the ends justified the means?"

"Yes," replied Steven, with a shrug.

"Then let's continue to trust in Mr. Morgan and the rest of *our friends* to make the right choices for our country, and us."

Steven slowed as they approached the intersection of Interstate 78. "Look over there, Katie, we must be getting closer to home!" They both laughed. The Samuel Adams Brewery rested quietly to their left.

"Not quite home, but a taste of home. Boy, could I use a taste of a Sam Adams!"

"No drinking and driving, sir."

"Who's gonna stop me?" asked Steven as a Camaro swung around them, almost clipping their fender, and roared toward the interstate on-ramp. Steven blared the horn and applied his middle finger for emphasis. "Screw you!"

"Wow, that was close. Do you think he was late for work?"

"Forget him. So I hop on I-78?" asked Steven.

"Yes, and we take it around the Allentown-Bethlehem metropolis."

Steven drove a short distance, but the exit ramp to I-78 was blocked by a stalled eighteen-wheeler and a bread truck. "Now what?"

Katie thumbed through the map and replied, "Maybe we could go ahead and turn north now. The Pennsylvania Turnpike will take us to Scranton, and then we could avoid any traffic coming out of New York."

Steven stayed in the right lane and took the ramp. They passed the Camaro that cut them off earlier.

"Hey, watch it!" said Steven as he gave the driver a long glare. He slowed the Highlander as they approached a line of cars passing through the toll lanes.

"Surely they're not collecting money, right?"

"No kidding," started Steven. "I guess the state never stops collecting money from—"

Suddenly, the rear window of the Highlander exploded, sending pieces of glass into the backseat. A gunshot rang out as a bullet flew between them and blew out the windshield.

"Holy—!" screamed Steven, as he swiveled to push Katie down. "Duck!" Katie sank below the seat and drew her weapon. Steven pulled out his as well.

"Who is it?" Katie yelled as Steven veered the Highlander toward the concrete barriers lining the toll lanes. Another shot struck the side of the truck.

"The Camaro. Two guys, firing out the window. Hold on!"

Steven tried to navigate the truck through a gap in the barriers. More shots were fired, and one struck Steven in the right shoulder. Another hit his seatback and lodged in his back. The impact of the bullets slammed him against the steering wheel. He screamed in pain but kept driving into the grass. The Highlander came to a stop sideways in a ditch along a fence row. Steven slumped over the steering wheel—his head bleeding from embedded glass. His shirt was soaked in blood.

"Steven. Steven! Are you all right?" Katie was frantic. More bullets riddled the driver's side of the truck. She rolled out of the passenger door and took a position at the rear fender. Two men were approaching the truck, and she fired at them. One went down instantly. The other turned to run.

Katie returned to the truck to see about Steven. He was alive.

"I'm screwed," he groaned his typical *Stevenism*.

"Where are you shot?"

"Back and right shoulder." He wiped the blood off his face and looked out his window. "They're coming back, Katie."

Katie looked up as two of the men approached the truck with guns drawn. The third man, only wounded, was making his way to his feet.

"Come on, we have to go. Can you crawl across the armrest?"

"Yeah." She helped Steven out of the front seat, and they crossed through the ditch into the trees.

"Wait here," instructed Katie as she ran back towards the truck. She fired in the direction of the assailants to slow their progress toward them. She reached into the back of the hatch and grabbed a bag before turning back towards Steven. Two more warning shots gave her the time she needed to bound through the ditch into the woods. Steven lay motionless in a pile of blood-soaked leaves.

CHAPTER 41

Sunday, September 4, 2016
4:01 p.m.
Allentown, PA

Katie held Steven's wounds to reduce the bleeding and did her best to keep him calm. As he slipped in and out of consciousness, he tried to muster the strength to go after his attackers. She kept him quiet and still. Fortunately, the shooters didn't pursue them into the woods, electing instead to loot her truck.

After they had left, Katie assessed Steven's wounds. It was dangerous to return to the truck with the shooters approaching, but Katie had the presence of mind to grab her medical bag from the backseat. The contents of the bag and Katie's self-training would save Steven's life.

She quickly picked the bits of shattered glass out of his face and forehead with a sterile forceps. She cleaned the facial lacerations with Betadine using Steripad wipes. She avoided using hydrogen peroxide, which could cause damage to the skin. Together with the use of triple antibiotic ointment, she cleaned the wounds and bandaged his face where necessary.

The bullet wounds were more complicated than the facial lacerations. A .45 caliber slug was embedded in Steven's back. Fortunately, it was slowed by the impact against the window and its route through his driver's seatback. It was visible and not deeply embedded, which would have required a surgeon—*if there was such a thing anymore*. Contrary to popular opinion, typically formed by movies, not all bullets needed to be removed. It made for high drama on the big screen, but was not always necessary in practice. In the case of Steven's back, the bullet was visibly bulging just under the skin and causing him pain.

Katie pulled another sterilized forceps out of her medical bag. She told Steven to bite a broken tree branch while she separated the skin. She was able to remove the slug with the other forceps. She bandaged up that wound and turned her attention to his shoulder.

Again, luck was on their side, to an extent. The entry wound was small in comparison to the hole left by the .45 round. It was possible Steven was only shot with an ordinary .22-caliber bullet. It carried only a couple of hundred foot-pounds of energy compared to the .45-caliber round that impacted its target at nearly five hundred foot-pounds.

Katie's first thought was relief that he was shot in the shoulder and not near his vital organs. But she also knew the shoulder was a dangerous place to get shot. It contained vital arteries that fed the arm and parts of the back. There was also a significant nerve bundle that controlled arm function. Again, it wasn't like the movies where the hero takes a bullet to the arm and still manages to hold onto the airplane wing during takeoff.

Katie cleaned the entry and exit wounds thoroughly and then bandaged him up. She pulled a bottle of electrolyte water out of her medical bag and gave Steven several Advil. She also started a dose of Fish Mox—a standard form of amoxicillin used to treat bacteria in fish, but commonly used by preppers to stock their medical cabinets.

After another gulp of the electrolyte water, Steven was becoming more lucid. "So, Doc Holliday, am I gonna live?"

"Maybe," replied Katie as she suddenly became overwhelmed with emotion. She began to cry and muttered, "But only if you pay my bill."

Steven reached out with his left arm to hold her. He winced in pain, but Katie took advantage of the comfort.

"Let me find my credit card," he groaned.

"I love you, Steven," Katie was crying now. "I thought you were—dying. You just slumped over the wheel. Blood was everywhere." Katie's sobs were mixed with sniffles.

Steven chuckled and then coughed. "I'm not going anywhere, Katie O'Shea—except to Boston. I love you too."

Katie looked into Steven's eyes and knew he was going to be okay. She wiped her tears away and sat up to look around. It was getting dark.

"We have to find a place to rest for the night. Do you think you can walk?"

"Yes, but we also need another car. I guess that yours is trashed."

She stood up and brushed herself off. "They took everything, Steven, except the medical bag I grabbed."

"Glad you did, Doc. You saved my life with it."

Katie wanted to start crying again, but Steven lifted himself to his feet with the assistance of several curse words in a variety of languages, it seemed.

"Let's make our way through the woods and see about some shelter. Then we'll talk about a car." She helped him as they walked down a deer path and crossed a road that contained only sporadic traffic. They were certain the attackers were long gone, but Katie kept her weapon ready. She had one full magazine left and several rounds in her gun. Steven never got to fire a shot, so he had two full mags, and his 9mm was full.

"Now we're talkin'," said Steven as he gestured to a Land Rover dealership. "I think we should car shop first." He picked up the pace down a side street toward the back of the Land Rover of Allentown dealership.

"They have Jaguars too!" exclaimed Katie. They found a spot to sit and observe the car dealership from across the street. Whether to break in and steal a car was not an issue for them. They lived in a world without rule of law. Neither law enforcement nor helpful citizen came to their assistance while they were under attack at the toll booth. Survival was their number one priority, and transportation was the first order of business.

Katie stood up and checked her weapon. She turned to Steven and double-checked his bandages. "Cop a squat while I walk around the building. Let me make sure no rent-a-cops are hanging around."

"Come and get me before you go in, okay?"

"Of course," Katie replied. "This is our first major purchase as a couple."

"Yeah, yeah," said Steven as Katie walked into the darkness. He whispered loudly to her, "Land Rover."

"Jaguar," was her answer.

After fifteen minutes, she returned with a hammer. "I found this in the field behind the building. I think it will make a pretty good entry key to the service department door."

After taking a few precautionary moments to observe the surroundings, Steven and Katie made their way across the parking lot to the obscured service entrance.

"We're about to find out if the alarm system still works," said Katie as she smashed the plate-glass door. There was silence except for the shards of glass hitting the concrete floor. "We're in."

Leading the way, both Steven and Katie pulled their weapons in case there was a night watchman with a death wish. They went room to room, clearing the building.

"It's tempting to sleep on Mr. General Manager's comfy sofa for the night, but finding places to sleep is easy," said Steven. "Let's pick a model and get out of here."

Katie ran for the showroom like a young child. "First dibs! Jaguar is the winner!"

"No fair, brat, I'm like Swiss cheese with bullet holes," replied Steven as he struggled to keep up with her. "Besides, we have to do this the smart way."

"What the hell does that mean?" asked Katie defiantly as she stood next to a shiny new Jaguar coupe with her hands on her hips.

"We'll decide based upon which vehicle has the most gas in it," replied Steven.

Katie pondered this for a minute and knew Steven was right. They systematically walked through the showroom and checked for keys and the fuel level of each vehicle.

Steven proudly proclaimed himself the winner when he found a black Range Rover, supercharged model, containing a full tank. "Turn out the lights, the party is over."

"Everybody is a comedian," said Katie. "Let's see what else is of use in the building; then we'll hit the road." She tossed her medical bag in the back compartment together with a basic first aid kit she found in the service center. Steven gathered up bottled water and snacks from the break room. He changed out of his bloody clothes and put on a drab gray mechanics suit. With his bandaged face, he joked that he looked like Jason in the *Friday the Thirteenth* movies.

When they loaded up everything of use, they faced a quandary. "How do we get this thing out of here?" asked Katie.

Steven looked around and realized the cars were driven into the showroom through a roll-up glass door at the end of the building. *It was electric operated.*

"Ah hell," said Steven. "This thing doesn't have a manual override. It requires power."

"Now what?" Katie and Steven surveyed their options before Katie answered her question. "Looks like I get to drive my Jaguar after all. I'll drive it through the windows of that portico. You follow me out."

"Sounds like a plan." Steven hopped into the front seat of the Range Rover while Katie revved the engine of the Jaguar. She floored it and crashed through the glass. Steven followed after the glass and dust had settled.

Katie jumped into the passenger side, and Steven roared onto Tilghman Street towards the Pennsylvania Turnpike.

"Now we're talkin'!" shouted Steven. "Grand theft auto! What a rush!"

Just as Steven was tearing up the entrance ramp heading north, Katie socked him with the buzzkill.

"Pull over up here. I'm driving."

Steven snapped his head towards her and then grimaced from pain. "Hold up!" he protested.

"Doctor's orders," said Katie. "You've only got one good arm. Now pull over."

Steven dutifully pulled over.

They were back on the road again.

CHAPTER 42

Sunday, September 4, 2016
10:19 p.m.
Port Jervis, NY

Katie checked Steven's wounds every fifteen to thirty minutes but was pleased that her bandages held. They would have to be changed in the next couple of hours, and after what his body had endured, quality sleep was necessary. She cut through the heart of the Poconos to avoid traveling through downtown Scranton. The famed Pocono Raceway was dark as she passed it on Interstate 80. Traffic was light, and it was a welcome relief. Now Katie viewed every vehicle as a threat.

Turning eastbound toward the New York state line on I-84, she thought of her career. Katie's family had stressed the importance of her education as a child. They had taken an active role in her studies, as well as her after-school activities. She was destined to have a promising career in any field that caught her attention. But it was the events of 9/11 that captured her imagination and set her life's path. While her teenage girlfriends savored the attention of boys and fawned over the latest teen heartthrob, Katie dove into the geopolitical details of the attacks on that fateful day.

When she voiced her initial reaction at the dinner table one evening, her parents were horrified. She said the events of 9/11 were the single greatest attack on America in its history. She was in awe at what a handful of men could accomplish against the world's only superpower.

Naturally, her conclusions drew astonishment and admonition from her parents. She was told never to say that to anyone again.

Katie took their criticism, but it did not change her opinion. She studied the events of 9/11 from an unemotional, rational point of view. Without allowing feelings of sorrow for the victims or a sense of patriotism to cloud her judgment, Katie was willing to say out loud what so many would not. *9/11 was a big win for terrorism.*

Katie set her sights on a career in government. At fifteen, she wanted to be a spy. When she told her parents she wanted to attend the U.S. Naval Academy, they were proud. She met Steven in college, and they had been close friends over the years. Now, they were *going steady*. Katie laughed to herself—*if I can keep him alive.*

"I need coffee," grumbled her patient.

"Let me find a Starbucks for you, honey. I'm sure there's one around here somewhere."

"You don't understand. I need caffeine. My head is splitting."

"Okay, we're almost in New York. We need to find a place to pull over for the night and catch some winks. Caffeine is off the menu, but ibuprofen is the next best thing."

"Where are we?"

"We're near a small town called Port Jervis on the Delaware River. New Jersey is across the river, and New York is up ahead on the other side of town. I'll pull off after we cross the Delaware."

Steven closed his eyes again, and Katie caught a glimpse of his face in the headlights of a passing car. He was incredibly handsome. This man risked his life defending his country and then chose a career where he willingly put his life at risk for a paycheck. *Or did he do it because it was enjoyable?*

Katie pulled off at a nondescript exit called Mountain Road. At the bottom of the ramp, she looked down the road about half a mile and saw an illuminated parking lot.

"Steven, they might have power here."

He stirred himself upright and more alert. "Careful, Katie, I'm not in the mood for any surprises."

Katie cautiously approached the source of the light until she could see the Greeneville Fire Department. Two of its green roll-up doors were open, revealing a fire engine and a tanker. A few residents were milling around, talking to the uniformed firefighters.

"Whadya think?" asked Katie. They both studied the surroundings and the people having a conversation in the parking lot.

"Let's pull in and circle around to point the truck out in case we have to run. I'll see if they're friendly."

Katie slowly pulled into the paved lot and circled as if to leave. The group turned their attention toward them, and one of the firefighters managed a wave. Steven rolled down his window.

"Good evening," he started politely. "Is there a hospital nearby or an EMS?"

"No hospital, but we have some medical supplies here. We're also trained for most nonlethal wounds." The group approached the Range Rover without hesitation.

"My wounds are nonlethal, *so far*, although that was not the intent of the guys who tried to kill us." Steven looked at Katie and nodded. He opened the door to greet the welcoming committee, showing his hands to keep them visible.

"Wow, your face is messed up," said a woman in the group.

"Windshield, or back window pieces," started Steven. "Heck, maybe even side window pieces." Katie studied the crowd and determined they were not a threat. She shut off the engine and joined the group, keeping her weapon holstered and hidden by her shirt.

"My name is Steven, and this is my friend Katie. We're trying to get home to Boston, and we were doing pretty well until a bunch of thugs carjacked us at a toll booth in Allentown."

"Hi, everyone," said Katie.

"My name is Hector," said one of the firefighters. "I know that toll booth. It's the perfect choke point."

Katie perked up at the use of the military terminology, as did Steven.

"Are you military?"

"Retired recently," said Hector. "I was with the 77th Sustainment Brigade. We provided logistical support to 1st Battalion, 25th Marines."

"Wait, were you stationed at Devens? Recently?" asked Steven.

"I was until February. Do you know Fort Devens?"

"I do, Brad—I mean Colonel Bradlee is a very close friend of ours." The rest of the group started smiling as everyone let their guards down.

"He was our base commander. I still keep in touch with my friends there, especially Gunny Falcone."

"Holy—!" exclaimed Steven, catching himself. "Pardon my French, ma'am. Small world, isn't it? Hector, my full name is Lieutenant Commander Steven Sargent, United States Navy retired. I believe we have a lot to talk about."

"We sure do," replied Hector. He rolled up his sleeve to reveal a tattoo under his forearm—the five red and four white stripes of the Rebellious flag.

"Choose freedom?" asked Steven.

"Choose freedom," was the response from Hector and three of his friends in unison.

CHAPTER 43

Monday, September 5, 2016
8:30 a.m.
Port Jervis, New York

After a night of conversation and some medical attention for Steven, the two travelers slept hard. Only the roar of the six-hundred-horsepower Cummins engine stirred them awake on Monday morning. Steven smelled coffee.

He kissed Katie and whispered into her ear, "Wake up, gorgeous." He felt better after getting a full night's rest. He walked out of the fire hall's sleeping quarters and found Hector at the front entrance.

"Morning, Steven."

"Good morning. Do you guys have a call?"

"A big one, in fact," replied Hector. "There's been an explosion and a massive fire at the Indian Point Nuclear Plant in Buchanan."

"Whoa, that's serious."

"It could be. Several transformers in unit three have caught fire. Then there was an explosion in the main transformer of Indian Point two. It's all hands on deck, I'm afraid."

"Be careful, my friend," said Steven.

"I will. I have lots to live for," said Hector, pointing towards the kitchen, where two women were preparing food, and the smell of coffee reached Steven's nostrils. "That's my wife and daughter. They've made breakfast and will hold down the fort until we return."

Steven's first reaction was that of concern. "Aren't you afraid to leave them here alone?"

"I understand where you're coming from Steven, but we live in the country. Port Jervis is not New York City or even Allentown."

Hector gently touched Steven's shoulder. "We all know each other and look out for our neighbors. Also, there are plenty of *friends* around." Hector patted his forearm with the Rebellious flag tattoo.

With his right arm in a sling, Steven reached out with his left hand to shake Hector's. "Thank you for what you've done for us. The place to crash, the medical attention, and the coffee will give us a boost."

"You're welcome, Commander," said Hector. "There is one more thing, and please don't repeat this to my wife. I don't want her worried."

"Okay."

"Interstate 84 across the Hudson has been closed due to potential nuclear fallout. They've evacuated a ten-mile radius of Indian Point, which includes West Point."

"We need to head northeast into Connecticut, but avoid Hartford. What do you suggest?"

"Check the map and make your way to US 209 towards Poughkeepsie. You can cross there and then make your way across New York into Connecticut. You need to be aware that some towns are closing their borders to travelers. Border closings seem to be happening nationwide, according to what we hear on our ham radio units. I've written you a letter on our station letterhead, vouching for you and Katie. I have provided my *hamr* call letters in case anyone needs to confirm who you are."

"Thank you, Hector," said Steven.

"Also, please tell your brother thank you."

"Sarge?"

"Yes," replied Hector. "We've read his book *Choose Freedom*—more than once. It's an inspiration to us all. We love America—*as it was originally intended*. Here in Port Jervis, we'll do our part to make her exceptional again."

"Absolutely, buddy. Stay safe and *choose freedom!*"

CHAPTER 44

Monday, September 5, 2016
1:50 p.m.
Poughkeepsie, New York

Steven felt much better in the khakis and Realtree camo sweatshirt provided by Hector. The mechanic coveralls didn't fit him properly, and the look might attract attention as they made their way home. Steven rounded the curve of US 44, and they approached the Mid-Hudson Bridge. A delegation of law enforcement officers and two retired military bulldozers blocked the route into Poughkeepsie.

"Let's see if Hector's *passport* helps us cross the Hudson," said Steven. Steven approached the police barricade slowly and kept his hands on top of the wheel in plain view of the officers.

"There are snipers on the ridges to our left and right," said Katie. "Army bulldozers too. What are they expecting?" Steven glanced in both directions without being obvious or appearing nervous to the officers. Sheriff's deputies approached both sides of the Range Rover with their AR-15s held at low ready.

"Sir, the bridge is closed to through-traffic until further notice," said the officer whose name badge identified him as Deputy Mullinax. "We'll need you to turn your vehicle around and choose a route to the north. There's another bridge crossing at Red Hook— about fifteen miles from here."

"Good morning, Deputy," said Steven. "I understand your need for security, but we're low on fuel. Highway 44 provides a direct route to the north of Hartford. We can't afford any lost gas mileage for detours."

"I'm sorry, sir, but for the security purposes of our town, only identifiable residents are allowed to pass on the Mid-Hudson Bridge." Steven reached for the letter on the console, and both deputies immediately raised their weapons and shouted.

"Put your hands where we can see them, sir. Now!"

Steven raised his hands and placed them on the dashboard. "I have a letter I need you to read. That's all!"

"Both of you step out of the vehicle!" Two more deputies ran to the aid of their partners, with weapons drawn.

Steven looked at Katie and nodded. They both exited the truck with their hands held away from their bodies.

"We don't want any trouble," started Steven. "Please look at the letter, Deputy. It's there by the gearshift."

A few cars were lined up behind the Range Rover but were keeping their distance. The deputy visually confirmed that the other officers were in position, and he found the letter.

"Do you have some identification?"

"I do, it's in the console. But just be aware, my Glock is in there as well."

"Understood." Deputy Mullinax looked at Steven's identification and reread the letter. He walked away for a moment and called someone on his two-way radio. After a moment, he returned the letter and Steven's driver's license. "Weapons down."

"My apologies, sir," said Deputy Mullinax. "You can relax now. We're trying to avoid the types of incidents that have plagued other small towns."

"Thank you."

"Are you related to Professor Henry Sargent?"

"I am. He's my older brother."

"My brother, Michael Mullinax, is the county executive and a fan of your brother's writing. Apparently they met in Orlando last summer at a libertarian conference."

"Apparently, Sarge has made a lot of friends this year," said Steven. He adjusted his arm sling, where his Glock 26 subcompact was hidden. *No need for this yet.*

"His book made a big impression on a lot of us, which is part of the reason we're guarding this bridge. After the power went down, our world became a lot smaller. As odd as it may sound, the City of Poughkeepsie must maintain its borders first, and then we'll concern ourselves with the rest of New York and America. As my brother says, *sovereignty starts at home.*"

"He's right," said Steven. "Thank you for letting us cross." Steven was ready to continue.

"Yes, sir. You're welcome. Another patrol car will escort you across the bridge and to the east side of town. From there Route 44, or the Dutchess Turnpike, as it's also known, will take you directly to Hartford. It's about a hundred miles from here."

"Thank you, Deputy Mullinax." Steven and Katie got into the truck, and Deputy Mullinax leaned into the window and quietly said, "Choose freedom."

CHAPTER 45

Monday, September 5, 2016
11:21 p.m.
Sturbridge, MA

Katie and Steven continued their trek across the northern route of Connecticut. They didn't encounter any violence, but several of the towns they approached were establishing security checkpoints. Hector's passport helped most of the time. On other occasions, Steven and Katie were forced to detour. With his injury, they were not interested in conflict with local law enforcement or the ragtag militias that protected these small townships.

The extended amount of time necessary to travel across the state was not an issue except evidence of looting became more frequent, especially north of Hartford. More disabled vehicles were seen on the roadways, and travelers were seen walking or riding bicycles to reach their destinations.

"Mass-a-two-shits dead ahead." Katie laughed.

"Home sweet home," joined in Steven. "Home of the baked bean."

"All hail to Mass-a-two-shits!" exclaimed Katie as they crossed the state line on Interstate 84.

"I think we're getting slaphappy," said Steven. "As much as I'd like to coast right into Beantown tonight, it's not gonna happen." Steve tapped the fuel gauge for Katie to see the red *low fuel* indicator.

"We'll be lucky to make it to Sturbridge."

"Twenty miles?"

"Yep." They passed the rest area and welcome center as they approached Exit 1. "Let's sleep for the night so we'll be fresh when we hit Boston tomorrow. If things have deteriorated, we may have to fight our way to 100 Beacon."

"What about fuel?"

"I have a plan," replied Steven. "Hector gave me a siphon hose and taught me which vehicles are easiest to pull from. This Mobil truck stop might give us some options."

"What are we looking for?" asked Katie.

"Most vehicles from the nineties forward have anti-siphon devices that prevent you from inserting the rubber hose all the way to the fuel. You just end up sucking air. Older models are easier to work with, especially pickup trucks if you have a long siphon hose."

"Do we?"

"Yes—courtesy of Hector's Passport and Gas Theft, LLC." Steven laughed.

Katie was still perplexed. "Do you know the model years of pickup trucks?"

"Look for the most busted-up vehicles you can."

Steven and Katie drove through and caught the attention of a couple of truckers standing by their rigs. After another pass through, they realized there were too many eyes upon them.

"Too hot, Bonnie," said Steven. "Let's work our way up US 20, Worcester Road. Surely something will catch our eye."

"It needs to be soon, Clyde. We're on fumes."

They drove several miles along US 20 and then hit the crest of a hill. "Katie, this is our last chance. We can coast down this hill, but then we look for another car or walk the last seventy miles." Steven let off the gas and put the car in neutral. As they began to coast, Katie yelled for him to stop.

"Back there, a driveway up into the woods. There was a sign with orange lettering that read *Landscape Supply*."

Steven pulled over to the side of the road and shut off the engine. He didn't want the fuel lines to run completely dry.

"How did you see that in the dark?" he asked.

"They probably have solar landscape lighting. You know, as a sales tool."

Steven shrugged. *Made sense.* "I'll check it out. Wait here."

"No, Steven."

"What?"

"I won't wait here. This is not a job for a one-armed bandit. We'll go together." Katie jumped out of the truck, and Steven followed suit. They hopped over the concrete highway barriers and crossed the remaining two lanes of the road.

They circled around the back of the greenhouse and immediately found an empty gas can.

"Crap," said Steven. Katie crouched behind a hedgerow and pulled her weapon. She was looking in all directions.

"What?" she asked.

"I forgot the siphon hose."

"You dumbass," said Katie jokingly. "You suck at burglary. I'll be right back."

While Katie retrieved the siphon hose, Steven looked through the greenhouses and found nothing. There was a large shed with a roll-up door that was padlocked. He quietly tried a side door, and it was unlocked.

Katie returned. "Any luck?"

"Yeah. This door is unlocked. Let's be smart and clear the building."

"It'll be easier with this," said Katie, holding up one of the solar-powered landscape lights.

"God, I love you, Katie O'Shea."

"I know. Me first." Katie led the way in and swung left, and Steven took the right side. There was no other room inside, and they quickly determined it was unoccupied. But there were also no filled gas cans.

"Nothin' runs like a Deere, unless it's empty," said Steven as he siphoned the gas out of two John Deere lawn tractors and a push mower.

"It's not quite five gallons, but it should get us home," he said.

"Good. I picked up a few burglary tools in case we need them." She showed Steven a pry bar, a long screwdriver, and another set of bolt cutters. "You never know."

CHAPTER 46

Tuesday, September 6, 2016
9:13 a.m.
Framingham, MA

The decision to drive into Boston on the Massachusetts Turnpike was not an easy one. They could have easily turned north and sought the comfort and safety of Prescott Peninsula. But in their last communication with Sarge and Julia yesterday morning, they'd confirmed their plans were to return to 100 Beacon. Traffic came to a standstill as they approached the intersection with the Boston-Worcester Turnpike.

"They're diverting traffic off the Mass Turnpike for some reason," said Steven.

Katie studied the map. "We'll have to go through a toll booth."

"No way. Not in my lifetime." Steven pulled onto the shoulder and began driving through the grass along a utility easement.

Katie grabbed the dashboard. "Steven, the fence!" Steven revved the engine and drove through the chain-link fence—bouncing both of their heads off the ceiling.

"What fence?" he asked as he gunned the engine and the back of the Range Rover fishtailed through the pine needles. He bounced them along under the high-voltage lines—which no longer carried any voltage—until they came out on Oak Hill Road. "Which way?"

"Are you asking me?" asked Katie, rubbing the newly formed knot on her head.

"You're the navigator. Do you want me to ask Siri?"

"No, wiseguy. Hold on." Katie studied the map for a moment. "Turn right. We'll pick up Highway 20 again."

Katie directed Steven through the neighborhoods until they came out on Turnpike Road at an industrial park.

"Steven, look!" Katie pointed to their left, where three men were chasing a young woman dressed in a FedEx uniform. "We have to help her!"

"Katie," started Steven, "this could be a really bad idea."

"Yeah, for her! Stop. Turn here!"

Steven slid the Range Rover into a turn—barely avoiding a curb and hopping into a cluster of trees. The men were gaining on the woman as she ran through the Penske Truck Rental parking lot.

"She's headed for the FedEx building on the right. Fire a warning shot to slow them down."

Instead of a warning shot, Katie shot one in the back of the leg, bringing him down in a heap.

"Katie!" screamed Steven.

"No rules, remember?" she fired again, missing the other two men, who continued their pursuit. While their attention was directed at the assailants, a BMW sedan crashed into their rear bumper, sending the Range Rover into a spin. Steven overcorrected in an attempt to gain control and skidded to a stop. They were sideways in the middle of the road with the BMW barreling toward them. Katie calmly shot the driver and braced for the impact.

The BMW struck the right front quarter panel of the Range Rover. The truck did a complete revolution, and the BMW went airborne before hitting a telephone pole that almost split the car in two. Smoke and fluids poured out of their engine.

"Are you okay?" asked Steven. But Katie was halfway out of the truck before he got a response.

"Let's go!" Katie shouted, after confirming the driver of the BMW was dead. Again, without waiting for Steven, she began running towards the FedEx building.

"Dammit," muttered Steven as he grabbed his handguns and ran after Katie, who had disappeared through some trees in front of the building.

He caught up with her at the front entrance. The plate-glass window was broken open with a trash can. She turned to him and held up one finger to her lips—to indicate quiet.

Steven whispered, "Katie, this is not our fight."

"Yes, it is, Steven. I'm not gonna let that girl get raped or murdered. What if that was me in there?" Of course, she had a point. His shoulder was throbbing, and all of the bandages had fallen off his face at this point. *I could scare them away.*

With a deep breath and an exaggerated wince, Steven removed his sling.

"You're bleeding."

"We'll fix it later." He holstered the subcompact Glock and carried the other 9mm in his left hand. He was ambidextrous and very comfortable shooting with either hand. "Follow me and listen for sounds. They won't be able to stay quiet."

"I think they're more interested in their prey than their hunters," said Katie.

They entered the lobby of the FedEx facility. Behind the counter, there were two swinging doors. Steven surmised the woman would run into the larger space—the warehouse—which might provide more places to hide. He nodded toward the set of doors on the left and Katie followed. They both crouched as they entered the massive sixty-thousand-square-foot building.

"Great," whispered Steven. "Needle in a haystack." It was pitch black inside.

"It's dark. It benefits someone who is familiar with the building."

"Let's wait here a moment until our eyes adjust to the darkness. We can use the slivers of light coming through the top of the steel roll-up doors as our guide."

A crash to their right caught their attention. Then they heard the metallic sound of wheels spinning.

"The package conveyor belt," said Steven.

"Come out, come out wherever you are!" shouted one of the men.

"Yeah, we just want to play," said the other.

Steven worked his way along the wall behind the offices. Katie was right behind him, constantly looking forward and then back, to ensure no one caught them off guard.

"Come on, girlfriend. We'll have a good time. You know you want some of this!" The men continued to taunt the woman while allowing Steven and Katie to draw a bead on their voices.

Steven found the conveyer belt that was the source of the earlier noise and decided to follow it into the center of the building. The FedEx panel trucks obscured any light emitting from the exterior doors. He moved quietly to the tailgate of each truck as they followed the presumed path of the two men.

"Maybe she went through the other doors, man," said one of the men, his voice up ahead of Steven and Katie's position.

"No, dude, I saw those doors swingin'. She's in here somewhere and I ain't leavin' 'til I get me some."

Steven was almost upon them when some boxes fell behind him. The men suddenly turned and ran through the darkness, crashing Steven into the wheels of a truck.

"Gotcha!" screamed one of the men as he jumped on Steven and started swinging at his face. The other man jumped to his feet just in time to be killed by Katie with two shots to the chest. The woman's shriek from their left provided the distraction Steven needed to roll the heavier man off of him. Before he could pull his backup weapon, Katie put two rounds in the remaining man's chest. They were both dead.

Steven groaned. In the darkness, Katie leaned down to see if he was hurt. She could feel the blood seeping into his shirt.

"Are you okay?" asked Katie.

"Yeah. That guy was heavy. He ran over me like he didn't know I was standing there."

"Can you stand?"

Steven lifted himself up, but his knees gave way as he fell against the conveyor.

"Stay here," said Katie. She turned her attention to the woman with the hope of getting Steven help. "Hello, ma'am, my name is Katie O'Shea. Are you okay?"

Silence. Katie tried again.

"Ma'am, we're not here to hurt you. We just wanted to protect you from those men. Could you please let me know you're okay so I can take my friend outside and get him some help? He's badly hurt."

After a moment of brief silence, she replied, "I'm okay. Thank you."

"You're welcome. Do you have a flashlight? It's dark, and I need to get some medical supplies for Steven."

"Hold on." A door to one of the trucks opened and a light faintly illuminated an area near the office entrance. Then headlights from the vehicle turned on, making it much brighter. One by one, the woman walked down the row of FedEx vans waiting to be filled with packages and turned on their headlights. In just a few moments, it was bright as day inside.

She peered around the last van and looked at Steven and then Katie.

"Was he shot?"

"Yes, but not here. I have to get my bag from the truck. It was crashed by another man that I assume was with these two." Katie kicked the legs of the dead men. The girl put her hands to her mouth and began to cry.

"They were going to rape me," she sobbed. She sat on the sidestep of a truck.

"Not anymore," said Katie. "What's your name?"

"Valerie."

"Valerie, will you stay here with Steven while I get my medical supplies?" Steven's leg began to buckle, and he landed on the floor with his back to the conveyor.

"Yes."

Katie turned to Steven and checked his eyes and pulse. "Keep him awake."

CHAPTER 47

Wednesday, September 7, 2016
10:51 a.m.
Boston, MA

"I vote the bigger, the better," said Steven as he surveyed the FedEx fleet. His body had suffered a lot of trauma in the last forty-eight hours, but he was clearly rejuvenated by the night's rest. At this pace, he wondered if they would ever make it to Boston—in one piece.

Valerie, the young FedEx employee, had been waiting for her boyfriend to return. He was a FedEx supervisor, and they were the only two employees working at the facility on Saturday night when the power went off. He was going home to grab his guns and some supplies for the trip into Auburndale and her parents' home. She dutifully waited for three days and, out of boredom, left the confines of the FedEx facility to look around. That was when her troubles began.

"I agree," said Katie. "That crappy Range Rover got pushed around by a Beemer—*literally*."

Steven stopped in front of a twenty-four-foot panel truck. "How about this one?" he asked. "It's as big as a U-Haul."

"I don't care," replied Valerie. "I quit as of yesterday. I'll probably never see my last check."

Steven stifled a laugh and then realized the girl was serious. All she could think about was her last paycheck. There were two crashed cars and four dead bodies lying around and nobody cared. Day four after the collapse and nobody was surprised at the carnage he and Katie left behind. *Imagine what Day 44 will be like.*

"Come on, guys, let's go," said Katie. "Valerie, will you be able to drive this thing after you drop us off?"

"Oh no, you can have it," she replied. "Just drop me off in Auburndale near Woodland Road overpass. My parents live right down the street. I can easily walk from there."

"Let's roll, then," said Steven.

The trio made their way onto the Massachusetts Turnpike and into the city without incident. They dropped off Valerie as requested and exchanged hugs. Steven sensed that the young girl was grateful for her rescue, but still hadn't grasped the magnitude of the mess her country was in. He hesitated to leave her on the side of the turnpike, but she appeared to feel safe in familiar surroundings. *As did he.*

"Do we take the turnpike all the way into downtown and double back?" asked Katie.

"I say we get off sooner, before Prudential Center," replied Steven. "I don't want to go through the tunnel, and I'd like to avoid the toll booth at Storrow."

"That's understandable, but we have to go through a toll somewhere."

"Let's just do it here in Newton," said Steven. "I can catch Commonwealth and drive this big boy right up to Sarge's front door."

As they drove through Boston University and into Back Bay West, visual evidence of looting and collapse became more prevalent. Stalled cars were the norm, parked in all directions when they had run out of fuel. Storefront windows were broken more often than not. Even the historic Harvard Club was not immune, as smoke billowed out of its upper windows.

"What will be left of Boston when, or if, this ends?" asked Katie. Steven attempted to turn down Berkeley Street, but the road was blocked. He would have to go up to Boston Common and loop through.

"Sadly, I haven't thought about it. It's all about survival right now. I've already had my share of excitement."

He steered the truck out of Boston Common and westbound on Beacon. He encountered two stalled vehicles that created a tight squeeze as they drove through. Steven rose up in his seat to look at the abandoned cars on the sidewalk and in the turn lane. People were running and screaming near the entrance of 100 Beacon. He pulled to a stop in the crosswalk.

The sounds of gunshots reverberated off the buildings.

"Steven, they're shooting in front of our building!"

He inched the FedEx truck closer. "Looks like four to six hostiles behind those parked cars, shooting toward the entrance," said Steven.

"Is anybody returning fire?" asked Katie.

"I can't tell," he replied. "We've gotta do something."

"How many rounds do you have left?"

"A full mag in each. You?"

"Same here. I emptied the last of my backup mag in that fat ass who tackled you," said Katie.

Steven sat there for a moment as the gunfight continued.

"Why waste bullets when you have a tank?" Steven hit the gas and roared down Beacon Street. The attackers didn't notice him until the FedEx truck was on top of their position. Only the last two managed to jump over the vehicles out of harm's way. The other three were not quick enough as the front of the truck ran over them one by one—crushing them under the weight of the twin rear axles.

Steven screeched to a halt. Both he and Katie piled out of the driver's side door, keeping the truck between them and the surviving attackers. The two remaining shooters were caught in the crossfire. A rifle peeked out of the front entrance to the building and fired wildly in their direction, managing to shoot holes in the FedEx truck. Steven reflexively dove behind the wheel wells. Katie waited a moment for the gunfire to subside and then quickly joined him.

They crouched behind the wheels while several more shots flew in their direction.

"I know that isn't Sarge shooting from the building. That's pathetic."

"No doubt. What's the plan?" asked Katie.

"You take the back side, and I'll take the front of the truck. My first shot will be your signal to join in. I'm worried less about the two hostiles than I am the dumbass behind the front door. That idiot might get lucky and shoot one of us."

"Got it. But you're bleeding again."

"Yeah, I hit my shoulder diving for cover. Maybe I'm getting too old for this."

"Nah. You love it. And I love you. Let's not get killed when we're thirty feet from the house, okay?"

"Yeah, ready?"

Steven ran towards the front of the truck and gave Katie a moment to get in position. The shooters were hunched together between an SUV and a Mercedes. Katie would not have a clear shot because of the SUV. Steven walked in a crouch along the side of the FedEx truck. He couldn't get too close to the shooters because Katie might open fire and shoot him by mistake.

He knew they were scared. He played on their apprehension. Once in position, he rose up with his gun trained on their location.

"Pssst, hey!" The two men instinctively stood to see who was summoning them, and each received a shot to the chest. Steven shouted, "Hold your fire," as he ran forward and put a round in each of their heads.

Katie moved to join him with her weapon drawn.

"Just like *Duck Hunt* on Nintendo. Their heads popped up and down they went."

"Great job, thanks for waiting for me."

"The SUV blocked your line of fire. It was the best—" Suddenly a bullet flew over their head and impacted in the truck. Steven and Katie hit the pavement and crawled behind the SUV.

"Hostiles?" whispered Katie.

"No, it's the dumbass behind door number one." Steven rose and walked to the back of the bullet-ridden SUV.

"Hey, be careful!" exclaimed Katie.

"Screw this," said Steven. "I could walk right up the sidewalk and that dumbass couldn't hit me!"

"Wait for me." Katie ran up behind him. Steven walked into the open with his hands up.

"Hey, dumbass!" he shouted at the entrance. "We just saved your collective asses. How about not shooting us as your way of saying thanks?"

"I don't know you," shouted someone from behind the door. Steven saw movement in the windows to the left of the gate. He passed through the iron gates.

"I'm here to see my brother on the top floor. His name is Sargent. Now lower your weapons so nobody gets hurt. Fair enough?"

"How do we know you're not lying?" said an older man's voice from inside the lobby.

Steven was losing his patience. "Because there are five dead bodies out here and none of them have your name on it."

After a moment, Steven was told to come inside. Katie walked in but with her hands on her weapon.

The man inside the building used the barrel of the rifle to wave Steven inside, which was a mistake. The moment the barrel moved away from his body, Steven grabbed it from the man with his left hand and kicked his legs out from under him. Katie immediately covered the rest of the room.

"Hey, what did you do that for?" asked the man as he sat up against the wall.

"Because you shot at me, dumbass." Steven emptied the ammunition from the M1 onto the marble floor with a clink. Then he removed the magazine before handing the vintage gun back to the man on the floor. "Nice gun, though. It's older than me."

"Do you know why those men were attacking you?" asked Katie. An elderly woman came into the lobby from the stairwell and Katie wheeled to cover her.

"They were upset with the man on the top floor."

"Did the men say why?" asked Steven.

"No," replied the man on the floor. "They were furious. They just cursed at us and started shooting because we wouldn't open the door."

"Let's go," said Steven. "You people are going to have to learn to defend yourselves better. You can't stick your gun around the door like those fools in the Middle East and hope to hit anything." Steven led Katie up the stairwell. Halfway up the stairs he had to catch his breath. He looked down and saw that he was leaving a trail of blood.

"You need some stitches."

"I do, and beer too." Steven laughed, but it hurt his shoulder too much.

Katie went ahead to open the door and found Sarge and Julia waiting. Julia immediately hugged her, and Katie began to cry. Sarge pushed his way onto the landing.

"Katie, where's Steven? Where's my brother?"

Steven rounded the stairs, his shirt covered in blood.

"Did you miss me?"

PART FOUR

Bug Out

CHAPTER 48

Saturday, September 3, 2016
9:11 p.m.
Triple Q Ranch, Prescott Peninsula
Quabbin Reservoir, Massachusetts

The Quinns, J.J. and Sabs settled back into their chairs—relaxed after a fun evening of burgers and beer. The conversation, as it so often did, centered on prepping and the threats America faced. The two couples were not into the arts or the latest news from Hollywood. The home opener for the New England Patriots wasn't even a passing thought. They enjoyed their family, the Quinn girls, and their friends. Overall, they shared an interest in preparedness.

Donald once said being a prepper was not a hobby or an obsession. He believed they led a preparedness *lifestyle*. They were committed preppers. He and Susan hungered for more information on the subject. If they found a new survival tool or learned of an interesting food-storage item, they would incorporate it into their plan. They realized how fortunate they were to have the financial backing of the Boston Brahmin. Most in the preparedness community did not have the resources the Loyal Nine enjoyed. But the prepping principles were the same nonetheless—beans, bullets, and Band-Aids.

Donald learned to ignore the media and their condemnation of preppers as the tinfoil-hat crowd, hoarders, and right-wing nutjobs. Prepping was like insurance, he had explained to J.J. that afternoon several years ago while they watched the girls play in the pool. A responsible family might carry home, auto, and life insurance. Fortunately, they might never experience an auto accident or devastating tornado damage to their home. But they carried insurance to protect against these calamities nonetheless. Some sensible families stored sufficient food, water, and supplies to deal with the inconveniences of natural disasters. They espoused the FEMA rule of three days' stored supplies. Donald believed this level of preparedness, while prudent, was insufficient.

Committed prepping was insurance against those potentially world-changing, catastrophic events resulting in TEOTWAWKI—the end of the world as we know it. He believed many threats were facing the world, and America in particular. *The bigger they are, the harder they fall.* As the world became more technologically advanced and more reliant on the power grid for survival, the likelihood that a catastrophic grid-down event could bring America to its knees increased exponentially. An EMP, a solar flare, a nuclear bomb, or cyber attacks had all occurred in the past. Any of these could bring America to its knees.

For a moment, they enjoyed the silence of the Quabbin Reservoir. An occasional loon would make its presence known, but otherwise the Rheem air-conditioning unit behind One Prescott Peninsula was the only sound the two couples heard—*until they didn't.*

At first, what had happened didn't register on them. Air-conditioning units turned on and off as a matter of course. But one didn't realize the ambient sounds made by electrically powered appliances. Even sitting outside, in a place as remote and serene as Prescott Peninsula, the low hum from inside the building could be heard—*until it wasn't.*

"Hey, who turned off the lights inside?" asked Donald. He sat up on the edge of the Adirondack chair and looked around. "Do you think the girls are fooling around?"

"It could be. I'll check on them," replied Susan. Susan slipped on her flip-flops and made her way around Sabs's chair when she accidentally kicked over a beer.

"Hey, party foul." J.J. laughed.

"I'm sorry, Sabs," said Susan, looking at the dark sky and the new moon. "I can't see. A little moonlight would be nice."

J.J. leaned down and picked up the now half-empty bottle. "It was full too."

"Can I get you another beer, Sabs?" asked Susan.

"No, thanks," she replied.

Donald checked his watch. It was 9:13. "Maybe we should wind it up for the night. I'd like to go fishing in the morning. J.J., are you up for it?"

"You know, I'm not much for fishing. I'm too impatient. But I'll tag along and help you reel them in. I think the girls were going to explore the peninsula, so we can have some male bonding time."

Donald laughed. He was about to add something when Susan interrupted.

"Hey, guys! The power is out."

Instinctively, Donald looked up and saw nothing but stars. The weather was supposed to be beautiful all weekend. "Did you pay the bill?"

"Amusing," said Susan. "It's on autopay. The last thing I heard was the AC running. Maybe Holyoke Electric is having problems."

"Now we're camping out," Sabs laughed. She pushed herself out of the low-slung chair and began to pick up some dishes from the table. J.J. joined them.

"I guess we'll turn in early," said Donald, turning to J.J. "You wanna start around six in the morning?"

"Some vacation," interjected Sabs. She hugged J.J. around the waist.

"I'm used to oh-dark-thirty," replied J.J. "I'll meet you in the kitchen with coffee brewing."

As the three carried dishes and cooking utensils inside, a cell phone began to ring.

"That's mine," said Donald. "Susan, my phone is on the entry table. Do you see the display lit up? Can you see who it is?"

"Darn it!" shouted Susan, with an accompanying thud as she hit a piece of furniture in the dark. "I've got the phone, but I was too late. It reads *missed call*." Donald led the way into the large entry of the main building dubbed 1PP—One Prescott Peninsula.

"I'll get the lanterns and flashlights," he said. He found his way to the kitchen and set his stack of dishes in the sink. The building was not equipped with emergency lighting like a commercial building might be. Like so many of the projects commissioned by John Morgan on behalf of the Boston Brahmin, the entirety of the 1PP compound was built without permits or the prying eyes of governmental entities. Publicly, the complex was known as a shelter for families fleeing abusive domestic partners. In reality, it was a state-of-the-art bug-out location developed without cost being a factor. Despite the opulence, one of Donald's twenty-four-dollar Rayovac camping lanterns shed all the light he needed in the pantry. He grabbed a flashlight and another lantern.

J.J. and Sabs joined him in the kitchen. He provided them a lantern and a flashlight. "You guys can find your way to your bungalow with these. Hopefully, the power will come back on soon enough. If we keep the refrigerators and freezers closed through the night, our food should be fine."

"I agree," said J.J. "Tell Susan good night for us."

"I just got a text from Julia," yelled Susan from the open living area.

Donald led the way out of the kitchen and lit up Susan's face with his flashlight. He saw the look on her face. "What?"

"It reads—*grid down, long-lasting, be ready.*"

Donald leaned against a foyer table and set down his lantern. No one spoke until he broke the silence. "Try to call her."

"I already did. All circuits are busy."

"System is overloaded," Donald muttered. "Send back a text and ask her for details."

Susan began typing.

He turned to J.J. "Guys, would you mind grabbing a couple of the weather radios out of the pantry," asked Donald. "J.J., grab our two-way sets. We'll need to be ready to advise our security after we gather a few more details."

"I'm on it, buddy," replied J.J.

"Sabs, would you mind going downstairs and grabbing one of the satphones out of the Faraday cages."

"No problem, Donald," replied Sabs. "Weapons?"

Donald thought for a moment. Julia would not joke about something like this. The text message was cryptic, but they were in the city. She and Sarge had a lot of things to do to secure 100 Beacon.

"I think so. Sidearms for us, but not Susan. No need to frighten the girls."

Susan walked up to Donald after J.J. and Sabs left on their errands. "The message finally went out after several tries. Donald, what does this mean?"

"I don't know. Let's use every information-gathering tool available to us. Our cell phones are Verizon. We'll have J.J. try his AT&T network. The portable radios might shed some light. Let's give Julia and Sarge some time to get organized. I'm sure she'll have her satphone up and running shortly."

"What do we do in the meantime?"

"I need you to focus on the girls. As far as I'm concerned, let them sleep until morning. If the power is not back on, we'll kick on the generators for short periods of time. They won't even notice the change."

"Okay," she said. "Anything else I can do?"

J.J. returned from the kitchen with two radios. Donald took the Sony shortwave world band unit first.

"Monitor the Sony shortwave for any station, both in the States and abroad. Make notes. We get clear reception out here."

J.J. handed Donald the Midland GMRS two-way crank unit out of its box. Donald gave it to Susan. "The Midland will be useful for local communications. You'll be able to pick up radio stations, citizens band traffic, ham radio chatter, and local law enforcement."

"Do you want me to grab any of the computer equipment?" asked J.J.

"Not yet," replied Donald. "Let's make sure this isn't an EMP attack. There might be more incoming nukes. Let's not jump the gun and fry our stuff. Susan has plenty to listen to."

"All right, I'll go help Sabs," said J.J.

"Before you go, let me have your cell. Susan will continue to attempt contact with Sarge and Julia."

J.J. pulled his phone out of his pocket and gave it to an already overloaded Susan.

"Brad?" inquired J.J.

"He's next on my list," replied Donald. He turned as Sabs emerged from the hidden stairwell with three holstered weapons, a satphone, and a Mossberg Tactical shotgun.

"Just in case," she said as she handed the Mossberg to J.J. and distributed the weapons. Because they had trained together, each of the Loyal Nine knew their partner's favorite weapon and method of carry. Donald insisted in like calibers for their handguns and rifles. He would have preferred common brands as well, but some of the weapons connoisseurs had differences in opinions. Just like sports fans might argue over who the greatest quarterback of all time was, gun owners would endlessly debate the virtues of Glock versus Sig Sauer versus H & K. Regardless of brand, Donald insisted that everyone carry a full-size .45 caliber in a padded waist holster except for Sabs, who preferred a leg holster. He had thousands of rounds of .45 ammunition stored as well as multiple backups for their preferred weapons. The prepper rule of redundancy applied to security as well—*Three is two, two is one, one is none.*

Donald turned to J.J. and Sabs. "I need you guys to assess our *troop strength*—with humble apologies for being tongue-in-cheek. Who does Brad have assigned to us this weekend, and how many are in position?"

"It's not Falcone," replied J.J. "I think it might be Shore." Chief Warrant Officer Kyle Shore, along with Master Gunny Sergeant Frank Falcone, were Brad's two most trusted officers.

"Okay," started Donald. "Try to raise Shore on the radio and find out where he is. Advise him of the situation in person and help spread the word. We need to put our perimeter defenses on alert but without a bunch of radio chatter." He rubbed Susan's back and saw a look of concern on her face.

"If we can listen to others, they can listen to us. Let's maintain radio discipline."

"We're on it," said Sabs. J.J. and Sabs left with their flashlights. Donald thought quietly for a moment until he heard the Kawasaki Mule fire up and head up the trail toward the entry gate. It had been nearly half an hour. *We need information. Assess. Secure. Survive.*

CHAPTER 49

September 3, 2016
9:58 p.m.
1st Battalion, 25th Marines HQ
Fort Devens, Massachusetts

Brad paced back and forth in his office. Gunny Falcone and First Lieutenant Kurt Branson stood just inside the doorway. The generators at Fort Devens were fully operational, and activity on the compound was frantic. Rumors were rampant among the unit, and Brad was just now getting a full briefing.

"Yes, General, I understand." Brad looked at two of his trusted officers, who remained unflappable. Brad continued to pace and finally leaned against the credenza, seated between the American flag and the Standard—the flag of the United States Marine Corps. As he listened, he looked into the eyes of his men. *Were they ready for this?*

Brad quickly jumped up and repeated into the satellite phone, "DEFCON 2, sir? What intel do—" Brad was cut off.

"Yes, sir, I understand. I will watch for further communications." Brad ended the call and slumped into his desk chair. He set the phone on the desk and motioned for Falcone and Branson to sit as well.

"Sir, did I hear you correctly?" asked 1st LT Branson. "DEFCON 2?"

"That is correct, gentlemen," replied Brad. "First, the extent of the power outage is nationwide and extends into Canada and northern Mexico. Only Alaska, Hawaii, and Texas continue to have power."

"Sir, may I speak frankly?" asked Branson.

"Gentlemen, as I have said, we should maintain proper military decorum when in the presence of the others, but in private, we are a team. Always speak freely."

"Thank you, sir. DEFCON 2 indicates the Pentagon is preparing for a nuclear war. Were we nuked?"

"No. I'm told that an unknown source has perpetrated a sophisticated cyber attack on the majority of the nation's power grid. The general did not say we were arming the nukes. He said the Joint Chiefs declared DEFCON 2 out of an abundance of caution."

"Is this because of the Russian sub activity off the East Coast?" asked Gunny Falcone.

"Probably," replied Brad. "Over the summer, the Russians have expanded their presence in the Arctic region. A cyber attack could be a harbinger of war. Time will tell. Under these circumstances, DEFCON 2 is not necessarily a bad idea. I'm just surprised the President agreed with the designation. He typically doesn't like to ruffle feathers."

"You mean, he cowers to the Russians," said Branson.

"I get it, Branson. He's still our Commander-in-Chief," said Brad.

"You said speak freely. You know me, sir."

Brad stood up and observed the activity on the base. Marines scurried about like ants, stopping to exchange information before hustling to their next stop. He wondered how many of these Marines would ask to leave or simply walk away from their post to be with their families.

"There's more," started Brad. "The general told me to prepare for orders regarding domestic deployment. They are going to call up all reservists, and we will be given orders regarding the use of troops locally."

"What do you mean by *locally*?" asked Branson.

"The general said to expect National Guard units and Marine battalions to work in concert. We may deploy to Boston to assist local law enforcement."

"Martial law?" asked Gunny Falcone.

"Not yet, but it sure sounds like they're getting ready for a declaration," replied Brad.

"On American soil," said Branson, shaking his head in disgust.

"It sure looks that way," said Brad. "Listen, we know each other well enough. We've discussed the fact the United States is in social and economic decline. Our country is a ticking time bomb waiting to explode. While all shocks to our way of life may not put the nation over the edge, a major blow like this cyber attack taking down the grid will be devastating."

"Not all explosives are the same," said Branson, who was trained in explosive ordnance disposal. His job required steady nerves and a calm demeanor. "I've worked in a wide variety of environments, and clearly there is a difference between dynamite and Semtex. You have to be extremely careful with dynamite. Semtex can be tossed around or thrown into a fire, and nothing will happen—until the right detonator is used. America is the same way. This country is up to its eyeballs in Semtex. No electricity for an undetermined amount of time is just the detonator required to blow the good ole US of A all to hell."

"Branson has a way with words, doesn't he?" Gunny Falcone laughed.

"He certainly does," replied Brad.

"It's like a delivery truck," Branson continued. "You can keep chuckin' Semtex into the back of it like those monkeys who work for UPS toss packages, and nothing will happen. Without the right detonator, it's as harmless as a truckload of apple butter. But you add the right detonator, like this cyber attack, and we're one click of the mouse away from collapse. *BOOM!*"

"Suppose the intel you received is correct," said Gunny Falcone. "If this grid-down event is extensive, it could take months or years to repair. Grocery store shelves are only a few days away from being empty under normal circumstances. Even if they could open tomorrow, the shelves will be wiped out within a couple of hours. Hell, the looters will probably clean them out tonight."

"I read that only about two percent of the population in America lives on farms," said Branson. "That means less than five million people have the means to feed themselves. And they're heavily dependent on fuel to operate their machinery. It's only a matter of time until the diesel tanks run dry."

"Consider the effect on America's stature in the world," said Brad. "Our country was already on its economic last leg. The Chinese were actively devaluing our currency. Our ability to prop up the dollar based upon its link to oil has declined. The petrodollar was on the way out the door already. It's been a house of cards for some time."

"Think of people who are drug dependent," added Branson. "How are all of these people who rely upon their Prozac and Zoloft going to keep their act together? People who have diabetes won't be able to receive their insulin. Where will they get their meds? How long will it take for them to get desperate?"

"All good points, gentlemen, but my concern is the societal collapse aspect," said Brad. "The general clearly alluded to martial law. America's moral decline is about to catch up with her. During the Great Depression, there was surprisingly little crime, other than Mafia-related incidents. People were raised with a clear definition of morality—what is right and wrong. Compared to then, our society today is undisciplined, unrealistic, and selfish."

"Hell, look at Christmas shoppers," said Branson. "The day after Thanksgiving, two hundred and sixty million people descend on stores at four in the frickin' mornin'. They scratch and claw, stampede, and murder over the latest television. Americans will kill each other over iPhones and Michael Jordan basketball shoes. Imagine when the reality of life with no power sets in."

"Yep," said Gunny Falcone. "They'll look to the government— FEMA. That will be an epic fail. Then, they'll loot their local stores."

"Then they'll turn on their neighbors," added Brad. "When that option is exhausted, if they're still alive, there will be a mass exodus from the cities because they will be unlivable. They'll be looking for vast open spaces, less violence, and the farmers who can supply them with food."

"Do they think they're gonna be greeted with open arms?" asked Branson rhetorically. "Farmers and the country folks won't stand for that."

"A friend of mine said he doesn't fear the collapse event itself, it's the way people react that causes him the most concern," said Brad.

"I get that," started Gunny Falcone. "If martial law is declared, what in the hell do the rules of engagement look like?"

Brad leaned back in his chair and stared outside, contemplating all of this. "Even without martial law, are there any rules left?"

CHAPTER 50

Sunday, September 4, 2016
6:36 p.m.
Triple Q Ranch, Prescott Peninsula
Quabbin Reservoir, Massachusetts

The sun was beginning to set to the west of Prescott Peninsula. There was a lot of activity at the Triple Q Ranch, so named because of its development by Donald and Susan Quinn, on land located at Quabbin Reservoir. The facility was designed with a long-term grid collapse in mind. Donald considered that to be the worst-case scenario that they could survive. Obviously, extinction events were different. In a mass extinction—or biotic crisis, using more scientific terms—there was a rapid and widespread loss of life on every evolutionary level. The most well-known of these occurred in the Jurassic period, which was caused by an asteroid impact and increased volcanic activity. During this period, the majority of life on Earth became extinct. No one could prepare for an extinction event.

Donald studied the next level of catastrophic events and decided the Triple Q Ranch could keep them alive for a period of time, but eventually food would run out. The most likely example was an explosion of the Yellowstone supervolcano. Yellowstone last erupted six hundred and forty thousand years ago. Scientists had determined that the Yellowstone supervolcano erupted in cycles, and that it was *due*.

An eruption would create a nuclear winter—a period of eight to ten years of substantially cooler temperatures and depleted ozone. It would be impossible to grow food in the United States and tough to breathe. The best option for the occupants of 1PP would be to survive until they could evacuate the fallout.

A grid-down collapse event was *manageable* in Donald's mind. He had ten years of food stored. Unless contaminated, the Quabbin Reservoir could provide more than enough water and freshwater fish to sustain them. He planned to harness the energy of the sun to power the Generac generators. The facility was built like a fortress. Donald had an open checkbook, and he used it.

A few luxuries were implemented in the last two weeks. Thermal-imaging cameras that could detect heat sources in the forest were installed around the perimeter of 1PP. They were hidden in trees, bird boxes, and tree stumps. A blast film was added to the windows to prevent them from shattering during an explosion.

Donald was also concerned with prying eyes and ears from above. He thought about what would happen to America after the collapse. *Will our adversaries look to take advantage of our weak condition? Will our government survive? If so, will we be restored to the freedoms contemplated by our forefathers, or will a tyrannical government rule with an iron fist?*

He thought about this at length and decided to err on the side of caution. He contacted a company called Conductive Composites based in Utah. The company created a nickel-carbon material that was both flexible and robust. It was flexible enough to be formed into wallpaper and sturdy enough to shield electronic devices from an EMP—whether nuclear or solar generated.

There was an added benefit. Donald set aside a communications room on the second floor of 1PP. Designed more like a Faraday room than a cage, the Conductive Composite wallpaper blocked satellites or ground-based listening devices from gathering information.

Donald spent the day trying to create a sense of normalcy for Susan and the girls. Brad doubled the military presence on Prescott Peninsula. All perimeter security measures were put into place without incident from outside intruders. Donald worked with a couple of the Marines and J.J. to set up the solar array. He reiterated the importance of sound and light discipline to everyone. There was no need to garner attention from the residents across the reservoir.

He knew that time would come, but he wanted to have his security team in place first.

He spoke to both Julia and Sarge. It appeared they were on track. Although Donald had not heard from John Morgan, he knew Sarge was working diligently to gather up the Boston Brahmin and bring them to the safety of 100 Beacon. There were no immediate plans to deliver them to Prescott Peninsula.

"Daddy, Daddy!" exclaimed Rebecca and Penny as they rushed out of the trail in the woods. "Look what we found!" The girls held out their dirt-covered hands and displayed a variety of pieces of flint or quartz and a couple of complete arrowheads.

"Wow, girls, where did you find these?"

"We walked and walked through the forest and didn't see anything," said Penny. "Then we found a stream and started making mud pies. That's when Becca found the first arrowhead."

"I found the first one, Daddy!" Rebecca proudly proclaimed. "It stuck me in the finger when I made my pie!"

"Let me see those muddy paws," said Donald as he examined his seven-year-old daughter's hands. "I don't see any boo-boos."

"It didn't hurt," said Rebecca. "Penny and I are going to make necklaces."

"Yeah," chimed in Penny. "Pretty Indian princesses we will be." Susan and Sabs caught up with the two bundles of energy.

"Not until you have baths, young ladies," said Susan. She turned to Donald and mouthed the words, "Do we have hot water?"

"We do," he replied. "I just shut off the generators, but the hot water should be good to go." Donald looked at them both and asked where their weapons were.

"We didn't think that we'd need them today," said Susan. "Besides, we had our sheepdogs nearby." Two of Brad's Marines entered the clearing. At Steven's suggestion, they wore a combination of khaki and Walmart camo—hunting apparel made by either Realtree or Mossy Oak. Donald agreed the soldiers would be less conspicuous by not wearing their issued MARPAT—Marine pattern digital camouflage. As much as possible, Donald and the security team tried to give the appearance of random hunters to anyone on a fishing boat or the banks opposite the reservoir.

"Come on, girls," said Susan. "Let's get you, and your arrowheads, presentable for dinner. Give your daddy a kiss!" Donald kneeled down to accept their generous, muddy hugs. He didn't mind. Every day that passed would become more dangerous for the girls to play in the woods. Let them make the most of it now.

He watched them bound up the stairs, and he turned to Sabs.

"Did they ask any questions?" asked Donald. He and Susan would have to talk to the girls about this. They were old enough to know that school was supposed to start on Tuesday. Donald and Susan had discussed homeschooling the girls, but when the nationally known Winsor School expanded their academic program to include all grades from first through the twelfth, the Quinns decided to enroll them there. With less than five hundred students, all female, the Winsor School was designed to instill confidence and competence in their female students. The girls would miss their school, the teachers, and their friends. Donald would have to address this with Susan by tomorrow.

"Not at all, Donald," replied Sabs. "I don't think they realize anything is wrong."

"What about the presence of the *sheepdogs*?" asked Donald, nodding toward the soldiers, who now had their eyes trained on the surrounding forest as night settled in.

"Not a problem. One of the guys said their job was to protect them from *lions, and tigers, and bears.*"

Donald laughed. "Oh my!"

"That's the exact reaction the girls had," said Sabs. "They immediately started singing and running down the trail. We had to hurry to keep up."

"That's great," said Donald, his mind wandering. "Susan and I will have to have a talk with them tomorrow sometime."

J.J. joined them and gave Sabs a kiss on the cheek. Donald never thought J.J. would be affectionate. He carried a lot of anger from his family relationship, his service in Iraq, and his postwar battles on behalf of wounded veterans. Donald verily believed that J.J. was at peace for the first time in his life. The way Sabs glowed when J.J. was around proved the feeling was mutual.

A sound caught Donald's attention. He walked into the clearing and tried to determine what the sound was. The soldiers, who heard it as well, immediately closed ranks around Donald, J.J. and Sabs.

Whop—whop—whop. As the noise grew louder, it was evident a helicopter was coming closer. The soldiers' radios came to life as the security team prepared for a potential hostile encounter.

"Inside!" ordered one of the Marines. Donald leaped up the steps and took a position by the rail. Two more Marines came running out of the woods and began waving instructions.

"I'll go with Susan and the girls," said Sabs. As she ran inside, J.J. emerged with the shotgun. He handed Donald his .45 and a pair of night-vision binoculars. The helicopter circled the building that was barely visible but didn't attempt a landing.

Donald studied the chopper and shouted into his two-way radio, "Hold fire. Repeat. Hold Fire!" He grabbed J.J. by the arm. "Grab the lanterns and flashlights. We need to give him a landing zone."

"Who is it?"

"John Morgan."

CHAPTER 51

Monday, September 5, 2016
9:22 a.m.
Triple Q Ranch, Prescott Peninsula
Quabbin Reservoir, Massachusetts

The night before, Morgan's pilot had expertly set the Sikorsky S-76 on the area illuminated by the lanterns and flashlights. Unbeknownst to Abbie, the helicopter was within moments of being out of fuel. She did not speak to her father during the first leg of the return home until they stopped for fuel at Seymour Johnson Air Force Base in North Carolina. She was too emotional and angry for idle conversation. Nor was she interested in his explanation.

The remainder of the long trip consisted of his asking her questions about what she'd observed in Tallahassee and during her journey across Florida. Her responses were terse. *Didn't he understand that these were my last hours with Drew?*

It helped Abbie to talk it out with Susan. Abbie appreciated Susan listening and offering condolences. Susan meant no harm and was trying to give comfort, but some of the things she said made it worse. *Be strong. He's in a better place. There's a reason for everything. He knew the risks of protecting you.* Susan was doing her best to *fix* Abbie's grief. The loss of Drew could not be *fixed*.

Abbie prepared herself a bowl of oatmeal and walked toward the forest. She loved Quabbin Reservoir. During the summer of her first senatorial campaign, she'd crossed the state in a Volkswagen convertible. Driving herself, she arranged to meet with local politicians in small towns like nearby Holyoke, Northampton, and Amherst. She wanted to overcome the stigma of being a *rich daddy's girl.* Wearing casual clothes and driving herself to the meet-and-greets was a hit. She was no longer Abigail Morgan, candidate for the United States Senate. She became *Abbie.*

"Abigail, good morning," said Morgan, who joined her with a bowl of oatmeal. "It has been a long time since I enjoyed oatmeal. I suppose it will become the norm for a while."

Abbie remained quiet. She spooned into the bowl of porridge, secretly wishing *Papa Bear* would leave her alone. He did not.

"I know that my explanations are falling on deaf ears. I won't try to make you understand the difficult decisions I have made. But I hope that you know, as your father, your safety will always take priority over any matter we face."

"Why did we leave Drew behind?" Abbie blurted out.

"I am sorry about that, Abigail. I will forever appreciate his heroics in saving you and shielding you from harm. But the pilot said we were at risk of being stranded. We would have met the same fate had we not left."

You mean the pilot that was whisked away in the middle of the night by one of Brad's men? How convenient.

Abbie took a deep breath and finally turned to look her father in the eye for the first time in twenty-four hours.

"I loved him, Father, and this will hurt me for a long, long time," started Abbie, fighting back the tears. Somehow, she regained her composure. "I don't want to discuss the events of yesterday with you ever again. There are no words to help me overcome the loss of Drew."

Morgan nodded his head. "I am sorry, dear."

"I know," replied Abbie. "The country is in trouble, Father. It has been for some time. This attack, whatever it is, could destroy America."

Morgan relaxed, and a sense of relief came over his face.

You're welcome, Father. I've let you off the hook.

"For the last several years, we've gone through a period of tumult and upheaval," said Morgan. "One might say that America has survived periods like this before."

"This has been different," interrupted Abbie. "Our politics, culture, education, economics and religious beliefs became so polarized that our nation could no longer resolve its differences. The America created by our forefathers—*our ancestors*—was ceasing to exist."

Morgan took Abbie's empty bowl and put it with his. He led her toward a picnic table, where they sat next to each other.

"The impact of our disarray is not restricted to our borders," said Morgan. "Our country has become the center of global politics and economics. I believe the growing global conflicts are directly related to America's failure to govern ourselves, caused in part by the polarization you mention."

"Well, I guess it doesn't matter anymore, does it?"

"But it does, Abigail. America is due for a revolution. We have reached a point of crisis where our republic will disintegrate due to lack of cooperation, or our woes will be addressed by a drastic change resulting in a revolution. Sadly, this cyber attack may be the catalyst our nation needs to either come together as one or eliminate through attrition those who cannot survive."

"What do you mean by that, Father?" asked Abbie.

"When faced with adversity, as my father would say, some people have the ability to hitch up their pants and deal with a problem head-on. When this country was founded, Americans were self-reliant and strived for self-sufficiency. The assistance of the government was a necessary evil, not a crutch to help them get through life. Compare that to the Americans of today. Over half of them are on some form of government subsidy to meet their necessities. When faced with a natural disaster—whether hurricane, tornado, or earthquake, most people look to the government for help. When this country was at its strongest, Americans looked to themselves first, then to their community or church."

"We were self-reliant," added Abbie.

"Yes, dear, and we looked to each other for assistance in a time of need, not the government."

"So which direction is our nation headed—revolution or self-sufficiency?" asked Abbie.

"It depends. It could require one to effectuate the other. Our nation has been through this before, although not of this magnitude. From the 1800s until the Civil War, the battle over states' rights was raging. History has been rewritten in this respect. Our nation was designed to be a Republic—a form of government that places power in the hands of the people. It was never intended to become this massive bureaucracy with power centralized in Washington. The Southern states fought over the issue of states' rights—with slavery being the impetus."

"That's not the version taught to high school history students," added Abbie.

"Correct," answered Morgan. "George Orwell, discussing the teaching of history, once said in Joseph Stalin's Soviet Union, yesterday's weather could be changed by decree. In the name of political correctness, America is not immune from this totalitarian impulse either." Morgan took in a deep breath and let out a sigh.

He continued. "Following the Great Depression, our country rallied around itself during a time of war. Having a common enemy allowed Americans to put aside any differences they had out of a sense of patriotism. In my opinion, that was the high point of our country's moral greatness. It has declined steadily since."

"So what happens now?" asked Abbie.

"Our nation has endured many problems," responded Morgan. "It shall survive the collapse of its societal morals and values as well. Americans will rally to help each other, or they will perish waiting on an inept and overburdened government to take care of them. If people of like mind rally to a life of self-reliance like our forefathers, I believe we will come out stronger than ever. If the people choose to look to the government for help, they will perish."

"The cyber attack acts as a reset of sorts, doesn't it?" asked Abbie.

"I couldn't have said it better, dear."

The two sat quietly for several minutes. There was activity around 1PP as the soldiers took turns eating breakfast. Otherwise, Quabbin Reservoir was serene and beautiful. Abbie broke the silence. She turned towards her father and took his hand. She knew he was troubled, downcast.

"Thank you, Father. I feel better." A smile found his face, which warmed her heart. *He means well.*

"Am I interrupting?" said Donald, as he interrupted their moment.

"No. No, Donald. Of course not," replied Abbie.

"I would like to show you both something," said Donald. Donald picked up their bowls and led them toward 1PP. "Abbie, it's been a while since you were here. Sir, we haven't discussed the final preparations I've implemented. I hope you approve."

"Well, Mr. Quinn," started Morgan, "I am confident you have spent our money wisely."

"Let's just say that I spent it wisely, and timely. Follow me, please."

Abbie took her father's arm as they followed Donald. She wanted to make it clear to everyone that she and her father were okay. *There is no room for family discord during the apocalypse.*

Donald led them inside and gave the empty bowls of oatmeal to Penny in the kitchen. Morgan and Abbie waited for him at the hidden passage.

After they descended the spiral staircase to the underground levels, Donald showed them the updated library, a dedicated room for hydroponic gardening, and a newly created war room of sorts. This space controlled all of the security cameras and communications within the compound. Within a few days, it would also be connected to the audio-visual system at 100 Beacon. Donald described each room in great detail as they made their way through the underground bunker.

"Everything is state of the art," said Donald. "There is one last thing I would like to show you in the library." He led them back into the room and removed a large Webster's Dictionary from the shelf. Behind it was a compartment door that contained a biometric entry device similar to the touchpads installed at 100 Beacon.

"I will program this for both of you today," said Donald as he placed his palm on the touch pad. A series of gears and locks sprang to life behind them. After the sounds had subsided, one of the bookcases popped forward slightly.

"Very James Bond." Abbie laughed.

Donald smiled as he slipped past them to the partially opened bookcase.

He turned it ninety degrees, revealing a passage and a thick glass door. "This glass door, made by Armortex, is blast proof. It's designed to absorb the energy generated by the bomb blast and disperse it. The explosion is more likely to kill the attacker than it is to breach the door."

Donald walked up to an eye scanner and pressed a button. "This entry device scans both the retina and the iris. Ocular-based identification reads the most unique form of our physiological characteristics—the eyes. As Abbie knows, one of my concerns at 100 Beacon is that an assailant could gain access to the upper floors by removing our hand to access the keypad."

"Mr. Quinn, is that likely?" asked Morgan.

"Sir, I try not to overlook any possibilities. Ocular-based identification removes that risk. You cannot remove an eyeball and open the locks to this door."

"Why is this so important here, Donald?" asked Abbie. Donald looked into the lenses, and the door locks released. He led them inside.

"Because of this." Donald stood out of the way to allow Morgan and Abbie entry to the vault.

"My God," exclaimed Abbie. "Is this real?"

"Of course it is, my dear," answered Morgan. "Well done, Mr. Quinn." Morgan slowly walked down the twelve-foot span of one-kilogram fine gold bars from Switzerland. Abbie walked in the other direction, randomly picking up similarly stamped one-kilogram bars of silver.

"These are heavy," said Abbie, holding the roughly thirty-five-ounce silver bar. "How much is this worth?"

"We purchased the majority of this when market conditions

favored it, did we not, Mr. Quinn?" asked Morgan.

"Yes, sir. The silver was purchased at approximately fifteen dollars per ounce, and the gold was one thousand one hundred dollars per ounce. The silver bar you're holding was worth five hundred dollars or so at the time of purchase. It's probably worth four times that now."

"More, Mr. Quinn. Much more."

Abbie walked around the room in amazement. She tried to fathom the value of the gold and silver that was stacked to the ten-foot ceiling. She ran her fingers through her hair and gathered the courage to ask.

"How much?"

"More than one hundred million dollars initial cost," replied Donald. "Today's value is unknown."

Abbie looked at her father. *He was calculating.*

He muttered, "Much more."

CHAPTER 52

Monday, September 5, 2016
11:11 a.m.
1st Battalion, 25th Marines HQ
Fort Devens, Massachusetts

Brad entered the briefing room and immediately told his men *at ease*. A courier had arrived via helicopter from the USNORTHCOM at Peterson AFB in Colorado. Since the *cyber event*, as the White House insisted the cyber attack be called, the Defense Department had become leery of the security of their communications. Also, Homeland Security was playing a more active role in the military's decision making. This made Brad nervous. When Brad entered the briefing room and found Agent Joe Pearson of the Federal Protective Services standing at the head of the table, red flags began to wave furiously.

"Hello, Colonel Bradlee," greeted Pearson.

Brad nodded as he walked to his regular chair at the head of the conference table.

"You might recall that we met last April in your office."

I remember. You had a lot to say about *insurrection.*

"I do. What brings our friends from FPS to Fort Devens? Aren't there federal buildings to protect?"

Some of Brad's staff shifted uneasily in their chairs. Brad had no intention of making Pearson's job easy.

"That's why I'm here, Colonel. As you know, our worst fears have been realized. The cyber event has damaged our critical infrastructure from coast to coast. Only the Texas Interconnection remains intact in the lower forty-eight."

"We've heard. How can we help you?"

"Homeland Security is reassigning certain assets to assist the military with its new role in light of the cyber event. Over the next several days, FPS advisors will be assigned to strategic military installations to serve in an advisory role to the base commanders." *Here it comes.*

"I have two more installation briefings to conduct, and then I will be returning to Fort Devens to assist you on behalf of Homeland Security." *Fabulous.*

"That is very kind of you, Agent Pearson, but my accomplished staff is capable, and we have always followed the orders issued to us like good soldiers. I believe there are some facilities where a man of your talents can be more useful."

Pearson took off his glasses and set them on a file folder he dropped on the conference table. He became antagonistic. "Colonel, I recall my April visit with you as if it was the other day. You have a way of using humor to make your points. Agent Nemechek made a similar assessment. I hope you understand this. My assignment to you by Homeland Security, which carries the full weight of the President behind it, is not an offer. It is an order, sir. I hope that you can respect that, and we can work together accordingly."

Brad studied Pearson for a moment and then leaned back in his chair and laughed. His aides were unsure how to react.

"Well, Agent Pearson, welcome aboard. I have never refused an order, regardless of how asinine it is. It is my duty as a soldier. Now, can we get down to business and the substance of this briefing so you can be on your merry way?" Brad's sarcasm garnered chuckles from his fellow soldiers.

"Yes, please," replied Pearson. "There is much to discuss."

The only thing to discuss is how to keep you the out of my way. "Well, let's get to it, shall we?" asked Brad as he nodded to his aides.

"Okay," started Pearson as he distributed briefing folders to everyone in the room. "We have actionable intelligence from Clear Air Force Base in Alaska that fishing trawlers are reporting an increase in Russian vessel activity near the Aleutian Islands. We have tracked Russian troop movement into their newly established Arctic military facilities. By our best estimate, they have deployed one hundred eighty thousand troops, two hundred and twenty aircraft, forty-nine ships, and two dozen submarines to the region. These new troop movements come in addition to the submarines that have been patrolling our Atlantic seaboard for months."

"I am aware the Russians have established an Arctic Joint Strategic Command," said Brad, who was more serious now. "Some reports claimed this was military posturing as part of Putin's desire to show off his military might. Another theory is the Russians were protecting their valuable oil fields above the Arctic Circle. What do you think, Agent Pearson?"

"Well, I don't know what Russia is thinking," replied Pearson. "It's likely they were just protecting their economic interests."

"From whom? Who is threatening the Russian oil fields in the Arctic?"

"Uhm, I don't know that anyone is," replied Pearson. "Most likely he's showing his capabilities as a deterrent."

"Okay. What else do you have for us?" *This is a waste of time. He came here under the guise of an intel briefing. FPS and Homeland Security have other things on their mind.*

Pearson distributed another folder marked *FEMA Region I*. The country was divided into ten regions. Region I included Maine, New Hampshire, Vermont, Massachusetts, Rhode Island, and Connecticut.

"Homeland Security will be directing you to secure the FEMA Regional Offices on High Street in Boston. You will assist in the protection of personnel and assets as the High Street facility plays a more expansive role in the recovery effort."

"A couple of things, Agent Pearson," began Brad. "When is this to take place?"

"By Wednesday at the latest," replied Pearson. "What else?"

"Why am I receiving orders from Homeland Security and not USCENTCOM?"

Pearson stood and began to gather his briefcase. Apparently, the briefing was over. "Colonel, the President has issued a series of executive orders regarding the safety of our nation and the protection of its citizens. Reserve units such as yours will play an integral role in providing a uniformed response in these trying times. The President believes a unit such as yours will be ideally suited for this purpose."

"What purpose is that, Agent Pearson?"

"I will be able to provide you greater detail about the new mission of the 25th Marine Regiment when I return on Thursday afternoon." Pearson began to walk out of the briefing room when he suddenly stopped.

"Oh, one more thing, Colonel," said Pearson, turning slowly to address Brad. "The President, by executive order, has commuted the sentences of all federal inmates below the penitentiary classification. We are no longer able to house and feed them. Please advise the warden of the local federal prison camp to release all inmates in his custody."

There were nearly a quarter of a million federal inmates in the Bureau of Prison's system. With the stroke of a pen, the President just released ninety-six percent of them.

"Where will they go?" asked Brad.

"That's not your problem," replied Pearson. "Just tell them to go."

CHAPTER 53

Monday, September 5, 2016
5:26 p.m.
Triple Q Ranch, Prescott Peninsula
Quabbin Reservoir, Massachusetts

Brad's Humvee pulled up to the entry gate to Prescott Peninsula. He instructed his driver to wait a moment, and he hopped out to address his men. CWO Shore greeted him.

"Good evening, sir!" said Shore as he saluted his colonel. Brad snapped a salute in return. "I'll have the gate opened for you."

"Thank you, Shore," said Brad. "Have you had any incidents?" Brad walked up and down the entry gate and surveyed the surroundings.

"Our first one occurred this morning, sir," replied Shore, following closely behind. "Two men dressed in hunting gear rode up to the gate on four-wheelers. They made small talk but did ask some questions. We responded as ordered, sir."

"You told them you were private contractors protecting the families?"

"Yes, sir. They didn't seem to question our statements, sir."

"Okay, good. Carry on, Shore." Brad headed back towards his Humvee.

"Sir, there is one more thing about the two men. They inquired about the helicopter. They apparently noticed the chopper's arrival last night as well as its lack of departure. Just an FYI, sir."

Brad nodded and got into the truck. Morgan's arrival by helicopter caused unneeded exposure to 1PP. When the power was off, any noise was exaggerated. The noise from the rotors probably reverberated from one side of the reservoir to the other. Brad hoped that wouldn't come back to bite them in the ass.

As Brad's convoy entered the clearing at 1PP, he was greeted by everyone, including Mr. Morgan. Brad had limited contact with John Morgan in the past. His uncle, Samuel Bradlee, played an active role in keeping Brad in charge of the 25th Marines. It was his uncle's close relationship with Mr. Morgan that helped Brad rise to battalion commander status at the fairly young age of forty.

Brad hopped out and greeted Mr. Morgan first. "Hello, sir, it's a pleasure to see you again."

"Yes, Colonel, it is my pleasure as well," said Morgan. "My friend, Samuel, has always spoken highly of you. I am very impressed with the security you have provided for this facility. Your men are top notch."

"Thank you, Mr. Morgan. In fact, I have another dozen men joining the team tonight."

"Excellent," said Morgan. Brad waved to the rest of the Loyal Nine and Sabs. He addressed his men, who gathered around. "Corporal, have the men refuel that chopper and then secure the fuel tanker in a suitable location in the woods, but not too close to any structure."

"Hi, Brad," greeted Donald. The men shook hands. "I like the fuel truck. But we no longer have our pilot."

"We do now." Brad smiled. "I brought more men in with me, and two of them are checked out on the old Sikorsky HRS Chickasaws. They tell me flying the Chickasaw is like driving a John Deere compared to the S76, which is like a Mercedes. But they all have collective levers, cyclic sticks, and anti-torque pedals. It's like riding a bicycle."

"Sounds good to me," said Donald. "You never know if we might need this thing at some point."

"I agree. When I learned of the chopper's landing, my initial reaction was not positive. Then I thought of the usefulness the Sikorsky could have to us. So I brought the tanker with me to refuel this bird. We'll conveniently forget the fuel truck when we leave in the morning."

"Come in, Brad," said J.J. as he put his arm around Brad's shoulders. The two men had become better acquainted during the build-out of Prescott Peninsula. They seemed to enjoy exchanging war stories. "We'll buy you a drink."

"Pour away, my friend. Listen up, everybody, there's lots to discuss," started Brad. "Before we get started, how are Sarge and Julia coming along?"

Susan spoke up because she had continued to maintain communications with Julia. "Everything is on schedule. Sarge was picking up Mr. Morgan's associates, and they should all be at 100 Beacon by tonight, or tomorrow morning at the latest. I believe Mr. and Mrs. Endicott were the only ones not accounted for."

"What?" asked Morgan.

"I'm sorry, sir, I thought you knew. As of my last communication with Julia, Sarge has not been able to contact the Endicotts. If he is unsuccessful by tomorrow morning, he plans on going to their residence."

"Keep me informed," said Morgan.

"Yes, sir," replied Susan. The group made their way into the large living area, where the Quinn girls were coloring.

"Uncle Brad!" shouted the girls in unison. They ran to give him a hug. Brad was a career military man who rarely had time for a date, much less a wife and kids. He chose to live vicariously through the Quinns. He was immediately handed a crayon drawing by the youngest Quinn.

"Look. I drew a picture of Mr. Morgan's helo-chopper," said Rebecca.

"I drew one too," chimed in Penny. "We don't have to go to school for a while, so Mommy said we have to practice our artwork every day. This is our first *no-more-school* school project."

"Well, you two have done a fine job, don't you think, sir?" said Brad as he handed Rebecca's drawing to Mr. Morgan.

"You sure have," he said as he rubbed the child on the head and handed her back the drawing.

"Girls," started Sabs, "why don't we go into the kitchen and see what Private Wilson has on tonight's menu. Maybe she has some mac and cheese!"

"Yeah! Our favorite!" exclaimed the girls. Sabs led them out of the room so the adults could spend some time getting up to speed.

J.J. grabbed a bottle of Glenlivet from the cabinet and poured glasses for everyone.

"Toast," said Donald. Each of the group clinked glasses except Susan, who didn't partake of alcohol.

"Tell us what you've learned, Brad," said Donald.

Donald relayed the briefing with Agent Pearson, and everyone agreed the President was taking unprecedented control over the military. He was apparently looking to centralize power over both military and law enforcement functions. Mr. Morgan was the first to raise the issue of Agent Pearson's role and the role of FPS in general.

"What do you make of Homeland Security's involvement?" asked Morgan.

"I believe Homeland Security has been looking for an opportunity like this one for a long time—and I mean years," replied Brad. "When Jade Helm was first announced by the Pentagon, I thought it would be a continuation of regular military training exercises in the past. But Jade Helm went further. By taking place across seven states, the most conservative of which were labeled hostile, Jade Helm expanded the size and scope of previous exercises. Many, myself included, saw this as a way to condition Americans to accept a military presence on our streets."

"I looked at Jade Helm as a prelude to martial law," said Susan. "This would not be the first time a major false-flag operation was undertaken while training exercises were being conducted. In '95, a few hours before the Oklahoma City bombing of the federal building, an ATF bomb squad was seen holding an anti-terror drill there. Later, it came out that despite the FBI- and ATF-maintained offices in the building, none of their personnel were injured in the blast."

"Isn't that a little conspiratorial, Mrs. Quinn?" asked Morgan.

"However it is labeled, the facts speak for themselves. Here's another example. As the hijacked airliners were headed toward the Pentagon and the World Trade Centers on 9/11, NORAD interceptor jets designated for just such an attack were hundreds of miles away, preoccupied with their training exercise."

"I recall something similar in London in'05," added J.J. "At the time of the London subway bombings, a training exercise was taking place by a private contractor on another train concurrently with the placement of the actual bombs by Pakistanis."

"These false-flag events aren't uncommon and have been used throughout history to gain an advantage politically and militarily," said Brad. "It's impossible to tell whether this is a false-flag event. My biggest concern at this point is the potential use of our military as law enforcement agents on U.S. soil."

"Isn't that prohibited by the Constitution?" asked Susan.

"Not exactly," replied Brad. "The Posse Comitatus Act was passed to prevent our military personnel from being used in traditional law enforcement functions on American soil. In fact, our Congress has repeatedly upheld the law, including following Hurricane Katrina. New Orleans was so out of control that Congress considered a law permitting an exception to the Act in cases of significant natural disasters. Although it was passed, it was repealed shortly after that."

"Assuming Jade Helm was a dress rehearsal for the imposition of martial law in America, the timing is certainly suspect, don't you think?" Susan asked rhetorically. "I mean, we're in the middle of the largest military exercise on the streets of America since the Civil War, and a cyber attack takes down our power grid. Pretty coincidental."

"The circumstances do seem odd," said Abbie finally. Brad noticed that she was quiet, but assumed it was due to the loss of Drew Jackson. Morgan shot her a glance. *What's that all about?*

"All I know is the declaration of martial law is synonymous with the suspension of our Constitutional rights," said Susan. "Americans should rise up in arms if that happens." The group sat quietly for a moment and then Morgan spoke up. He finished his drink and indicated for J.J. to pour him another.

"Assuming, *arguendo*, that Jade Helm was an extensive military exercise for the very circumstances we find ourselves in today, Mrs. Quinn, would you prefer chaos or control?" Morgan sat back in his chair and studied Susan. She seemed unfazed by the question.

Susan, taking a deep breath, looked Morgan directly in the eye and answered, "If given the choice between losing my constitutional rights—and the freedoms those rights afford me—in the name of controlling the chaos to which you refer, I'll choose freedom."

CHAPTER 54

Tuesday, September 6, 2016
10:15 a.m.
1st Battalion, 25th Marines HQ
Fort Devens, Massachusetts

"Gentlemen, I'm going to give you both the option to go home and turn away from what we have set into motion," said Brad to his two most trusted officers—Gunny Falcone and CWO Shore. "The actions we take today may ensure our survival and the potential security of the future leaders of our nation. But to some, our actions may constitute treason. I want you to have the opportunity to leave. Go home to your families or friends. I will understand and say that I am proud to have served as your commanding officer."

Gunny Falcone walked a few paces away and then returned to Brad. "Forgetting the fact that there's nothing out there for me, I wouldn't leave. I am loyal to you, this unit, and America. I believe wholeheartedly in what we're doing. Regardless of my suspicions surrounding the events that brought us here, I will continue to devote my life to protecting the Constitution."

"I'm in, hondo percent!" said Shore. *Hondo* was Shore's way of saying one hundred.

"Gentlemen, I'm humbled by your loyalty and couldn't be prouder to serve with you. We have a limited amount of time to logistically reposition our assets. When that jackass Pearson returns on Thursday, he'll find a facility at quarter strength in both troops and firepower. Agreed?"

"Absolutely, Colonel," replied Gunny Falcone.

"Good. The first order of business is to speak personally with each of the Mechanics. Look them in the eye. Confirm their commitment while keeping them on a need-to-know basis. Over the next two days, they'll gather up the critical assets and weaponry necessary to maintain this unit at battalion strength, but housed in a different location. By dusk tomorrow evening, we'll start quietly rolling out of here under the auspices of traveling to Boston to assist local law enforcement and for the protection of those FEMA idiots. In reality, we'll move the Mechanics to Prescott Peninsula."

"We'll make it happen, sir!" said Shore.

"I've been in contact with our fellow patriots and oath keepers throughout the military community," said Brad. "They're all making similar arrangements. How many soldiers will follow in our cause is unknown. But those in the Pentagon and the so-called *Western White House* who underestimate the number of soldiers who will stand by the Constitution against all enemies, foreign and domestic, will do so at their peril. I believe there are far more military personnel who will defy tyrannical orders infringing upon the constitutional rights of freedom-loving Americans than there are those who will blindly follow such orders. As for those who don't stand with us, let's hope they go home to their families rather than stand against us."

"Sir, once we pull out, what will you do?" asked Gunny Falcone. Brad had thought of this extensively. His battalion would lose more than half its personnel and deployable assets over the next forty-eight hours. Someone would need to provide Agent Pearson an explanation.

"I'll stay here and keep Pearson occupied. There are already defections across the country. More soldiers go AWOL every day. He won't be surprised."

"What about the equipment and weaponry?" asked Shore.

"For one thing, he doesn't know what we're supposed to have. I trust that you two can make the records look like a pile of incoherent garbage?"

"They already do." Gunny Falcone laughed.

"Great, I guess," said Brad. "Remember, he's not military. He's a pencil-pushing prick that's learning on the job. As this thing continues, which I believe it might for months to come, he will grow bored and either move on or go home himself."

"Maybe you can take him to Boston and tell him to wait on a street corner in Roxbury," said Shore. "He can explain to the locals that he's from the government, and he's there to help." All of the men laughed at Shore's bastardized quotation of President Ronald Reagan's famous statement.

In a 1986 news conference, President Reagan famously said *the nine most terrifying words in the English language are: I'm from the government, and I'm here to help.*

Brad thought for a moment. *Yeah, maybe that's what I'll do.*

CHAPTER 55

Tuesday, September 6, 2016
7:13 p.m.
Triple Q Ranch, Prescott Peninsula
Quabbin Reservoir, Massachusetts

"Hey, girls, guess what?" asked Susan. Rebecca and Penny came over to where she was sitting with Sabs on the couch. They were all ears.

"What do we get if we guess it right?" asked Penny.

Susan laughed at the young negotiator. "Well, you'll probably never guess, but I can tell you it'll be loads of fun for you girls!"

"Tell us now! Tell us now!" exclaimed a hopping Rebecca. The girls looked up at their mom like baby chicks would plead for that big fat worm in her mouth. *Chirp, chirp, chirp.*

Sabs laughed and commented, "There is no end to their enthusiasm."

"Very true," said Susan. She pulled the girls in close. "Tomorrow, we'll be getting lots of visitors to stay with us, and one of them has a cute little French bulldog—Winnie the Frenchie."

"Is it for us?" asked Rebecca innocently.

"No, but I'm sure they'll let you play with her lots. How does that sound?"

"Are you serious?" asked soon-to-be teenager Penny.

"Yes, honey, sometime tomorrow you'll have a new playmate!"

"Awesome!" exclaimed Rebecca.

J.J. entered the room, holding a couple of board games. "Ladies, who's up for a game of Chutes and Ladders or Sorry?"

Donald and Susan discussed the possibilities of having to bug out with children. If you had a family with children, a bug-out situation was not as simple as grabbing your bags and hitting the front door. They recognized that kids were not wired for quick, organized reaction. Their needs were far more complicated than adults. One regret Susan had was not teaching the girls more about the possibilities of a disaster and a prolonged stay away from home. When she and Donald sat down with the girls on Monday, it went better than expected. Oddly, it was Rebecca, who was fairly new to school at age seven, who protested the most. She was very social, and not being around children for an extended period would take its toll on her.

Children of every age need to be adequately sheltered, well-fed, and entertained. This last aspect of prepping was overlooked by many. The Quinns made a habit of playing board games together once a week—*Friday night game night*. Whenever the family took a liking to a particular game, Susan bought one for 100 Beacon and a backup for 1PP. Lately, the game of the week was either Sorry or Chutes and Ladders. It appeared J.J. was up to the task.

"I wanna play Sorry!" exclaimed Penny. She ran to J.J.'s side as if being first in line would guarantee her choice.

"No," protested Rebecca. "I never win. I want to play Chutes and Ladders!"

J.J. looked at the women and shrugged. Susan smiled and shrugged back.

Sabs laughed and whispered, "He's in a pickle now." Both women clammed up, leaving the negotiation up to J.J.

"Okay, I'll make a deal with you guys," started J.J. "We'll play both games if you let me read a bedtime story to you tonight. How's that?"

"Deal!" the girls responded in unison. They grabbed J.J. by the arm and escorted him toward the kitchen. As they walked away, the negotiations escalated.

"J.J., I want you to read us Harry Potter."

"No, please read *Charlotte's Web* again."

"Not two nights in a row. Bad form!"

"How about *Peter Pan*?"

"Yeah!"

Susan laughed and leaned back on the sofa. Sabs did the same and grabbed a pillow to snuggle. After they were done laughing, Susan spoke.

"J.J. is great with the girls. He has changed so much over the last several years. I'll never forget the first few times he came over to the house. He wanted to bring the girls a gift, but he was never quite sure of what was age appropriate. He must have gauged their reaction and studied popular gifts for young girls on the Internet. The gifts became huge hits with the girls, as did J.J. Donald and I began to wonder if he was coming to visit us or play with Becca and Penny."

Sabs propped her right leg on the table and then crossed it with her prosthetic leg. She appeared to unconsciously tap her left leg with her prosthetic left arm. *Or was it deliberate?*

"The girls always appear thankful for the love and attention they are given," said Sabs. "Material things don't seem to rule their lives."

"As the girls learned to speak, we taught them four words to help them learn communication skills—*please, thank you, all done,* and *more.*"

"More?"

"That is comical, isn't it? We spend our days trying to teach them to be thankful, yet we encourage them to use the word *more.* However, that enabled us to teach them the meaning of the word *no.*"

"Makes sense," said Sabs.

"We live in a world of selfishness and entitlement. We wanted to raise the girls to be aware of the basics they might take for granted, the opportunities they are given, and the experiences they enjoy. Believe it or not, we knew it would prepare the girls for a situation like the one we're in now. By teaching them to appreciate the basics, they live a life of humility, generosity, and happiness. It'll serve them well if they have to grow up in a post-apocalyptic world."

Susan drank some of her water and listened to the playful banter coming from the kitchen. Sabs was silent for a moment, and then Susan noticed she was crying.

"Sabs, are you okay?"

"Yes," she replied, once again tapping her left arm on her left leg. "It's ironic that I lost my arm and leg saving children. On the one hand, it was the greatest moment of my life. On the other hand, not so much. For years afterward, while I was thankful to be alive, I held a bitterness of what I was left with. By saving those children, I thought I'd never get a chance to hold kids of my own."

"Sabs, you did a great thing in Fallujah that day. You're a real hero."

Sabs continued. "Now I have J.J. in my life, and I see how much he enjoys your girls. My dream has been to find a man who loves me unconditionally like he does, and have beautiful babies with him." Sabs began to sob now, unable to control the tears.

"Honey, what's wrong?"

"I'm pregnant."

CHAPTER 56

Wednesday, September 7, 2016
7:13 a.m.
Triple Q Ranch, Prescott Peninsula
Quabbin Reservoir, Massachusetts

"Rise and shine with a good cup of joe," said Abbie to J.J. and Sabs on the front porch of 1PP. They toasted their cups to Abbie.

"Good morning," replied J.J.

"You guys look serious this morning," said Abbie. "Everything okay?" She leaned against the railing and enjoyed a sip. If it weren't for the circumstances, 1PP would be a very relaxing place.

"It's fine," replied Sabs. "J.J. is being overprotective." Sabs finished off her coffee and stood up.

"Brad had to pull the bulk of the security detail to gather up your dad's friends and to clean out Devens," said J.J. "Sabs volunteered for gate duty to fill the void." J.J. crossed his arms and stared into the woods. He was obviously upset.

"Listen. Going on patrol with the guys is routine and probably a one time thing *although* I am perfectly capable, you know. I will always be a soldier."

"I get that, Sabs, but there has been more activity at the gate since the helicopter's arrival." *Ouch.*

"I'm sorry about that, J.J.," defended Abbie. "My father said we had just enough fuel to get here, and the drive from Norwood would have been very dangerous. The south side of Boston was falling apart Saturday night. Twenty-four hours later would have been worse."

"Please don't get me wrong, Abbie," said J.J., staring intently at the Sikorsky. "That chopper landing here Monday night might as well have been *the rockets' red glare*. In a world with no electricity, a sound as unique as a helicopter probably drew attention from miles around. I've already heard that men have approached the front gate with questions."

"Wayward hunters, J.J.," interrupted Sabs. "Stop making Abbie feel bad." The front porch was filled with awkward silence. J.J. shifted uneasily in his chair as Sabs got her gear together. Abbie chose to remain silent. *He was right, of course.*

"I'm sorry, Abbie," said J.J. finally. "And I'm sorry to you too, Sabs. I was out of line."

Sabs walked over to J.J. and pulled his head against her hip. She scruffed his hair like he was a child.

"I am a soldier. I have some limitations that, thanks to you, J.J., enable me to continue to be what I am—a *sheepdog*. Somebody has to be on the front line. I have every confidence in the people I love to take care of themselves, but none of you have ever been in combat. You may not be capable of killing another human being, whether in self-defense or otherwise."

"What do you mean by *sheepdog*?" asked Abbie.

"Most Americans sleep safely in their beds at night, knowing that someone like me is willing to die for their safety, and some choose to deny there are bad people out there ready to do them harm," replied Sabs. "The sheep pretend the wolf will never come for them. But the sheepdog lives for the opportunity to protect the sheep when that day comes."

"I see," said Abbie.

"I don't mean anything negative by referring to anyone as sheep," continued Sabs. "You can look at it as the egg of one of these beautiful woodpeckers we hear right now. Inside, it's vulnerable and unable to protect itself. But on the outside, its shell is tough— enabling it to survive. A soldier is like that tough shell exterior."

"It's a dangerous world," added Abbie.

"Then you must know the world is full of wolves," said Sabs. "The wolves will feed on the sheep without mercy. Just like the wolves, some evil people are capable of indescribable horror to their fellow man. J.J., you've seen it."

"I have."

"Then there are the sheepdogs, like me. I live to protect my flock of sheep. I dare the wolf to confront me. That will be ingrained in me for the rest of my life."

Sabs stood tall and proud. J.J. stood and hugged her.

"I love you," he whispered in her ear as he held her tight. "Be safe."

"I love you too, Doc."

Branson pulled up on a four-wheeler. "Ready to roll, del Toro?"

"Roger that, L-T."

"I'll see you guys later!" shouted Sabs as she bounded down the stairs to join 1st LT Branson.

"Go tend to your flock," mumbled J.J.

CHAPTER 57

Wednesday, September 7, 2016
11:23 a.m.
Triple Q Ranch, Prescott Peninsula
Quabbin Reservoir, Massachusetts

Susan joined Abbie in the kitchen to help prepare a lunch of white beans and fish dip. The Quabbin Reservoir was fed primarily by the Swift River. With nearly two hundred miles of shoreline and over twenty-five thousand acres of water, it was the largest freshwater lake in Massachusetts. Trout and bass were the most common fish in the reservoir and were easily caught from the shore. Donald and J.J. incorporated shore fishing as part of their morning ritual. They didn't take out a boat to avoid drawing attention. Thus far, Steven's fleet of specially retrofitted Stroker boats was not needed.

Susan chopped the garlic while Abbie prepared the smoked fish. Some cannellini beans, olive oil, and Wheat Thins finished off the hearty spread. The ladies made some small talk while they moved about the kitchen. The girls were off in the woods with J.J., looking for more arrowheads. Donald was monitoring communications traffic and scouring the Internet via the Hughes satellite system.

"Do you think the Brahmin will like our setup here?" asked Susan.

"They'd better," replied Abbie. "I can't imagine any acceptable alternative in the country right now, except maybe Texas."

"They still have power, so I guess they dodged a bullet. Donald picked up some ham radio chatter from down that way. Governor Abbott ordered the border closed."

"The Mexican border is already closed. Do you mean the state's borders?"

"Yes. According to the reports, Texas Rangers have been dispatched to every major entry point and are turning people away unless they can prove residency," replied Susan.

"Wow. I know Greg. He doesn't mess around. Sometimes I wonder if he's extra tough because he was a former prosecutor or because he's a paraplegic and wants to prove his mettle. Either way, he doesn't take any crap."

"What do you think about him closing the border?" asked Susan.

"Technically, it's his state to protect, but I can't see the President standing for it." Abbie finished unwrapping the fish and placed it into a food processor to puree. Susan added her share of the ingredients. Before they started the processor, Abbie looked around to see if they were alone.

"Susan, I've been having nightmares."

Susan wiped her hands and took Abbie's hands in hers. "Oh no. Abbie, is it about Drew?"

Abbie's eyes welled up with tears. "I don't know if it's the pressure of all of this, but I'm having trouble sleeping at night. I share the bungalow with my father, and I've woken up more than once crying. The first night he didn't say anything, but I can tell that I'm upsetting him."

"Abbie, you have every right to be upset. Drew was an exceptional man, especially to you."

"We became so close that night, Susan. We both admitted that we were in love. But there was no time to enjoy the moment. We were in a race against time, and there was one dangerous obstacle after another."

"I know, Abbie, and I'm very sorry. The passage of time might make it better. Would it help to get you another place to sleep? With the arrival of your father's friends, we can rearrange the bungalow assignments."

Abbie thought for a moment and wiped the tears from her cheeks. "No, but thank you. I'll get over it. I just keep replaying the final moments over and over again. He was reaching out to me, shouting *love you, love you.*" Abbie started crying again.

"At least you can hold on to those final words. He obviously loved you very much, Abbie. He saved your life."

Susan wiped Abbie's tears for her and gave her a long hug. Susan knew Abbie's loss was just the first to be consoled. Abbie finally pulled away and regained her composure.

"I know, Susan. I just don't understand why it's bothering me so much. It's like an endless loop of a video. I dream the same thing repeatedly. I just miss him, you know?"

"I do," replied Susan. They both shared a nervous laugh and returned to the food processor. Susan hit the puree button that created a noise loud enough to wake the dead. So loud, in fact, they did not hear the sounds of gunfire outside.

CHAPTER 58

Wednesday, September 7, 2016
11:35 a.m.
Triple Q Ranch, Prescott Peninsula
Quabbin Reservoir, Massachusetts

"Susan! J.J.! Anybody!" yelled Donald as he came running down the stairs from the communications room. "Susan!"

Abbie and Susan ran out of the kitchen to meet Donald. "What is it? What's wrong?"

"Where's J.J.?" he shouted.

"He's in the woods with the girls, looking for arrowheads. Are the girls okay? What is it, Donald?" Susan begged for an answer.

Donald caught his breath and steadied himself. "There's been a shooting. It's Sabs. She's been shot, and it's serious." Abbie fell against the wall and covered her mouth.

"We need J.J. now!" he shouted.

"Abbie, get him," said Susan. "You know the creek where they usually go, right?"

Abbie meekly nodded her head.

"Abbie! Can you get them?" yelled Donald.

"Yes. Yes, of course," she replied and ran towards the front door.

"Come on, Susan, we need to get the room ready." Donald began to run for the hallway leading to their version of an ER.

"Donald, wait!" Susan urgently whispered to him. "Listen to me. She's pregnant!"

Donald stopped dead in his tracks. "Who? Abbie?"

"No, Sabs is pregnant, and J.J. doesn't know. Nobody knows but you and me."

"Oh my God. Susan, she's been shot in the chest. We have to tell him."

"No, we can't. It will make the shock on his system worse. It's bad enough that he has to be the one to save her."

Donald stopped for a moment to process this. *Would it make J.J. try any harder to save her life? Would it be an undue distraction?* The distant sound of four-wheelers approaching 1PP shook him back into reality. "I'll figure it out. Prepare the room for him. You remember what to do?"

"Of course. I've practiced with J.J. several times."

Morgan emerged from downstairs. "Mr. Quinn, what is going on?" he asked.

"Sir, there has been a shooting at the entry gate. Sabina has been shot in the chest. I have to go."

"What can I do to help?" Morgan asked as Donald ran for the door.

"Please continue to monitor the communications room. If there are continued signs of trouble, such as a coordinated attack, please get me." Morgan stood for a moment and walked slowly up the stairs. Donald didn't wait for a reply. He grabbed two poufs and propped open the front doors. *This can't be happening. What do I do?*

J.J. came rushing out of the south trail that led into the forest. Abbie and the girls were a moment behind him.

"Donald! What's happened to Sabs?" asked J.J. Despite being in reasonably good shape for his age, J.J. was breathing heavily and bent over with his hands on his knees to catch his breath. Donald put his hands on his shoulders.

"They're bringing her in," started Donald. "Catch your breath until they get here. Abbie!" Donald went to meet Abbie and his daughters.

"Daddy, what's wrong?" asked Penny, tears of emotion streaming down her cheeks. Donald kneeled down to her level and pulled her and Rebecca close to him. *What if it was my daughter who was shot?* "Come here, girls. J.J. has to help someone. I need you two to go with Abbie for a while, okay?"

"Okay, Daddy." Abbie looked down at Donald and nodded her head.

"Come on, you guys," said Abbie. "You haven't seen my bungalow yet." She led them behind 1PP just as Donald heard the distinctive roar of the Humvee from the front gate racing down the gravel road. He turned his attention to J.J.

"J.J., here's what I know. Two sets of men on four-wheelers approached the front gate and began to question Sabs and Lieutenant Branson. Things got out of hand, but the men left. Branson called some other men to patrol the front security fencing when the men returned and tried to break through the barriers."

"Donald, what happened to Sabs?" J.J. was frantic.

"Shots were fired, and Sabs took a bullet to the chest."

J.J. looked dazed. "How could this happen?"

"J.J., you have to get a hold of yourself. She needs you." The Humvee roared into the clearing and parked in front of the steps leading into 1PP. The Marines on the four-wheelers took up defensive positions. J.J. ran towards the back of the truck as Branson emerged from the passenger side. As if a light switch had been turned on, J.J. became all business.

"What've we got, Branson?" J.J. allowed two of the soldiers to slide a portable gurney out of the back gate. Sabs was covered with blood, but it appeared to have been stopped. She was barely conscious.

"Sir, she took a single GSW to the chest. Probably a .308 or Winchester .270."

"Exit wound?"

"Couldn't find one, sir. Single entry, which I treated with CELOX."

J.J. nodded with approval.

As a combat field surgeon specializing in traumatic wounds, he understood the importance of time. Hemorrhage was responsible for half of combat deaths. In combat, it often took hours to transport casualties off the battlefield to a mobile surgical unit. Also, the hazardous nature of the forward combat zones made it dangerous for medical personnel to provide the requisite attention to the wounded. A standard known as the *platinum five minutes* was adopted by emergency medical personnel. The theory was that a time-critical patient, such as Sabs, should only spend five minutes in the combat zone until she was seen by the trauma surgeon. Branson's use of CELOX, a highly respected hemostatic agent, along with assigning one of his men to maintain pressure on the wound, greatly enhanced the possibilities for her survival.

Sabs was now in the *golden hour*—that critical time needed by the surgeon to stabilize the patient and begin life-saving treatment. The clock was ticking for J.J.

"Let's get her inside," said J.J. The men carried the gurney into the entrance and quickly got her settled on the surgeon's table prepared by an awaiting Susan. Donald followed to lend assistance.

"Thank you, gentlemen," said Donald as he dismissed the two soldiers and closed the door behind them. He pulled together two curtains and applied the Velcro closures. He tried to give J.J. a sterile environment in which to work. Susan was scrubbed in and wore a surgical gown and hat. She had no training other than what she'd studied online and what she'd learned from J.J.

After J.J. had washed up, he approached Sabs and touched her cheek. She began to stir awake and moaned.

"I'm going to take care of you, my brave girl. Please be strong."

Sabs's eyes started to flicker in and out of consciousness. She raised her hand and motioned for J.J. to come closer. She began to cough, and a trickle of blood came out of the side of her mouth before she spoke. "Please save us."

Susan looked at Donald over her mask, and he shook his head side to side. A tear ran down Susan's cheek.

"Stay with me, soldier. I'll fix you up. Stay strong, Sabs. I love you."

Sabs passed out as J.J. brushed the hair out of her face. J.J. was back to being all business.

"Okay, Susan, are you ready?"

Susan nodded.

"Donald, just in case, I need you to scrub in. We may need an extra set of hands."

Donald rushed to the sink and got ready without responding. He was still wrestling with telling J.J. about her pregnancy.

"Susan, help me cut these clothes off her. Donald, grab those mylar blankets and the hospital warming blankets from the cabinet over the sink. We have to keep her warm to prevent her from going into shock. Branson did an excellent job in stopping the bleeding."

Donald returned to the table and assisted J.J. in packing both sides of Sabs with blankets.

"You can't necessarily rely on visual entry and exit wounds. Sometimes the bullet can hit a bone, fragment, and then ricochet throughout the body. We don't have the benefits of an x-ray machine, so we have to look for other indicators of difficult breathing or abdominal pain." As they gently rolled her over, J.J. inspected her body for other entry or exit wounds. There were none.

"Okay, let's keep her covered up. The gunshot wound is severe enough. Death from hypothermia would be tragic." J.J. retrieved the electronic blood pressure unit from the shelf and handed it to Susan. "Monitor this, Susan. Check her pulse and let me know what you find."

Donald watched J.J. work. He admired his friend for what he'd been through in his life. Now J.J. was trying to save the woman he loved. J.J. turned his attention to the wound. He removed the CELOX gauze.

"With a chest wound, two of my biggest concerns are spinal damage and damage to the lungs," started J.J. He put his ear to her chest and listened intently. "If you hear a sucking sound coming from the wound, there's damage to the lung. The concern is allowing too much air in, or out, leading to a collapsed lung." J.J. nodded and smiled. Apparently, he was satisfied.

"J.J., her pulse is sixty, and her blood pressure is one hundred four over sixty-one."

"Thanks, Susan. Her lung seems to be intact, and the fact that she raised her arm is a plus. Her body temperature is stable. Let me finish cleaning the wound, and then I'll need to make a decision."

"What about the bullet?" asked Donald.

"Unlike what you see on television where the characters risk everything to remove the bullet, it's not necessary for most circumstances. Without advanced x-ray capability, the bullet will be almost impossible to find. There are a lot of soldiers out there who still carry shrapnel in their bodies. We'll monitor her for signs of sepsis by watching her heart rate and fever. To ward off any problems, I'll set up an IV of antibiotics and—"

Suddenly, Sabs's body shook violently. Her jugular veins in her neck became distended. Her breathing became rapid as if she was gasping for air.

"Susan, what's her pulse?" shouted J.J.

"It's around a hundred. But her blood pressure has dropped. It's down to ninety over sixty."

"She's going into shock." J.J. held his fingers to her neck. He shook his head. "Please, Sabs. Please hold on."

Her head arched back, and her chest heaved.

"Blood pressure is eighty-two over fifty."

"Dammit, she's going into cardiogenic shock. The bullet, or a fragment, must have hit a ventricle. It must have found her heart. Please, Sabs! Hold on!"

Donald caught Susan's attention. He felt helpless. Sabs was dying, and J.J. didn't have what he needed to save her. Although they had incredible resources at their disposal, a bullet to the heart was not within their limited capabilities. Donald watched as she stopped breathing.

"J.J., no pulse!" exclaimed Susan.

"Please!" he shouted as he began CPR. He furiously began rapid, deep presses on the middle of her chest. His goal was one hundred uninterrupted chest presses per minute.

"Donald! Grab the defib out of the closet." As J.J. continued the chest presses, Donald retrieved the Philips HeartStart portable defibrillator and plugged it in.

"Donald, continue compressions while I prepare the machine.

Hurry!" Donald traded places with J.J. and continued pumping her heart.

He handed J.J. the defib unit, and J.J. made a few minor adjustments to the simple interface. He pulled the handles to activate the unit. He removed the white adhesive pads and placed one under her left breast across the rib cage and the other on her chest above her right breast.

"Stand clear, everyone," ordered J.J., who then took a deep breath. He pressed the flashing orange button. A shock was delivered to Sabs's body, and it heaved slightly off the table. J.J. looked at Susan with hopeful eyes.

"Nothing," she said.

J.J. immediately began hand compressions again. This time, his goal was thirty consecutive compressions, followed by forced breathing. Although mouth-to-mouth breathing was no longer considered necessary during the cardiopulmonary resuscitation process, J.J. was trying all available CPR methods. He tried thirty more compressions and breathing again.

Susan shook her head as she continued to monitor Sabs's pulse. She looked at Donald and shook her head.

"Stand clear. We have to try again!" J.J. reset the machine to its maximum two hundred joules and tried again. Again, her body was given a jolt. He followed up with thirty compressions and mouth-to-mouth breathing. It wasn't working. He repeated the process.

Finally, J.J. stopped. He looked defeated. He removed his surgical clothing and dropped them to the floor. He began to cry and lifted Sabs into his arms.

"You're the only love I have ever known. I'm so sorry I failed you." As he cried uncontrollably, Donald patted his friend on the back and Susan hugged them both. The death of Sabina del Toro was tragic. *She was one of the good guys.*

CHAPTER 59

Wednesday, September 7, 2016
4:13 p.m.
Triple Q Ranch, Prescott Peninsula
Quabbin Reservoir, Massachusetts

"The convoy is headed your way," announced First Lieutenant Branson announced over the two-way radio. Sabs died four hours ago, but it seemed like an eternity. Donald sat on the front porch of 1PP with a glass of Glenlivet. He and Susan hadn't said a word in about an hour. J.J. sat with his back to them at the edge of the woods. He alternated between sitting there and walking around the helicopter.

"Should we talk with him?" asked Donald. The loss of Sabs was a shock to all of them, but the situation at 1PP was fluid. Not only were the Boston Brahmin arriving, but Brad was increasing the number of soldiers on Prescott Peninsula to nearly four dozen. The Triple Q Ranch was rapidly developing into a community with a full platoon of United States Marines as its security force. First, J.J. needed time to grieve. But then there was the issue of Sabs's burial. A proper ceremony should be conducted. In the meantime, the disposition of a dead body was an important medical and hygienic matter. Unlike the pre-TEOTWAWKI world where a morgue was at one's disposal, a rapidly decomposing body could cause significant health risks to all of those who came in contact with it.

"I'll talk to him," said Susan. "I was closest to Sabs, but I can't tell him about the baby. It would send him over the edge."

"Agreed. Listen, her body is a real health risk. We need to place her in a body bag at the very least. A burial tonight would be ideal, but I suppose we can wait 'til morning. Will you bring it up to him, or do you want me to?"

"I'll do it," she replied. "I'm gonna take him for a walk in the woods. He seems bitter as well. The trucks are coming, and we don't need a scene." Susan walked to J.J. and carried a drink for him. Donald threw back the last of his scotch and prepared to greet the new residents.

"Mr. Quinn," said Morgan as he approached. He gestured towards J.J. "Is he doing any better?"

"I don't know, sir," replied Donald. "He hasn't been willing to talk with me about it. Susan is going to console him now."

"Let me know if there's anything I can do. The rest of my friends and associates are coming in now. I will make sure they understand the situation. Shall I speak with him?" *Not a good idea.*

"Perhaps a woman's shoulder is best for now, sir. But, thank you. You and I will have our hands full with our new arrivals. They'll experience quite a shock to their lifestyle."

"Indeed, Mr. Quinn. At first, they might look at this as an interesting adventure and an opportunity to socialize with each other. If this collapsed-grid situation persists, life outside Prescott Peninsula will get ugly. I hope they realize they're better off here than in Boston."

The first of several Humvees entered the clearing together with two troop carriers. Gunny Falcone approached Donald and Morgan first.

"Gentlemen," greeted Gunny Falcone. He turned as if to present a new car to a happy buyer. "Special delivery. Two truckloads of slightly grumpy Bostonians, who are no worse for wear."

"My name is John Morgan."

Gunny Falcone shook his hand. "Gunnery Sergeant Frank Falcone, sir. It's a pleasure."

"Chief Warrant Officer Kyle Shore, sir," said Shore, who joined the group. Morgan shook Shore's hand and then smiled as he saw familiar faces descend from the military transports.

"Gentlemen, sincerely, thank you for keeping my friends safe. Were there any difficulties?"

"Mr. Morgan, the city of Boston is under assault from within. Because of the detours and delays, it took us eight hours to make a two-hour trip." The delays caught Donald's attention. They monitored radio communications and the Internet round-the-clock, searching for updates. There was little information coming out of Boston. Sarge reported gunfire and looting, but nothing near 100 Beacon thus far.

"What did you see?" asked Donald.

"We sent one of the Humvees as an advance team to make sure the roads were clear. The Mass Turnpike was very busy in the morning. We elected to take the route to the north through Concord. Getting out of town was the most difficult part. There were several intersections blocked with stalled and burning vehicles. Most retail stores have been broken into. The city is becoming deserted."

"This is happening already?" asked Morgan.

"Yes, sir."

"I can add that reports from across the country are similar," added Donald. "Major cities are experiencing mayhem. There's a mass exodus for the perceived safety of rural towns. But the chatter we're receiving from ham radio operators is that these small towns are setting up roadblocks to deny access to the refugees."

"I'm astonished that this is happening already," said Morgan. "The power has only been out for a few days."

"True," said Donald. "But people are learning that the power isn't coming back anytime soon. Panic is setting in."

CHAPTER 60

Wednesday, September 7, 2016
7:13 p.m.
Triple Q Ranch, Prescott Peninsula
Quabbin Reservoir, Massachusetts

Susan finished up cleaning the kitchen with Millicent Winthrop and Estelle Peabody—Julia's aunt Stella. The evening went very well as the new arrivals got settled in their bungalows. The Winthrops graciously allowed Susan's children the opportunity to play with their French bulldog. It was a welcome distraction for the girls, who were unaware of the death of Sabs.

"Are you ladies sure you don't mind watching the girls while we view the presidential address this evening?"

"Not at all, Susan. Millie and I loathe that man. Don't we?"

"He's so full of crap," said eighty-year-old Mrs. Winthrop. "Whatever he says won't be the truth. I miss Ronald Reagan."

The three women made their way down the lighted path towards the Quinns' bungalow. Susan thought she heard voices near the edge of the woods, but she continued on her way. It was another beautiful night, and it was undoubtedly some of the soldiers talking about the day's events.

"Here we go," said Susan as she opened up the bungalow door. Inside, Abbie was on the floor with Rebecca and Penny, who were gleefully being entertained by Winnie the Frenchie. Abbie looked up at Susan, but there was a look of sadness on her face. She was doing her best to hide it for the benefit of the children. Abbie had experienced death twice in a short period. She was clearly troubled.

"Girls, Aunt Stella and Mrs. Winthrop are going to stay with you guys for a little while. I'll be in the main house if you need me, okay?"

"Okay, Mom," said Penny without looking up. Susan helped Abbie off the floor. "You two be good girls for them, please."

"Yes, Mom."

Susan stood with her hands on her hips as the girls continued to roll on the floor while Winnie gave them kisses. "They couldn't care less about me," Susan observed. She laughed. "Ladies, are you sure about this?"

"Don't you worry about them, dear," replied Aunt Stella. "They'll tucker out soon enough."

Susan and Abbie left the bungalow and started back towards 1PP. Susan heard the voices again. Her curiosity got the best of her.

"Oh shoot, Abbie, I forgot something. You go ahead without me. I'll catch up in a moment."

"Okay, but I need to talk with you," said Abbie. Susan paused, but then decided to investigate.

"I'll meet you on the front porch." Susan made her way towards her bungalow and then confirmed that Abbie was headed to 1PP. She removed her flip-flops and quickly moved toward the sounds of the voices. She quietly passed the empty bungalows. Everyone was gathering in the living area for the presidential address. She inched her way forward until she was around the edge of the bungalow where the men were speaking.

"John, what do you expect the President to say tonight?"

"I haven't spoken with him directly, Lawrence, but I have been in contact with David McDill, his former Chief of Staff."

"Former?"

"Yes, Walter. He's circling the wagons. He has replaced McDill with Victoria Blanchett as his Chief of Staff."

"His consigliere," interjected Lawrence Lowell.

"I saw this coming," said Morgan. "They are very close. We have to be prepared for moves like this."

"Is our man in place?" asked Walter Cabot.

"He is," replied Morgan. "I suspect tonight's address will be a shock to the nation, but it should go according to plan."

"Is there any chance of a double-cross, John?" asked Lowell.

"With this President, there is always that possibility."

Susan heard enough and quickly crossed the clearing toward 1PP. Donald walked out onto the front steps, looking for her. She ran up the steps to him, out of breath.

"Hey. Hey. Is everything okay? The girls?" asked Donald.

Susan was trying to catch her breath. She shook her head and held up her hands to quiet Donald. He helped her get steady on her feet. Her heart was racing. *This is incredible.*

"The girls are fine. I have to tell you something." Susan pulled Donald aside and whispered the content of the overheard conversation.

"Susan, are you sure?" he asked.

"I'm sure."

Abbie walked onto the porch. "Susan, can we talk, please?"

"Yes, honey, of course. Donald, would you excuse—"

Abbie held her hands up, indicating that Donald could stay. "It's okay, Susan. He can hear this." Before she could speak, her father ascended the stairs with Lowell and Cabot.

"Good evening all," said Morgan. "Has he started yet?"

"No, sir," replied Donald.

"Late as usual, I see," said Lowell.

"So typical." Cabot chuckled, shaking his head. The three men made their way through the double entry doors, leaving the Quinns alone with Abbie once again. Susan grabbed Abbie by the hands.

"Abbie, what is it?"

Abbie turned around to make sure they were alone. "Susan, I figured it out. I remember now."

"What, Abbie?" asked Donald. He and Susan leaned in to hear Abbie's words.

"I realize what Drew was shouting to me as my father closed the door of the helicopter."

"What was it?"

"He knew. Drew was shouting *he knew.*"

PART FIVE

Martial Law!

CHAPTER 61

Wednesday, September 7, 2016
7:18 p.m. EDT
Western White House
Honolulu, HI

The *blue goose*, the nickname for the large blue podium adorned with the seal of the President of the United States, stood empty for seventeen minutes past the hour. The White House press corps, who traveled with the President to Hawaii, was growing impatient. Typically, they would be standing, facing their respective network's cameras, killing time with their opinion of what the President was going to say. This time, it was different. There was only one camera. Network feeds were unnecessary, as there were no networks available to receive them.

Flanking the podium to the viewers' left was the United States flag. To the right was the flag of the President of the United States, which consisted of the presidential coat of arms on a dark blue background. Nothing from this live feed appeared out of the ordinary, although the President's address would be remembered as extraordinary.

The President, followed by General Mason J. Sears, the Chairman of the Joint Chiefs of Staff, approached the podium. He began.

"My fellow Americans and citizens of the world. Tonight I come to you under inexplicable circumstances. On Saturday, September 3rd, at approximately 9:11 p.m. Eastern Time, the United States fell victim to a vicious attack by an unknown enemy. At that moment, the vast majority of the nation's electrical grid, which provides electricity to nearly three hundred million Americans, was destroyed by an unprovoked cyber intrusion. At this time, forty-seven states, parts of northern Mexico, and southern Canada are without power. Only Texas, Alaska, and Hawaii have been spared.

"First, let me express my condolences to the wife and family of our Vice President. Join me as we mourn with them following his unfortunate death. I will say a few words in a moment about logistics and continuity of government.

"Today, we face a threat never before seen by this nation. As Commander-in-Chief, my highest priority is the security of the American people. Our military women and men have kept us safe from the terrorist threats of ISIL and al-Qaeda. Now we have threats to face from within. While our military forces protect us from further attempts to breach our sovereignty, we must remain vigilant as new risks emerge.

"Let me make two things clear. First, we will find the perpetrator of these attacks and bring them to justice. If this is found to be the actions of a terrorist, they will pay a high price. If this turns out to be a state-sponsored act, they will be brought before the United Nations and held to account. While we have not detected specific, credible evidence of who is responsible for this heinous act, make no mistake, we will.

"Second, we must now turn our attention to helping our fellow Americans during this critical period in our history. I know many Americans are concerned about their health and safety. Many are hungry and without proper shelter. Some folks are in need of life-saving medications. I want you to know that your government is making it a priority to help you through this as we work diligently to restore power.

"However, this burden will not rest on the government's shoulders alone. Tonight, I am executing a series of executive orders that will create the largest citizen-based recovery effort in modern history. Under the auspices of the Department of Homeland Security, and in conjunction with the Federal Emergency Management Agency, we are expanding the role of the Citizen Corps. The mission of the newly empowered Citizen Corps is simple. We will harness the power and resolve of every American citizen who wants to assist in the recovery effort, in order to make our communities safer, stronger, and better prepared to respond to any threats that may hinder the recovery effort. Most importantly, the Citizen Corps will save lives.

"Those Americans who join with me and become involved in the Citizen Corps will be rewarded with shelter, food, medicine, and a paying job. Those who make the Citizen Corps a success will be provided a significant role in the rebuilding of America as we weather this storm.

"I am issuing a call to action for all American citizens. Help your government help you. We have established a national network of state, local, and tribal Citizen Corps Councils. These councils will build on community strengths to implement the goals I establish for the rebuilding of America. You will be an integral part of carrying out a local strategy to assist your government, Citizen Corps leaders, and the newly constituted Council of Governors in restoring order and making sure every American has an equal opportunity to survive this calamity.

"I believe it is your personal responsibility as an American to unselfishly help your fellow man in their time of need. Do not delay. Find your local Citizen Corps leaders and visit one of the thousands of upcoming Citizen Corps Council meetings in your neighborhood. I know you will because it's the right thing to do.

"Now, let me address the important matter of continuity of government. With the assistance of the United States Pacific Command—USPACOM, my compound in Honolulu, Hawaii, will become the temporary White House. Until order and electrical power can be restored in Washington, D.C., Hawaii is better suited for conducting the business of the nation.

"With the unfortunate death of the Vice President, the next member of the government in line to the presidency is the Speaker of the House. At this time, the Speaker is unaccounted for in Wisconsin. The President pro tempore of the Senate, the next in line to the presidency, is also missing in his home state of Utah. As of this moment, the acting Vice President of the United States is the next official in line, Secretary of State John Kerry. At this point, Mr. Kerry is safe in an undisclosed military facility. Once it is clear that the nation is not under additional threats, he will join me here.

"With me today is General Mason J. Sears, Chairman of the Joint Chiefs of Staff, to make a statement. I have instructed him to recall all active-duty military, except those required for security at our international facilities, to return home. They should be here with their families, and to perform the duties necessary to protect and serve our citizens.

"The actions I have taken today are done with an overriding purpose—ensure the continuity of government and protect those among us who are the most vulnerable.

"I will take a few questions after General Sears makes his statement. Thank you."

CHAPTER 62

Wednesday, September 7, 2016
7:22 p.m. EDT
Western White House
Honolulu, HI

"My name is General Mason J. Sears, Chairman of the Joint Chiefs of Staff. The text of the following executive order will be delivered to you following the President's closing remarks. It will be delivered to the United States Postal Service for posting in a conspicuous place. It will also be made available through the offices of the Council of Governors as established in this executive order.

"It is my duty to read the following executive order in its entirety.

"This is Executive Order 13777. Dated September 7, 2016, entitled **DECLARATION OF MARTIAL LAW**.

"By the authority vested in me as President by the Constitution and the laws of the United States of America, including the Defense Production Act of 1950, as amended; Executive Order 13603 entered into the Federal Register on March 22, 2012; and in furtherance of National Security and Homeland Security Presidential Directive 51, herein Directive 51, signed by President George W. Bush on May 4, 2007; and in my capacity as Commander-in-Chief of the Armed Forces of the United States, it is hereby ordered as follows:

"PART I: PURPOSE, POLICY, AND
IMPLEMENTATION
"**Section 101**. *Purpose*. This Executive Order 13777 incorporates

all prior Executive Orders and Presidential Policy Directives that have been established to promulgate the decisions of the President on national and domestic security matters. This Executive Order 13777 establishes a comprehensive national policy on the continuity of the Federal Government. Through the establishment of ten regional Governor's offices, the Executive Branch will name a National Continuity Coordinator responsible for coordinating the development and implementation of Federal policies to ensure Continuity of Government and the ability to provide the citizens of America certain *National Essential Functions*, as prescribed from time to time by the President.

"**Section 102**. *Policy*. It is the policy of the United States to maintain a comprehensive and effective continuity capability composed of Continuity of Operations and Continuity of Government programs in order to ensure the preservation of our form of government under the Constitution and the continuing performance of National Essential Functions under all conditions. In addition, it is the duty of the United States to protect and serve our citizens. This Executive Order 13777 declares the United States to be in a state of Catastrophic Emergency, as that term is defined in Directive 51. A Catastrophic Emergency means any incident, regardless of location, that results in extraordinary levels of mass casualties, damage, or disruption severely affecting the United States population, infrastructure, environment, economy, or government functions. The authorities created in this Executive Order shall be used to strengthen our national defense preparedness, and to assist further federal, state, and local law enforcement during this Catastrophic Emergency.

"**Section 103**. *General Functions and Implementation*. All executive departments, agencies, and the newly constituted Council of Governor's offices responsible for plans and programs relating to national defense and domestic policing, shall:

(a) Assist in identifying the full spectrum of emergencies facing the Continuity of Operations, including all threats, foreign or domestic;

(b) Assess and report any individual or group of individuals who are actively opposing the provisions of this Executive Order;

(c) Be prepared, in the event of a potential threat to the Continuity of Government or the security of the United States, to take all actions deemed necessary and appropriate to ensure National Essential Functions.

"**Section 104**. *Implementation*. The Office of the President, in association with the cooperation of the National Security Council, and the Department of Homeland Security, and pursuant to Executive Order 13528 entered in the Federal Register on January 11, 2010, as amended and superseded herein, hereby establishes ten Regional Offices of the Council of Governors. The Council of Governors will be maintained in the existing regional offices of the Federal Emergency Management Agency and will be tasked with coordinating the efforts of the National Guard, the Citizens Corps, homeland defense, and the integration of State and Federal military activities within the United States. The Governors will be appointed by the Office of the President based upon merit, and without consideration of political party affiliation. These duly appointed Governors will report directly to, and serve at the pleasure of, the Office of the President.

"**PART II: SPECIFIC PROVISIONS**

"**Section 201**. *Generally*. In order to maintain security and order, and provide essential services to the citizens of America, curfews will be established and until further notice, there will be a suspension of certain provisions of the United States Constitution, including, but not limited to, civil law, civil rights, habeas corpus, and such other and general provisions as may be determined in the national interest by the Office of the President. Specifically, but without limitation, the following restrictions and suspensions are effective immediately—all determined to be in the best interests of the nation, and the safety, health, and general welfare of its citizens:

(a) The First Amendment right of free speech and the press are hereby restricted to the extent such speech or written word is deemed intended to incite a riot or hostilities against the United States. The right of assembly is hereby limited to not more than ten persons, in public or private. Specifically excepted from this provision is the right to freedom of religion in a designated house of worship for so long as such religious gathering is properly permitted by the Council of Governors, and monitored by its designated agent;

(b) The Second Amendment right to bear arms is suspended. All weapons, magazines, ammunition, and related accessories are hereby declared unlawful and shall be voluntarily, or forcibly, surrendered to law enforcement designated by the Council of Governors;

(c) The Third Amendment restriction of quartering soldiers in private homes is suspended. In order to assure an Enduring Constitutional Government, the nation's military personnel, members of law enforcement, and appropriately designated members of the Citizen Corps, will have the full force and effect of a soldier within the meaning of the Constitution. Housing for these specially appointed citizens will take priority over all others. Those citizens displaced from their homes will be provided suitable housing at the discretion of the Council of Governors, or its designees;

(d) The   Fourth   Amendment   right   against

unreasonable searches and seizures is hereby suspended. No citizen shall hinder or prevent any action or process in furtherance of the duties of those appointed by the Office of the President or the Council of Governors;

(e) The Fifth Amendment right to due process is suspended. All persons subject to appearance before the state and federal courts of the United States will now fall under the purview of the Military Tribunals of the United States;

(f) The Sixth Amendment right to a speedy trial is suspended as being an undue burden upon the Military Tribunals of the United States. The right to trial by jury, to be informed of the criminal charges against the person, the right to compel and confront witnesses, and to the assistance of counsel is not suspended. However, the Military Tribunals of the United States may delay the prosecution of individuals based upon the accused's insistence upon exercising these rights, and all defendants shall be so informed;

(g) The Seventh Amendment right to civil trials by jury is suspended;

(h) The Eighth Amendment forbidding the imposition of excessive bails or fines is suspended. Specifically, the right to bail is suspended;

(i) The Ninth Amendment clarifies that the specific individual rights not enumerated in the Constitution, such as the right to privacy, are given full force and effect as law. These rights may be suspended as deemed necessary by, and in the sole discretion of, the Office of the President and the Council of Governors, in the best interests of the nation, and the safety, health, and general welfare of its citizens;

(j) The Tenth Amendment is suspended. By the execution of this Executive Order 13777, all matters of governing shall reside within the Office of the President, the Council of Governors, or their designees.

"PART III: GENERAL PROVISIONS and PENALTIES

"Section 301. *Continuity Annexes.* The directives and the information contained herein shall be protected from unauthorized disclosure and alteration. The Continuity Annexes attached hereto are hereby incorporated herein and made a part of this Executive Order 13777 by reference. The Continuity Annexes are hereby designated *Classified* and shall be accorded appropriate handling, consistent with prior applicable Executive Orders.

"Section 302. *Force and Effect.* This Executive Order 13777 shall be implemented in a manner that is consistent with, and facilitates effective implementation of, provisions of the Constitution concerning the exercise of the powers of the Office of the Presidency, with the consultation of the Vice President, the Council of Governors and, as appropriate, their designees. Heads of local, state, and federal agencies shall be prepared at all times to implement the directives issued by the Office of the Presidency deemed necessary and appropriate for the health, safety, and welfare of American citizens and interests.

"Section 303. *Further Directives.* The Council of Governors, upon the direction of the Office of the President, is hereby authorized and empowered to issue such further regulations as they may deem necessary to carry out the purposes of this Executive Order 13777 and to issue licenses hereunder, through such officers or agencies as they may designate from time to time.

"Section 304. *Penalties for Violations.* Whoever willfully violates any provision of this Executive Order 13777, or any rule, regulation, or license issued thereunder, will be subject to imprisonment and asset forfeiture as deemed appropriate by the Military Tribunals of the

United States. In addition, any person who, owing allegiance to the United States, or otherwise, levies war against the United States, or adheres to their enemies, giving them aid and comfort, is guilty of treason. Such person shall be brought before the Military Tribunal of the United States, and if found guilty of treason against the United States, shall suffer the penalty of death.

Signed under hand and seal by the President of the United States on this seventh day of September 2016."

CHAPTER 63

Wednesday, September 7, 2016
7:33 p.m. EDT
Western White House
Honolulu, HI

The President retook the podium.

"Thank you, General Sears. Let me add one thing. It goes without saying that these actions are deemed necessary because of the position we have been placed in by this unprovoked attack. The provisions of the Declaration may appear onerous to some. They are not considered permanent. As soon as order is restored to my satisfaction, I will begin to rescind all or part of the Declaration as appropriate.

"Furthermore, although these provisions have gone into effect this evening at 7:00 p.m. Eastern Time, I recognize it may take several days for the content of the Declaration to be disseminated around the country. Under the direction of Homeland Security, the Council of Governors, and the Citizens Corps Council, we will distribute copies of the Declaration throughout the country. I have instructed General Sears to allow a grace period until Sunday night, December 11, for Americans to comply. Until Sunday evening, law enforcement and the military will be permitted to use their discretion in the enforcement of the Declaration, unless an immediate threat of loss of life or damage to federal property is at stake. In that case, they should act accordingly.

"Now, I will take a few questions before I get back to work. Jim Acosta."

Jim Acosta of CNN News stood and asked, "Mr. President, could you provide any details on the damage sustained to the power grid, and are you prepared to give the American people a time frame for its repair?"

"Thank you, Jim. We are working with Homeland Security and local utilities to assess the extent of the damage. Because of the massive impact of the cyber intrusions, both computer technology and electrical transformers have been destroyed. Some of these transformers are unique to the particular location in which they were used. This may require the construction of new replacements. It will take days and possibly weeks to provide a final assessment. In addition to protecting the American people, these repairs are our utmost priority.

"Pete."

"Thank you, Mr. President. Peter Alexander, NBC News. We are receiving reports that Governor Greg Abbott has closed the Texas borders to any nonresidents. Further, he has deployed the National Guard to apprehend all non-U.S. citizens and forcibly deport them to Mexico. First, has Governor Abbott committed an act of treason by closing the state's borders? Second, is the deportation of foreign nationals in direct contravention of your immigration policy?"

"Governor Abbott has no legal basis for closing access to the State of Texas to any individual lawfully residing in this country, including those who entered our country looking for a better life. Now, whether the actions of Governor Abbott give rise to an act of treason in the eyes of the Attorney General is not for me to decide. I have contacted the governor, and we had a very frank conversation. I told him that his extreme actions constituted a betrayal and disloyalty to his country. He should be welcoming his fellow Americans into Texas so that Texans can do their part in the recovery effort."

"Follow-up question, Mr. President. If Governor Abbott refuses to heed your request, what are your options?"

"It's too early to address the specifics, Pete. I want to give the governor time to do the right thing. Just know that all options are on the table."

"Major Garrett, CBS." Garrett stood to address the President.

"Mr. President, along the same line as the previous question. Is there any truth to the fact that the U.S. Border Patrol agents are being recalled to handle other duties?"

"That is true, Major. Our number one priority is providing assistance to our citizens. This attack was perpetrated on America, but large parts of northern Mexico were affected by the collapse of the power grid. That is not their fault. If allowing our borders to remain open helps those folks affected by our problems, then so be it. And, let me say this as well. I have been in contact with Mexican President Enrique Pena Nieto, who is willing to consider a limited number of our refugees to come to Mexico in exchange for our removing the draconian and onerous barriers we have placed between our nations. I agree with him, and the recall of the Border Patrol agents is in furtherance of this policy."

"Let me see. Peter Baker, *New York Times*. Peter."

"Thank you, Mr. President. Are you able to comment at all on intelligence as to the possible motive or perpetrators?"

"The investigation is ongoing, and the events are fluid. Over the last several days, I have been in contact with our NATO allies who have agreed to provide assistance in the relief effort as well as the investigation. I have opened diplomatic channels with the Russians and the Chinese. As of date, no one has claimed responsibility for this, nor has any military power made a move against us."

Still standing, Baker pressed for more. "But, Mr. President, we have reports indicating the Russian military has amassed a significant number of forces and military assets at their Arctic facility. Also, Russian submarines openly patrol just outside our territorial waters on both the Atlantic seaboard and the Pacific coast. Could the Russians have used this cyber attack as the beginning of an invasion of the United States?"

"Before the event, there were no military hostilities between our two nations. We have no reason to believe that President Putin would be so foolish as to invade the United States. If he does, I intend to invoke Article Five of the North Atlantic Treaty, which states that an attack on one ally shall be considered an attack on all.

We will defend ourselves as appropriate.

"Next up, Luis Ramirez, Voice of America Radio."

"Mr. President, you mentioned the United Nations in your opening remarks. Has the UN offered any support in the recovery effort?"

"Yes, thank you, Luis. I should have expanded on that earlier. Whenever there is a disaster or a humanitarian catastrophe, the United Nations is on the ground providing relief, support, and assistance. Our situation is no different. Through the coordinated efforts of our Department of Homeland Security and Secretary-General Ban Ki-moon, the United Nations will be providing aid throughout the nation in primarily heavily populated urban centers. Also, while our forces help maintain stability across the nation, the UN has committed a sizable peacekeeping force, who will work with the Citizen Corps Councils in more rural parts of the country. We are fortunate to have this asset to help reduce tensions in troubled areas.

"Jonathan."

Jonathan Karl of ABC News addressed the President next. "Mr. President, the Chinese are formally demanding that the dollar no longer is considered the world's reserve currency. They insist that our currency is now worthless without sufficient gold reserves to back it up. How do you respond?"

"Jonathan, economic tensions have been building for a number of years between our country, the Russians, and the Chinese. Reserve currencies come and go. Arguably, under normal circumstances, the loss of reserve currency status would cause our imports to cost more, and our standard of living would go down. Many argue that our standard of living is too high. Under the present circumstances, the standard of living is the least of our problems. If they wish to devalue the dollar and take away our reserve currency status, so be it.

"Julie Pace, Associated Press."

"Thank you, Mr. President. The Associated Press is reporting that the Federal Bureau of Prisons is preparing to release inmates currently housed in its prison system. Is that correct?"

"Yes, Julie. The federal government no longer has the personnel nor the requisite provisions to feed and provide medical care for the already overburdened federal prison system. Therefore, I have commuted all sentences of those inmates below the penitentiary level. Also, to assist these able-bodied Americans to transition back into society, such that it is, we are encouraging them to contact their local Citizen Corps Council to volunteer for work. While they will not be paid a salary commensurate with others, they will be housed, fed, and provided medical treatment. I am told this will be effectuated by the end of this week.

"Last question."

Ed Henry of FoxNews stood up. "Mr. President, if I may."

"Well, Ed, you don't seem to have left me a choice, now have you?" The President bristled, his lips pursed.

"Mr. President, you have declared martial law on a nationwide basis for the first time since the Civil War. You have suspended habeas corpus that will enable the government to seize property or detain persons in violation of their civil rights. Further, by using the United States military on American soil in a law enforcement capacity, you arguably run afoul of the Posse Comitatus Act, which has been in effect for one hundred and forty years."

"Is there a question coming, Ed? I have lots of work to do."

"Sir, it appears you have violated prior precedent followed by your predecessors in office and several established court rulings of the United States Supreme Court. What is your response to this?"

"Well, it's simple, actually. I am the President, and they're not. If someone objects to the way I am handling my job, they can sue me. But in case you haven't noticed, the lights are out at the Supreme Court building."

The President walked away from the podium without saying another word.

CHAPTER 64

Wednesday, September 7, 2016
7:45 p.m. EDT
Western White House
Honolulu, HI

General Sears stood to the side of the stage and listened to the President's final comments in astonishment. His aide, Vice Admiral Kurt Klemons, approached General Sears with his satphone.

"General, an urgent phone call for you, sir," said Klemons. "It's John Morgan, sir." General Sears took the phone from his trusted aide and walked to a secluded corner away from prying ears.

"Yes, John." The four words that General Sears heard from John Morgan were plain and simple—yet chilling.

The end begins tomorrow.

The saga will continue in FALSE FLAG.

Continue reading to get a sneak peek at the first few chapters.

THANK YOU FOR READING MARTIAL LAW!

If you enjoyed it, I'd be grateful if you'd take a moment to write a short review (just a few words are needed) and post it on Amazon. Amazon uses complicated algorithms to determine what books are recommended to readers. Sales are, of course, a factor, but so are the quantities of reviews my books get. By taking a few seconds to leave a review, you help me out, and also help new readers learn about my work.

And before you go…

SIGN UP for Bobby Akart's mailing list to receive special offers, bonus content, and you'll be the first to receive news about new releases in the Doomsday series:

eepurl.com/bYqq3L

VISIT Amazon.com/BobbyAkart for more information on his next project, as well as his completed words: the Doomsday series, the Yellowstone series, the Lone Star series, the Pandemic series, the Blackout series, the Boston Brahmin series and the Prepping for Tomorrow series totaling nearly forty novels, including over thirty Amazon #1 Bestsellers in forty-plus fiction and nonfiction genres.

Visit Bobby Akart's website for informative blog entries on preparedness, writing, and a behind-the-scenes look into his novels.

BobbyAkart.com

READ ON FOR A BONUS EXCERPT from

FALSE FLAG

Book Four in The Boston Brahmin Series.

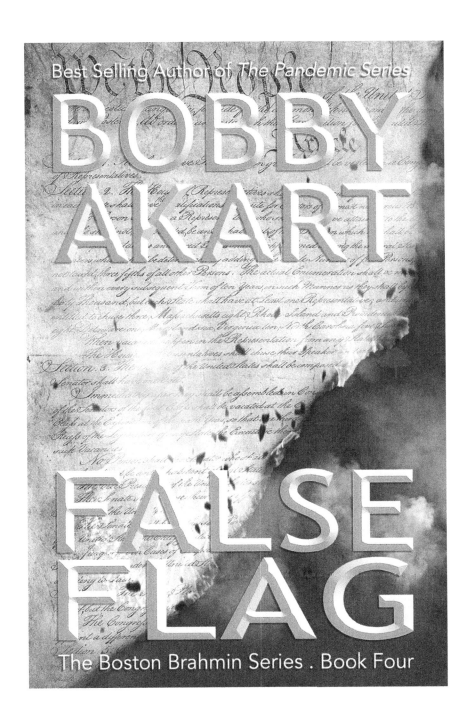

Best Selling Author of *The Pandemic Series*

BOBBY
AKART

FALSE
FLAG

The Boston Brahmin Series . Book Four

EXCERPT FROM *FALSE FLAG*

CHAPTER 1

Thursday, September 8, 2016
4:05 a.m.
265 First Street
Cambridge, Massachusetts

COGAS, combined gas and steam, permeated the nearly thirty-mile labyrinth of steel pipeline under the streets of Boston's government facilities, hospitals, businesses, and residential neighborhoods. The Kendall Cogeneration Station, located on the banks of the Charles River in Cambridge, was billed as a sustainable and energy-efficient alternative following the closure of the Pilgrim Nuclear Generating Station.

Cogeneration is the process of combining steam heat with power by recycling waste heat and converting it into stored thermal energy. It was hailed as an environmentally friendly method of energy production that improved air quality and reduced carbon emissions. One official, who praised the project as being consistent with the President's desire to protect the environment, also proclaimed Kendall Station as the beating heart and arteries of the cities power generating system.

The nearly sixty-year-old Kendall Station was retrofitted with industrial jet engines which utilized more than one million gallons of fuel oil stored at their facility across the Charles River from Massachusetts General Hospital. The French company which designed the system proudly proclaimed that the Kendall Station was positioned to jump-start the electrical grid following a blackout.

City officials pressured the company to bring the plant back online. After all, the plant was designed to function following a blackout just like this one. In the early morning hours of day five, after much of America was thrust into darkness, the Boston-based electrical engineering team at Kendall Station believed they had a solution which would refire the jet engines, immediately allowing the plant to produce two hundred fifty-six megawatts of electricity and one million, two hundred thousand pounds per hour of steam. Relying upon satellite phone guidance from the expert troubleshooting team based in France, they initiated the necessary steps to return power to Cambridge and much of Boston.

As with all appliances, incidents with gas fueled engines and turbines typically occur during start sequences. The newer cogeneration plants in Europe—France and Denmark in particular— contained sophisticated auxiliary equipment, sensors, and control systems for the purposes of purging pressurized air within the network of piping. The latest technology incorporated into the European plants had large exhaust systems capable of handling significant volumes of stored COGAS upon the restart sequence. It was recommended that forced ventilation continue at idling of the jet engines during the start-up process as high concentrations of unburnt gas can accumulate within the exhaust system and throughout the pipeline distribution network.

The team initiated the startup sequence, but the turbines did not rotate. The engineers tried again, but nothing happened as the system misfired. They waited, heeding the warning to limit the number of start attempts. The team, and their French counterparts, was concentrating entirely on the firing of the jet engines. They did not focus on the requisite purging of combustible gases contained within the exhaust system and the pipeline network.

The team tried again, and again. With each attempt, high

concentrations of unburnt hydrocarbons backed up throughout the system. When the powerful jet engines finally fired for a moment, the team cheered and shared high-fives. But after the engines groaned to a halt, dejection was the mood.

During the brief operation of the turbines, combustible gases were forced through the pipelines from Cambridge to the west, throughout Boston across the river. The steel pipes swelled, and the gases looked for a place to release—*to purge*.

Within moments, the *beating heart and arteries* of the Boston power grid had an aneurysm.

CHAPTER 2

Thursday, September 8, 2016
5:51 a.m.
100 Beacon
Boston, Massachusetts

Sarge stood alone on the rooftop of 100 Beacon, staring across Cambridge in wonder of the darkness and the deafening silence that had overtaken his hometown, as Beantown was devoid of vehicle traffic. Ordinarily, Storrow Drive would be awake with commuters making their way downtown. The never-ending low hum of the vehicular traffic on the Mass Turnpike to his south would be evidence of Americans going about their lives, scurrying from one important destination to another.

Was this the new normal?

It had only been a few days since the cyber attack took away power and water from two hundred and ninety million Americans. America went from a nation enjoying Saturday night dinner dates or sporting events, to a country struggling to survive—under the specter of martial law.

Sarge was incredulous as he watched the arrogance of the President's press conference the night before. He was too wound up to sleep and took Julia's shift patrolling the rooftop and the rest of the top three floors of 100 Beacon.

Although information was limited, Sarge was privy to communications via the expansive network set up by Julia. Within a day of the grid collapse, they were fully informed. For other Americans, information was scarce. *Not knowing* consumed them initially. Then the realities that America was a *powerless* nation set in— as did the panic. On this sixth day, survival was all that mattered to most.

I knew this would happen!

Sarge's lectures at Harvard Kennedy covered a variety of subjects, including national defense, global governance, and the subject of world economics. He tried to be impartial in his discussions, but it was impossible to avoid inserting his world view when exploring these concepts. He warned his class about the fragility of society and the dangerous threats that one nation could pose to another. He talked about advanced weaponry like electromagnetic pulse weapons, bioterror, and, of course, cyber warfare. *Did his students prepare?* Doubtful. Sarge knew that most Americans who were interested enough to advanced their level of knowledge on these subjects still had enough doubt in their minds regarding the realities of these threats. Sarge had no doubt, and he prepared accordingly.

He ambled along the building's rooftop, periodically looking over the edge for signs of activity along the street. He kicked a pebble into one of the roof's scuppers and listened as it found its way down the drainpipe to the ground eleven stories below. He stopped and stared out across Boston Common to the southeast. It was completely deserted.

So this is what TEOTWAWKI looks like.

Sarge thought about this for a moment—the end of the world as we know it. *It doesn't have to mean it's the end of the world.* The situation was bad for most, but it could be worse. Sarge was exceedingly concerned about the events surrounding the cyber attack. He'd observed the increased Russian military activity along the U.S. coastal waters. Putin had amassed an army in the Arctic. All signs pointed toward a potential incursion onto American soil. It was the Russians modus operandi to use cyber attacks as a precursor to war. Estonia, Georgia, Ukraine, and Turkey had all experienced Russia's use of cyber warfare to collapse their financial institutions and critical infrastructure in advance of military action. With Americans losing hope every day, the country was weakened. Sarge hoped that the military was prepared for every contingency.

If the Russians are preparing for World War III, why is the President using American soldiers to clamp down on our constitutional rights by declaring martial law?

Sarge watched the sun begin to peek through the skyscrapers of Boston, bearing names like John Hancock, Prudential, and the Federal Reserve. Sarge doubted that John Hancock would find anything prudent about the Federal Reserve.

The situation throughout the country was dire. In the large urban centers, the impact was felt immediately. Opportunists seized the night, taking advantage of a shocked populace and an outgunned law enforcement community. As despair spread across the nation, even midsized cities felt the impact. Julia was able to confirm that although rural areas experienced the collapse of the grid, thus far they had been spared from the collapse of society.

Where do we go from here?

With the arrival of Steven and Katie yesterday, Sarge was able to lift that concern out of his mind. They had been out of communication for days, and despite Steven's extraordinary capabilities, Sarge was worried about his brother. His *making an entrance* was both theatrical and typical for Steven. *My brother is a magnet for excitement.* After a brief conversation, and some dinner, Steven started on the rest he needed to heal his gunshot wound. At some point, the four of them would have to discuss their future. There were so many issues to address.

Should they stay at 100 Beacon or travel to the rural safety of Prescott Peninsula?

If they remained in Boston, did they hunker down and react to events, or did they become active in any rebuilding effort?

But a troubling question hung over his head like a dark cloud. *Who caused this, and how long will it last?*

"Do we just try to survive?" asked Sarge aloud. He glanced down at the front entrance and then up and down Beacon Street, which was free from activity. The sun was getting brighter and he looked toward Cambridge. He wondered whether he would ever teach again.

He thought about the students he had taught over the last ten years. Then, his thoughts were interrupted.

CHAPTER 3

Thursday, September 8, 2016
6:13 a.m.
100 Beacon
Boston, Massachusetts

Intuitively, Sarge sensed it first. He felt it coming. Inexplicably, Sarge knew it would be devastating. In the relative quiet of Cambridge across the Charles River, a hissing sound filled the air. A gaggle of Canadian geese, which had been resting on the muddy bank of the river, suddenly took flight. Sarge brought his AR-15 to low ready as the first explosions shook the building.

A geyser of hot steam broke through Amherst Street, which traversed east to west through the heart of MIT. A shower of mud and flying debris rose into the dark sky until it was eye level to Sarge. The cloud of steam continued skyward and then a second explosion occurred to the east. Sarge ducked and then ran past the hot tub towards the cloud undulating into the morning sun.

The height and breadth of this explosion obliterated his view of Mass General, which was less than a mile away. The entire complex was engulfed in smoke. Drivers, apparently startled by the events, hit each other on Storrow and careened down an embankment towards The Esplanade.

Another explosion occurred across the river near the Charles River Dam. As 100 Beacon shook from the blast, Sarge ducked again and looked towards the sky. *Are we being bombed?* Then another violent eruption shook the ground. This time, a large crater formed at the base of the Longfellow Bridge connecting Cambridge to downtown Boston. A towering cloud of swirling steam rose into the sky for nearly four hundred feet.

Car alarms were sounding all around. Then another explosion came from the downtown area. Steam rose into the sky, taller than the newly completed Millennium Tower, which stood seven hundred feet above ground. For a brief moment, the rising sun was obscured by the debris, and then the winds created gaps allowing the light to shine through.

Sarge was mesmerized. It reminded him of a scene from the *Apocalypse Now* movie. The sound of collapsing concrete and steel snapped him out of his trance as he looked back towards Cambridge. Another blast widened the crater at the Longfellow Bridge. The structure had been compromised, and the central span of the bridge was giving way.

Panicked, some drivers were attempting to back off the bridge, but the steam swallowed them from view. Others frantically turned back towards the billowing steam that surrounded Mass General. Suddenly, the bridge gave way as the structure and deck of a two-hundred-foot span of Longfellow Bridge collapsed into the Charles River. At least a dozen cars sank to the bottom, only the red illuminated taillights indicating their path to the murky depths below.

A vehicle on the south side of the bridge caught fire. A pickup pulling a trailer rested precariously against the guardrail of the collapsed structure, near the burning car. Sarge could hear the screams of motorists on the bridge, attempting to escape the collapse.

"What's happening, Sarge?" screamed Steven as he ran onto the rooftop with Julia and Katie close behind. The sun was rising and their view of the carnage was getting better.

"Are you okay, Sarge?" asked Julia as she reached Sarge's side. The four of them looked from Boston to the east across the Charles to Cambridge in the west. The sky was dense with steam, silt, and flying debris. Longfellow Bridge continued to creak as it struggled to stand.

"I've counted at least a dozen explosions," said Sarge. "Look at the steam rising out of the ground." Sarge directed their attention to the massive craters left by the escaping steam and debris. Another vehicle crash distracted them momentarily.

"Were we bombed?" asked Julia. She was trembling as she hung on to Sarge's arm. She was badly shaken by this, or the culmination of the entire situation.

"No," replied Sarge. "I saw it. I mean, I felt it coming." Sarge looked at the ground, looking for the right words.

"What do you mean, bro?" asked Steven.

"I mean, I could tell something was about to happen, and then the ground began to erupt," said Sarge. He loosened his grip on his rifle and slung it over his shoulder. He turned his attention to Julia and gave her a reassuring look. "Something happened underground. It looks like a bad day at Yellowstone Park."

Moisture and debris began to fall on them from the north as the winds picked up. Steven shielded his eyes and looked around.

"Maybe we should get inside," said Steven. "I don't know what this stuff is, but it could be toxic." The four of them turned toward the stairwell when one final massive blast knocked them to the roof deck. The sound was deafening. Katie and Julia screamed as the guys scrambled to cover them.

In Cambridge, the Kendall Cogeneration Station, the latest-and-greatest innovation in green-energy production, disintegrated and took three city blocks with it. Lights out, for a long time.

CHAPTER 4

Thursday, September 8, 2016
8:42 a.m.
100 Beacon
Boston, Massachusetts

Julia stood at the window and watched as the clouds of debris began to dissipate. For over two hours, their views of Boston and Cambridge were obstructed. The reinforced windows Sarge had installed during the initial renovation of 100 Beacon withstood the blast, but the residents of the lower floors were not so fortunate. Virtually all of the windows on the east and north sides of the surrounding buildings were shattered, throwing bits and pieces of plate glass to the sidewalk below.

A pipeline explosion like this had happened before. In the summer of 2007, an underground steam pipe exploded during the evening rush hour at the Grand Central Terminal. Steam, mud, and pieces of concrete were hurled forty stories into the Manhattan sky. Dozens of people were injured during the blast, primarily from the panic at the busy intersection. The carnage Julia was observing was much worse. There were immense craters spewing steam in every direction of the city.

She tried not to be overwhelmed, but despair did cross her mind from time to time. She was safe, and they'd sufficiently prepared for a collapse event just like this one. But Julia wrestled with her concern for others. People aimlessly walked along the sidewalk, appearing lost and disoriented. Not only had they lost the lives they were accustomed to, but now their homes were destroyed. *Haven't people suffered enough?*

Katie joined her and stood silently for a moment, taking it all in. Finally, Julia spoke.

"This is unimaginable, Katie. Look at these buildings. This is not Ukraine or some city in the Middle East. This is our home, Boston. It looks like it's been bombed." Julia pressed her palms against the window, unconsciously trying to reach out.

"I know, Julia," said Katie. "We're very lucky." Katie put her hand on Julia's shoulder in an attempt to comfort her.

"It's not that we're lucky, Katie. We knew our country faced threats, and we prepared accordingly. But no one could have expected *this*." Julia drew a line across the glass with her index finger, tracing the destruction from Cambridge to the north all the way to downtown Boston, where steam still billowed skyward. "We have to do something."

The stairwell door slammed, and Julia heard the guys' voices as they approached. She couldn't hide her emotions and a few tears streamed down her face. As Sarge and Steven approached, in an attempt to stay strong, she tried to cover her face.

Sarge knew her too well, however. "Honey, what's wrong?" he asked.

Julia tried, but couldn't contain her feelings any longer. She broke down crying. "Sarge, we have to do something for them." She sniffled out the words, waving her arm towards the windows. "They didn't deserve this. Is it fair for us to hide up here in our *fortified penthouses* while so many innocent people are suffering out there?" Julia couldn't hide her sarcasm.

Steven started to speak, but Katie grabbed his arm and pulled him back. Sarge took Julia in his arms and held her until she recovered. Julia had held it together during these first six days. The fast pace in which events occurred and the large amount of activity at 100 Beacon had kept her from focusing on the reality.

"I understand where you're coming from," said Sarge, breaking the tension. "This is a conversation that is overdue. But now that Steven and Katie are safe with us, let's talk. Okay?"

Julia, still sniffling, wiped her eyes with her sleeves and nodded.

The four made their way to the couches. Katie grabbed a bottle of water for Julia, who held it against her neck. Without the generator running, the interior of 100 Beacon was stuffy and warm. This had a calming effect on her.

"It's very dangerous out there, Julia," started Steven. "I've been shot a few times, but never on American soil. I knew things would suck after the collapse, but I didn't expect to be shooting at each other within days of it happening."

"I know, Steven," said Julia. "But what are we supposed to be doing?"

"Surviving," replied Steven. He slumped back into the sofa, wincing as his shoulder hit the padding.

"We are, but where do we go from here?" asked Julia. "I guess I'm just trying to get an overall view of what we're supposed to be doing." She looked to Sarge for guidance, as she was having trouble finding the words to express her feelings. Sarge rescued her.

"Listen, guys, let's not put too much pressure on ourselves right now to set a course for our lives," said Sarge. "First, let's be thankful we're still alive. Steven was shot and survived. These two were in three gunfights in five days. I was chased by people who clearly wanted to kill me—just because I made the mistake of driving through their neighborhood!"

"That's right," added Steven. "The situation is only going to get more dangerous. As people get more desperate, they will become a threat."

"And obviously, gangs are starting to form," said Katie. "The opportunists out there know there is strength in numbers. It's a matter of time before looting gets out of hand."

Julia listened to their words, but her focus was still on the injured and the people displaced from their homes. "I know all that," Julia said. "It's a matter of time before our neighbors, or thugs, try to beat our doors down. Isn't there something we can do right now, today, for the people who just had their asses blown up?" Julia shouted the last part of her statement. She could tell that the consensus was to stay put. Her gut told her she should try to help others. It would come back to them someday.

The room was silent for a few awkward moments. Sarge stood and walked towards the windows, hands in his pockets. Shaking his head, he turned and spoke.

"My, no, our number one priority is survival and staying safe. This may sound crass and insensitive, but those people out there are not our problem. Our decisions need to be practical, considering the risk versus the reward. There are—"

Julia interrupted. "What if we were the ones suffering from injuries? Look at Mass General. It's like a war zone! What's the harm in going over to offer a helping hand? I'm not saying we have to give up our food or guns or precious medical supplies. Let's just, you know, help somebody!"

Katie and Steven remained silent, and wisely so. Sarge would always be the one to make decisions for the group. This responsibility carried a heavy burden, especially after the collapse of society. Julia stared at him. She would not go against his wishes, but she would not be happy if he turned down her pleas.

"What I was about to say was," started Sarge, "there are bigger plans for us down the road. I'm not entirely certain about what caused these events, but that conversation can be held another time. I do know this. The Declaration of Martial Law by the President came quickly, as if prearranged. Steven and Katie's observations of National Guard placement in Washington was organized at warp speed. There are aspects of this that stink to high heaven. If my hunch is correct, I believe we will play a significant role in saving Boston and maybe our nation. But, in any event, we have to maintain our humanity."

Sarge walked back to the window, where the view of the city was becoming clearer. Julia joined him and held him around his waist. She whispered into his ear.

"I love you, Sarge. Let's see if we can help them. Even if it's just one."

THANK YOU FOR READING THIS EXCERPT OF False Flag, book four of The Boston Brahmin Series. You may purchase FALSE FLAG on Amazon or by visiting www.BobbyAkart.com.

SIGN UP FOR EMAIL UPDATES and receive free advance reading copies, updates on new releases, special offers, and bonus content. You can contact Bobby directly by email (BobbyAkart@gmail.com) or through his website:

www.BobbyAkart.com

Made in the USA
Monee, IL
10 September 2022

13734271R00194